"I wouldn't want anyone else but you as the mother of my kids, Jill,"

Greg said, his voice briefly unsteady. "You're doing a great job." He reached out and took her hand.

She couldn't speak for a moment, holding his hand. Such a strong, capable hand, she thought.

Long ago she had heard that in a love match there was a lover and a beloved. In this one, Greg was the beloved and she was the lover, always seeking, always reaching out.

Only you don't know it. I'm always here. I always will be. Oh, dear God, please help Greg see how much I love him....

VIRGINIA MYERS

Virginia Myers has been writing since childhood. As an adult she has published ten novels, contemporary and historical, for the general market. She has now written two novels for the inspirational market.

Active in the writing community, Virginia developed a course in popular novel writing, which she has taught in several Washington colleges. She has lectured, taught writing workshops and served for two years on the board of trustees of the Pacific Northwest Writers Conference.

She lives in Seattle, Washington, where she is active in her community and a faithful worker in her church.

Helpmate
Virginia Myers

Love Inspired®

Published by Steeple Hill Books™

STEEPLE HILL BOOKS

Steeple
Hill™

ISBN 0-373-87036-1

HELPMATE

Copyright © 1998 by Virginia Myers

This edition published by arrangement with Steeple Hill Books.

® and TM are trademarks of Steeple Hill Books, used under license. Trademarks indicated with ® are registered in the United States Patent and Trademark Office, the Canadian Trade Marks Office and in other countries.

Printed in U.S.A.

Train up a child in the way he should go, and even when he is old he will not depart from it.

—*Proverbs* 22:6

To all young mothers everywhere. You have the high privilege and appalling duty of shaping the world, because your children will *be* the world.

Chapter One

The lunch crowd at the Tacky Shack Café had thinned out. Consuela, Jill's assistant hostess and cashier, had given Jill a thumbs-up sign as she shut the cash register drawer and picked up the counter phone on the first ring. Business had been good at the Shack from day one. Connie was quick and excellent at her job. Jill was glad she had hired her. Connie and Felix, Jill's cook, were an odd pair, but their marriage seemed to work.

As usual now, Jill thought of Greg with a sense of unease. Why couldn't her own marriage be as carefree and easygoing as Connie's? She lowered the blinds in the main dining room against the afternoon glare. Seattle's short summer was hot this year. People constantly complained about it.

Come back to me, Greg. Don't run away to your silly boat and retreat into yourself. I never know what you're thinking anymore. Two more customers entered, squinting a bit as they came in from the bright outdoors. Jill went to seat them, since Connie was still on the phone. She hoped they wouldn't order the sesame chicken salad that Felix did so well, as they had sold out early.

"Jill!"

She turned quickly, startled at the sharpness in Connie's usually soft Hispanic voice. And Connie's face looked oddly pinched. What now? With a sense of urgency Jill hurried back to the counter, preparing herself for another crisis of some sort. As Connie handed her the phone she clasped her hands over her mouth. Then sudden panic rushed through her. A personal call!

Not my children. Oh, please, not my children.

"Yes? Hello?"

"Is this Mrs. Rhys?" A woman's voice asked briskly.

Jill paused for a split second. She always used her own name, Jill Bennett, for business. But she was Mrs. Rhys, too. *Oh, not Greg.*

The brisk voice tried to sound reassuring. "Mrs. Rhys, this is the Seattle Police Department. First let me tell you that your little girl is in good hands at—"

"Which little girl?" Jill gripped the phone with a familiar rush of panic. "I have two little girls. Laurie? Megan? And where is Ben, my little boy?" *My children are at their day care center. Safe. Cared for.*

There was a pause at the other end of the line, the rustle of paper. "Yes. Here it is. The child is Megan Ann Rhys? Aged two years, seven months? Is that your little girl?"

"Yes!"

Megan, the tiny image of herself at that age. Same dark hair, same dark eyes, and definitely the wide Bennett grin. Megan, their unpredictable child, who just last night had discovered lipstick and painted her face. Megan, whose latest game was to take off her shoes and socks and throw them away. Disjointed images darted through Jill's mind. The supermarket man in the green apron, handing over two small sandals and a sock. *Ma'am, I think your little girl left these over in Produce.* And Greg's voice, as he helped get the children ready for day care. *No, sleepyhead, put your arm through here. You're not a morning person, are you? No, through here, baby.* Megan, the only one in the family who could make Greg smile these days.

"What happened to Megan?" The phone was slippery in her hand and she gripped it more tightly.

"There was an accident, Mrs. Rhys. But Megan is doing well. She's at Harborview Medical Trauma Center." The voice was kind. "Harborview is famous for its trauma center, but the doctor thinks you should come down."

"Yes. Yes, of course," Jill said quickly. "What... happened?" She realized that she was praying silently, pleading with God. *Please keep my little girl safe, please, please.*

There was another brief pause, more paper rustling.

"It appears, according to the report, that she was left in the day care van until almost noon, and it's a hot day—"

"*Why!* Why was she left in the van!" Oh, stupid question.

"Uh—let me see. The caregiver, it says here, stated that the child fell asleep in the back of the van. And when the caregiver took the other children into the center she forgot Megan, because she couldn't see her and—"

"She *forgot* Megan! *Forgot!* What *happened* to Megan in the van!" Jill's mind felt numb. People at a nearby table were howling with laughter at a joke. She strained to hear the voice on the other end of the phone. Words came through. Very hot today. The inside of a closed van. Heat prostration. Exhaustion. Then the laughter diminished, and she could hear more clearly. "Mrs. Rhys, are you all right? Can you drive? We can send a car for you if—''

"No. Thank you. I can drive. I'm all right." Jill spoke with an effort. She had started to shake, and couldn't seem to hang up the phone. Connie reached over and took it and put it back. Another disjointed image crossed her mind. A TV newscaster talking about a recent cruelty-to-animals story. *It is unwise to leave your pet in a locked car with the windows closed. An outside temperature of seventy degrees can reach over a hundred and twenty degrees inside the car....*

"Jill, are you okay?" Connie's voice was low, guarded. Nearby customers were noticing that something was wrong. Jill heard her own voice reply, sounding matter-of-fact.

"Yes. It's Meggie. She's had an accident. She's down at Harborview. I'm going down there. Can you manage here?"

"Yes, of course. Do you want Felix to drive you? The rush is about over."

"No. Thanks. I'll be fine." *I'm Jill Bennett. I can do anything I set out to do. I'm a big success. Everybody says so. But my little girl needed me and I wasn't there. I just want to hold my little girl. To see that she'll be fine. Dear Lord, please. She has to be.*

But when she got to the hospital she found she couldn't hold Megan yet. Megan was asleep, looking pathetically small in the hospital bed. She was still in the trauma center, in a curtained-off area of some sort, connected to various pieces of hospital equipment. Jill tried to shut out the sounds of urgent activity beyond the curtain. She was very aware of the IV needle in Megan's small hand, the liquid dripping down a tube, methodically letting something healing into her child's veins. She stared for a hypnotized moment at the monitor on the other side of the bed, with the little throbbing green line, telling anyone who looked that Megan's small heart was beating.

Greg's mother, Laura Rhys, sat at the bedside. She rose as Jill entered. She was a tall woman with the same strong-featured face Greg had, but her fair hair was beginning to gray. Would Greg's hair gray in the same way? He would look so elegant when he went gray.

"They called the wrong Mrs. Rhys first, so I gave the police your work number."

"The day care place has my work number," Jill said woodenly, feeling as she always did the underlying antagonism between them. Greg was Laura's only child and she would never forgive Jill for taking him away.

"But you will recall they also have mine. Take this chair. I've been sitting too long."

"No, thanks. I don't mind standing," Jill said awkwardly. The day care center did have Laura's number, because sometimes the children needed things when Greg was not available and business was hectic at the Shack. Laura lived nearby and was retired, so had some extra time to help out. *Mother, can you take the kids down for their booster shots today? Jill has three parties booked at the Shack and I can never get away at tax time.* Be fair. They had both used Laura. She had pushed her own responsibilities onto the older woman. Jill wished for an urgent moment that things were...what? Different. Better somehow, but she didn't know how. She just wasn't sure yet.

"I asked, are you going to stay here?" Laura's cool voice penetrated Jill's mind and she looked up from Megan's small sleeping form. "Someone should be here when Meggie wakes. If you're staying, I'll go. I've al-

ready missed half a meeting at the church that I'm supposed to chair.''

"Yes, yes, you go ahead. And thank you." Somehow
Laura always made her feel like a confused adolescent.
"I'm sorry you've missed—"

"They'll survive." Laura looked older today. She
picked up her handbag from the floor beside the chair.
"Push that bell and tell the nurse to get the doctor. He'll
explain about Megan. He says she'll be fine, but it was
close. They got her body temperature cooled down to nor-
mal, but she's still suffering from dehydration and exhaustion. It seems she woke up and tried to get out of the
van...but couldn't.'' The last was added deliberately, with
an underlying tone of accusation. Jill felt sick, trying to
shut out the mental image of Meggie crying as she struggled to get out of the hot van.

Laura, now widowed, had worked alongside her husband in their property-management business, and had
raised her son and run their perfect home with no problems. She had been openly critical of the way Jill ran her
home and raised her children.

"Thank you for coming down," Jill said politely. "Did
you call Greg?" Dumb question. Of course she had called
Greg.

"Of course I called Greg. He's out of the office with a
client, en route someplace. As soon as he calls back he'll
get the message.''

When Laura had gone, Jill sat down in the bedside
chair, her legs feeling weak. She reached over and
touched a strand of Megan's dark hair on the pillow. It
felt wet and sticky.

And when Greg did get here, what would he say? What
was happening to their marriage? What was happening to
their lives? Sometimes she felt the only thing still holding

them together was Greg's devotion to their children. *I can't lose Greg.* Sometimes she woke up in the predawn hours and listened to his breathing next to her. *Dear God, make Greg love me as he used to.*

But now, with his demanding job at the CPA firm, and her work at the Shack, and three children, there was never any *time* for just the two of them. What little time Greg did have he seemed to want to spend on his sailboat that he loved so much. Sometimes he took five-year-old Laurie with him. She had named their first child after Laura as a placating gesture that hadn't worked.

Now four-year-old Ben had conned him into taking him, also. Jill had the feeling that Greg might have preferred to go alone, but he wouldn't deny the children. Maybe she shouldn't have pushed him into starting their family so soon, but her sister, Kate, had children, and she couldn't wait to have a family of her own. And too often now she caught Greg staring off into space, his mind a thousand miles away from their chaotic home. Too often now she sensed his feeling of entrapment.

It had taken Greg years to build his boat. Woodworking had always been his love. He had studied marine engineering independently and the *Far Horizon,* when he had finished building her, was a superb sailboat. He never missed a meeting of the Wooden Boat Association, and each year at the annual Parade of Boats on the beautiful Sound, the *Far Horizon* sailed proudly with all the others. He was justifiably pleased with his accomplishment. He'd started building her during college. *We'll sail across to Kauai, just the two of us.* And he had stood at the wheel, laughing, the wind plastering his wet shirt against his strong chest. What had happened to just-the-two-of-us? Was he yearning for some far horizon of his own? Without her? Without the children? Without the daily hassle?

The daily crisis? Would this be the final crisis? *Greg, I can't go on like this. I'm beaten. I give up. I can't do it all. I'm not Laura.*

Greg had been so proud of her success. He had encouraged her to return to college between babies, to study restaurant management. *Go for it,* he had said. And together they had decorated the Shack. It was a small old frame cottage in what was now a mixed small business and residential district neighborhood in the northeast end of the city. He'd done most of the renovating for her and taken off the wooden shutters as she directed, and had wanted to nail them all back on with precision. She'd had to argue to get him to put them all back crookedly. *But that's part of my plan,* she had said, laughing. *You see, they're all going to be different colors.*

The finished effect was delightful and he'd loved it. The sparkling white of the cottage itself, with each of the shutters a different shade, pink, yellow, aqua, lavender, all crooked and awry. It looked like some enchanted place in a picture book.

"You've got to admit people will *notice* it," she had said, wiping her paint-stained hands with a turpentine wet rag.

"I'd say they can't *not* notice it," Greg had agreed. "It gives you a kind of I-don't-think-we're-in-Kansas-anymore-Toto feeling."

She had hired Felix Alarcon as cook. Felix and she had been classmates in the restaurant management program. Felix was a superb cook. He and Connie wanted to have their own place some day when they could afford it. Felix and Connie—she recalled once again how they never seemed to have any trouble with their marriage. Felix was twice Connie's age and they had each brought a child to the marriage. Somehow things seemed to work for them.

Megan made a small sound, part moan and part sigh. Jill reached over and touched her hand, and Megan slowly opened her eyes and smiled.

"Mommy."

A welling of relief flooded through Jill. "Yes, baby, it's Mommy."

"Go home now. Okay?" Megan started to get up.

"Not yet. I don't think we can go yet, Meggie. We have to wait to see the doctor." Remembering suddenly what Laura had said, Jill reached over and pushed the nurse's bell.

Megan's small mouth set firmly. "No shots. Okay."

"No. I don't think this is the kind of doctor who gives shots. Besides, you've already had your shots."

There was a sound at the door and Jill looked up, expecting the nurse. She felt a rush of dread. It was Greg.

Not yet. She couldn't tell him yet.

But Greg gave her a moment's reprieve. He headed straight for the bed. Megan had drifted into sleep again. Jill observed him, as she always did, seeing everything about him. His fair hair was just a shade too long. He needed a haircut. She often had to remind him. He was competing on the job with several bright new people. And he was wearing the same shirt he had worn yesterday. Had she remembered to send the laundry? Early in their marriage she had kept up his wardrobe—he didn't have much clothes sense. He really needed a couple of new suits.

He glanced up at her, his expression carefully neutral. They quarreled so easily these days.

"I talked to the doctor out in the hall. He'll be in in a few minutes. He says they can release Meggie as soon as the paperwork is finished. Do you have my insurance card?"

"Yes."

Megan opened her eyes and murmured, "Daddy," and closed them again. Jill let out a soft sigh. *Kiss me, Greg. She's my little girl, too. I was afraid, Greg. I was so afraid.* But he didn't kiss her. He seldom did now unless prompted.

"Are you going to stay here for a while? I really need to get back," he was saying.

"Yes," she answered woodenly. "I'll stay." She quelled a sudden panic. How could she stay? Dinner hour was the busiest time in the Tacky Shack. Who could she get in to help?

"Greg, we have to talk." She hadn't intended to say that.

Greg paused a moment and then answered carefully, as if weighing each word so as not to say too much, or the wrong thing.

"I'm sorry, but I have two appointments to get through, but I can be home by six. Will that do?"

"Yes. I guess so." She had noticed a flicker of anger come and go quickly in his cool gray eyes. She could never fault him for not helping. He was the one who picked the children up from day care every day but Monday, when the Shack was closed. It was he who picked up their casserole-and-salad dinners from Felix at the Shack, fed, bathed and put them to bed. He complained only rarely, usually making a joke of it. He was fed up with *Green Eggs and Ham*, Megan's favorite Dr. Seuss book. He was going through the good doctor's books three times, once with each child.

Jill tried again. "Greg, we do have to talk seriously tonight. We can't take the chance of something like this happening again. I want—" She paused. She couldn't say it. Not yet. She sensed his defenses rising.

"As I recall, you selected this day care center," he said levelly.

"Mommy?" Megan's voice startled them. She was awake again. Greg's attention turned to her.

Jill wondered again if she could hire an evening assistant manager for the Shack's dinner trade. Getting a good person would cost the earth, and Laura would have plenty to say about that. She was very protective of Greg and had made it very clear to Jill that she thought a wife should pull her own weight financially. Then she felt Greg behind her, his hands on her shoulders.

"I'll see you at six," he said. "And we'll talk after the kids are down for the night." She hated it when he used that tone, his voice low, still very polite. He was humoring her. Well, whether he liked it or not, they would have to talk. Suddenly she felt very tired. But she couldn't be tired. There wasn't time. She sensed his absence as soon as he was gone, leaving her alone with Megan. Megan's eyes were still on her.

"We're going home in a little while, baby." She pushed back Megan's dark hair. "Can Mommy use your phone?"

"My phone?"

"Yes. I think that's your little table there, with the water jug and tissues on it. Mommy has to make some calls."

With Megan's sleepy eyes following her, Jill dialed the restaurant. Connie couldn't handle the dinner hour seating and the take-away counter. Just two months ago she had put in the take-away, featuring Felix's casseroles and splendid salads. It had been an immediate success with working people who didn't want to cook or go out after working all day.

She spent a half hour on the phone, placating an increasingly fretful Megan between calls. She managed to get the extra waitress who had worked at the Shack before, which would be easier on Connie. She talked with both Connie and Felix again, giving instructions, settling minor questions.

The doctor came in to speak to her about Megan, and when she started to dress Megan to take her home she found that Meggie had apparently vomited while in the van and whoever had undressed her in the emergency room had just wiped it away. Jill sponged it off as well as she could in the rest room, but Meggie still smelled and was upset about it. She didn't understand why Jill couldn't change her into clean clothes. Balancing a fretful Meggie on her hip, Jill signed the various papers provided for the insurance.

Tired, and holding back tears—*she would not cry*—she finally got the spare child's car seat from the trunk of the car and strapped Megan in it, with Meggie complaining loudly about wanting to get home in the blink of an eye so she could watch her favorite video. Increasingly frustrated and with anger building, Jill determined to drive right over to the day care center and give them a piece of her mind before she went home. Jill sighed. The house was such a mess. Maybe she'd have time to do some housekeeping before Greg arrived. It really needed a good cleaning. Twice she had hired a cleaning service, but each time the place began to look good she regretted spending the money and canceled the service.

Then, still fighting tears, she found herself on the freeway, looking for the drop-off exit for West Seattle. She didn't dare face the day care people yet. She might say too much. Better to talk a while with Kate, her sister. Kate was the steady one, the little plodder. Jill, though the younger, had been the brainy sister, the one with ambition—and where had it gotten her? Kate had, or seemed to have, a much more peaceful and contented life. Since Megan seemed fine now, Jill thought it would be all right to stop at Kate's for just a short visit.

Kate's little house, nestled between two larger, newer ones, looked shabbier than ever. She wondered if the roof was all right for the coming winter. She'd given Kate some money last year for a patch. Widowed a few years ago, Kate lived precariously with her two children on her husband's insurance. It was touch and go for her, but she never complained. Jill wished again that they didn't live so far apart. Kate caring for all the kids might have been a solution, but with Seattle's bumper-to-bumper gridlock during rush hours it was impossible. *No,* she thought. *I want to take care of my own.* She was actually facing it for the first time. She wanted to be with them as they grew, as their personalities formed. There was an odd, empty feeling in the pit of her stomach. Neither Greg nor Laura would understand.

She turned the car into Kate's driveway. Kate's house was on a slight promontory. From the living-room windows you could see the coming and going of the Fauntleroy Ferry, making its slow way across the green-blue or gray water, leaving behind it a wide shallow wake. Getting Megan out of the back seat, Jill went around to the back door of the cottage. Kate was probably in the kitchen. She did all her own cooking from scratch, including bread, because it was cheaper that way, and she had to watch every penny.

Jill opened the door of the service porch. "Hi, Katie. It's me," she called out.

"Jill—come on in!" Kate's voice sang out happily. "Whatever brought you over here at this time of day? I'm in the kitchen up to my elbows in flour."

And she was. As Jill came into the kitchen she felt a
rush of affection. Kate was so *Kate*. She might be prettier
if she bothered to work at it, but not Kate. Her light brown
hair was pulled back into a ponytail, secured by a simple
rubber band. Her rather round little face was free of any
makeup. Dad had always called her his little Campbell
Soup kid. She wore, as usual, a loose print cotton blouse,
faded from many washings, and an equally faded denim
skirt, which she had made out of denim jeans. Without
seeing her feet, Jill knew they would be in worn tennis
shoes, the cheapest kind from the local discount store. Her
sturdy little hands, covered with flour now, were pressing
a lump of dough onto a sheet of waxed paper. Little shreds
of dough clung to her fingers as she tore off another sheet
to press down on top.

"Sit down. I'll be through in a minute. What on earth
brings you over here at this time of day?" She took up
her rolling pin and began to gently roll out the dough
between the sheets of paper. It was the only way she could
handle her short, delicious pie dough without tearing it.
"You came at the right time. I'm making rhubarb pies
today for the freezer. You wouldn't believe my rhubarb
crop this year. How'd you know I was making these?"

"Lucky guess," Jill said, sitting down in one of the
kitchen chairs and putting Meggie next to her. Rhubarb
pie was Greg's favorite.

"Here, Meggie, you can have this," said Kate, and she
handed Megan a small lump of leftover dough, scraping
it from the bowl and shaping it into a roundish lump.
Meggie, kneeling on her chair, began to pummel her lump
with concentration. Jill wished she had remembered to
wash Meggie's hands.

"Since you're here, you can take a couple of these
home for Greg," Kate said, carefully putting the circle of

dough in the last pie tin, and crumpling up the sticky waxed paper she had peeled off. "And I'll give you a care package of fresh veggies before you go. You wouldn't believe my tomatoes. They're ripening faster than we can eat them. I gave my next-door neighbor some yesterday. I mean, I gave them to his housekeeper."

"Thanks," Jill said. Kate loved giving her produce. It was about all she could give. There was only a year's difference in their ages, and they had always been close. Jill was often able to give Kate money to help out with unexpected bills, so she welcomed any chance to help Jill in return.

"What's that funny smell? Did Megan spit up?"

"Yes. I'll tell you about it. I got pretty upset."

"I threw up," Megan said angrily. "In the van. On the seat. All over," she added with satisfaction.

"Well, peel off her clothes and run them through the washer," Kate said. "She can't get cold on a day like this."

Here was sanity. Control. Directions to follow. With an almost loving look around Kate's shabby old kitchen, Jill did as she was told. Then, to the churning sound of the ten-year-old washer on the back porch, she told Kate about the nearly fatal accident.

Kate was horrified. "What's going to happen to the nitwit responsible for this?" she asked. "Shouldn't there be some charge? Endangerment of a child? Neglect of a child? There must be something!"

"Van too hot," Meggie said angrily, pummeling her grimy lump of dough.

"I suppose there is, but that's the least of my worries. Greg was upset, of course, and Laura was there. Hyper-critical, as always."

Kate ignored the comment about Laura, and Jill felt a

slight annoyance. Kate could always see the other side, could somehow find sympathy for Laura, widowed, clinging to her only son. Jill was sorry she had mentioned Laura.

"I can't go on like this," she said, and stopped at hearing the slight quaver in her voice. Kate looked at her keenly, then turned to wash her hands at the sink. As she dried them she sat down opposite Jill.

"What do you mean?"

"I mean I'm thinking of quitting work. Selling out the restaurant. I'm thinking about raising my own kids—the way you are. Sometimes I think I don't...even know my kids anymore. I think...Greg sees more of them than I do." She faltered to a stop at the expression on Kate's face.

"But you worked so hard. The Tacky Shack is such a...such an *achievement*. You worked so hard...so long. Both you and Greg. How could you...give it up? Oh, Jill. I think you just got frightened today and discouraged. Nothing is easy, but you mustn't give up your work. You're so brainy. You're such an...such an overachiever. How could you *not* overachieve. You'd go crazy cooped up all day with nothing to challenge you, with nobody to talk to but the kids."

"I don't think so," Jill said steadily. "This is not a quick decision, Katie. I've been thinking about it for quite a while, but I need your help."

"Of course," Kate said immediately. "Anything. But *how!*"

"Greg and I spend like there's no tomorrow. I really have no idea how to...*manage*...the way you do. And the first thing I think I have to do—before I talk to Greg—is to work out some kind of budget. I really have no idea how much it costs us to live.'' She felt a flush of embarrassment.

"Oh, wow," Kate said. "Lemme get a pencil and paper."

Chapter Two

Greg was at the door when Jill got home with Megan. It was almost six-thirty.

"Come on in. I've got dinner in the oven." He held the door for her.

Megan said, "Daddy," and reached out to him. He took her from Jill.

"Thanks, Greg. I'm sorry I'm late, but I was so frazzled at the hospital that I drove over to see Kate for a while. That always calms me down, but I should have remembered the going-home traffic. It took forever on the freeway from West Seattle."

"No problem. I gave the kids the rest of the graham crackers to prevent starvation. They're okay. What's that?"

"Oh, a rhubarb pie. Kate was making some for the freezer and she sent this for you. What's for dinner?"

"The kids wanted macaroni and cheese again," Greg said, taking the pie in his free hand. "But I got a fruit salad, too, to sort of balance out the vitamin thing. Last night you recall they wanted spaghetti."

Jill sighed. Greg was too indulgent with the kids. They should eat a more balanced diet. Growing children needed more than pasta or beans and franks, another favorite.

As Greg went back to the kitchen with Megan and the pie, Jill looked around their disordered living room, so different from Kate's. The comparison was shocking. This carpet hadn't been vacuumed for days. Dust lay thick on the furniture. The coffee table was piled high with magazines, junk mail, yellow plastic bits from Ben's construction blocks, a sticky cappuccino cup from her own unwinding period last night about midnight after she'd closed the Shack, and one of Megan's patent leather dress shoes.

This place is going to look like *House Beautiful*, she thought determinedly as she went into the kitchen. Why aren't we eating in the dining room? Dining rooms are for dining. But in their hasty, hurry-up life it was easier to eat near the oven and the dishwasher.

"Dinner's on," Greg called to the other two children, and both Ben and Laurie came running from their rooms, heading for the kitchen. Greg already had Megan on her booster seat with a bowl of macaroni and cheese in front of her.

"Ben got into trouble today at day care," Laurie was saying as she got into her chair. "He didn't clean his plate at lunch, and I did, and I get to be table monitor tomorrow. I don't think Ben will ever get to be monitor." Laurie's voice held that familiar whining note that Jill was beginning to notice. She wished Laurie wasn't such a tattletale.

"Okay," Greg said. "No time for squabbling. Time to eat. Dig in, kids."

Jill sat down gazing thoughtfully around the table at her family. Greg, looking tired and harassed. Yes, he did need a haircut. Laurie, starting to eat but looking sulky at her father's implied reprimand. Four-year-old Ben, not eating yet but looking off dreamily into space, as his father often did. What long thoughts did a four-year-old boy ponder? And since when, Jill thought, had five-year-old Laurie taken over family discipline? And Megan, ignoring it all, concentrating on shoving large spoonfuls of food into her small mouth, having already smeared it all over her chin.

Jill watched Greg reach over and wipe Meggie's chin then turn with a sigh and look down into his own plate.

"Didn't you want macaroni and cheese?" Jill asked suddenly. The kids always clamored for what they wanted, but did anybody think about what Greg wanted?

Startled, Greg looked up from his dinner. "Me? No, I'm a carnivore. I would like—some day, maybe—my own personal steak. Or maybe just that great meat loaf your mother used to make. But you know kids. Tomorrow we'll probably be back to beans and franks. Or maybe we'll just skip Felix and go to McDonald's."

"I'm sorry," Jill said simply.

Greg looked surprised, then shrugged. "Oh, well."

Jill started to eat her meal, but it could have been sawdust for all she tasted it. Life shouldn't be patient acceptance, a shrug and an "Oh, well." They were a family. Maybe they hadn't exactly planned it. Maybe they had rather blundered into it, but family they were, and life should be better than this. Laurie had been such a sweet-natured child. She didn't need to grow into a little shrew because she, as the oldest child, wasn't getting enough attention. Ben didn't need to escape into daydreams about cuddly TV characters who loved everybody. And Greg, after working all day, had a right to come home to a clean house, a happy family and a meal he enjoyed. And Meggie? Meggie's life should not be put at risk because she was carted around in a hot, stuffy van and had fallen asleep.

"How's Kate doing?" Greg asked, interrupting Jill's thoughts. "It was nice of her to send the pie."

"Fine. You know Kate. I'm supposed to call later and tell her about the day care problem. Is anything being done about the idiot who left Meggie in the van?"

Laurie interrupted. "Please! Don't talk about the van! We heard about it all day at day care!" She put her hand to her forehead in a dramatic gesture.

Ignoring her, Greg answered, "I've already talked to the police about it. I was going to tell you later. And I talked with the day care people. The prosecutor's office has to decide if any charge is to be placed, and if so, what. The day care worker has a good reputation. She's an experienced caregiver. This is the first blot on her record. She's devastated by what happened. She had to be sent home. So it's kind of a tricky situation."

"I see what you mean," Jill said slowly, putting down her fork. Greg was looking at her. Their eyes met. And a clear understanding passed between them, without spoken words. It was almost like old times.

He gave a slight smile. "I know. My first reaction was to fight tooth and claw, protecting my young, but I've made mistakes with the kids, too. Last time I had Ben on the boat he almost went over the side. I grabbed him just in time."

Jill felt a slight lump in her throat. Greg was so good. Like Kate, he was willing to always give the benefit of the doubt. If she could stay home, it wouldn't matter if Meggie fell asleep in her car seat. Because Meggie wouldn't be in day care. Meggie would be safe with her mother. Jill began to rehearse in her mind what she would say to Greg after the children were in bed.

The endless meal was finally over, and while Greg bathed the children and got them through the going-to-bed routine, she cleared the table and put the dishes in the dishwasher. The kitchen floor felt sticky beneath the soles of her shoes. She knew she should clean it, but she didn't have the energy. Eventually the house was quiet. The children, having had a difficult day with the excitement about Megan, had mercifully gone to sleep quickly. She returned to the disordered living room to wait for Greg. She heard the shower go on in the master bathroom and then shut off, and Greg came into the room.

"Sorry," he said at the doorway. He had already taken off his shirt. "I'm beat. I guess I forgot you wanted to talk. Any reason we can't postpone it until tomorrow?"

"You think I'm not beat?" she asked.

"Okay. It's a given that we're both tired. Which tells me we should hit the sack. Then we can cope with it tomorrow with clearer heads. How about it?"

Jill swallowed, fighting tears. "I want to get past it tonight," she said steadily. "I need to have a talk with you and…you're not going to like it."

He sighed and sat down on the couch, pushing aside a stack of old newspapers. "Okay, what is it?"

"Today we almost lost Megan."

"I know." He shivered slightly and bowed his head, rubbing his hands over his bare arms as if he were cold, which he couldn't be in this weather. Maybe it was the same inward coldness she had felt ever since the phone call about Megan.

"What do you suggest?" He glanced up at her, his clear eyes questioning.

"I suggest I stop trying to be Wonder Woman and stay

home and raise our kids to adulthood and create a decent
home for you, for our family.''

"You mean run the Shack by remote control? You've
always said you had to *be* there, to oversee everything."

"No. I know that wouldn't work," Jill said. She wished
she had some water, for her mouth had gone dry. "I mean
sell out. To Felix and Connie. They want to own their
own place. They'd buy me out in a minute."

For what seemed a full sixty seconds he stared at her
as if she had lost her mind. "I don't believe this." He
shook his head. "After all your years of work! Jill, you're
still in shock about Meggie. You can't be serious. And
what would Felix use to pay you—play money?"

"I'd have to give them rather generous terms," she
conceded, "but they could borrow..." Her voice dwindled at the stubborn look on his face. He was shaking his
head.

"I knew we should have hit the sack. You just aren't
thinking straight. Jill, the Tacky Shack Café was your
dream for years. You—we both worked our tails off to
get it started. Now it's just beginning to pay off and you
want to throw it away?" There was the beginning of
Greg's slow anger, and Jill sent up a silent prayer. She
should have waited until he wasn't so tired and impatient.

"Okay, Greg, if you want to talk tomorrow I—"

"No way! I had no idea what you had in mind! Now
that it's out on the table, we're going to deal with it! When
did you get this crazy idea?"

She leaned back in her chair, feeling as if she wanted
to shrink out of sight.

"Actually, I've been thinking about it for some time. I
think we went too far, too fast—my fault, mostly. I was
the one who wanted to start our family. And...and..."

"I don't begrudge any woman wanting to start a family,

Jill. Maybe having three was a little much, but that's life. Things happen. But I thought we had it pretty well worked out. I thought we were doing...okay.'' His own voice dwindled away, and he looked off into space for a long moment.

"Actually, you don't, do you?" Jill asked gently. "Is this what you call living? Both of us running as fast as we can to stay in one place? Trading the kids back and forth. Living in this perpetual clutter and dirt. The only time we ever go out is to collect the dry cleaning, or pick up a prescription at the pharmacy, or shop the supermarket for breakfast stuff, or pick up ready-cooked food for our main meals. And me, on Monday, my day off. I spend most of it on the phone ordering restaurant supplies or making business calls. And Sundays, our wonderful Sundays, when we try to sneak a little extra sleep, because the Shack opens at noon Sundays, trying to shut out the kids quarreling in the living room about which cartoons to watch. And skipping church. I can't remember when we went to church last. Can you?"

He was looking at her intently. "No," he said slowly. "I can't. You have a kind of end-of-your-tether sound. You said you've been thinking about this a long time. I'm glad you finally mentioned it to *me*. No, scratch that. I don't mean to be sarcastic. But about all this thinking you've done, have you concluded anything? I guess what I'm asking is, how do we get *off* the treadmill? Or can we?"

"I think we can," Jill said carefully, unfolding Kate's estimated budget and handing it to him.

"What's this?" He reached out and took it.

"When I was at Kate's I talked to her about it. She's so good at managing...and we...worked out a monthly budget." She watched his experienced glance go down the careful list she and Kate had made. He was, after all, a certified public accountant. Maybe she should have talked it over with him first.

"Well, what do you think?" she asked as he looked up from the list.

"Am I supposed to give up my boat?"

"No! Of course not! What makes you say that?"

"Well, I can't put it in the garage, Jill. And you haven't even listed anything for moorage fees. And nothing for the ongoing upkeep. I spend real folding money when I'm down at the marina. Whoever it was who said that a boat is a hole in the water in which you pour money was right on target."

"Add that in, Greg. I don't want you to give up the boat. I would never ask you to do that."

"Good. Because if you did, we'd have the mother of all battles. I built that thing. It's part of my life!" He had raised his voice angrily, and he tossed the list onto the littered coffee table.

Jill wondered a bit sickly if the boat was the most important part of his life, the part that got him off—what had he called it? The treadmill? They both heard the slight sound at the hallway door, and turned to see that Megan was there, clad in nothing but a bedroom slipper on her left foot. She ran naked into the room and hit Greg on the knee.

"Don't be mad at Mommy!" she said, and started to cry.

"I'll find her nightgown," Jill said tiredly. She got up from her chair as Greg picked up Meggie to comfort her. Jill found the nightgown on the hallway floor, as well as the other slipper, and took them back into the living room. As she put the gown back on Meggie, she and Greg avoided looking at each other.

"I'm sorry I yelled," Greg said after a moment. "I know that quarreling parents upset kids. They assume blame. I remember..." He stopped. He almost never spoke of his own childhood, which, to hear about it from Laura, had been perfect. Jill didn't pursue it. She had learned long ago that Greg's loyalty to his mother was absolute, but she had sometimes wondered how he had fared as an only child, a latchkey kid. Had he felt lonely? Neglected? Unloved?

"Wait a minute," he said as she started to take Megan back to bed. They both knew the discussion was over for now, as it would take another bedtime story to put Meggie back to sleep again. "Let me think about this. I can tell you're dead serious. Let me see what I can work out about finances?"

She felt a flood of gratitude. "Would you?"

"Sure."

She turned away quickly. She didn't want to see that faraway look again. Not right now.

Jill was late getting to work the next morning because the day care van didn't stop for the children and she had to take them. It seemed that Laura, the day before, had told them that the Rhyses would find another day care facility, without mentioning it to Jill or Greg. Marsha, who ran the center, was profuse in her apologies for the problem with the van and Meggie, and delighted to have the Rhys children back. Jill tried to explain that she and Greg understood it was simply an accident. She even remembered to ask about the caregiver.

"Daisy? She's still at home. She's upset, of course, as there may be charges. Do you know anything about that, Mrs. Rhys?"

Jill, mentally counting the minutes, passed the responsibility over to Greg and cravenly said, "Give my husband a call. He's the one who talked with the police and everybody. He'll know more than I do."

"Daisy's not here?" Suddenly little Ben spoke up, looking around the large central playroom. He stood there frowning, a small image of Greg. "But Daisy's my best friend," he added forlornly. It stabbed Jill's heart. She wanted to pick him up, console him, and at the same time she was thinking, *My children should bond with me, not a caregiver who may drop out of their lives at any time.*

But there was no time. "I really have to go. I'm running late." And she managed to get away, almost running to her car so she could get to the Shack.

They had opened at nine o'clock sharp ever since they discovered that the surrounding businesses had employees who wanted a ten-o'clock coffee break. They came for the excellent coffee and Felix's delicious heated cinnamon rolls with a pat of melting butter on top. When she got to the Shack, she found that Connie and Felix had opened it and there was a line at the take-away counter and people were seated at some of the tables. Jill plunged into her day, forcing herself to put her personal life on hold.

It was a good business day. They sold out three of the entrées for lunch. Trade was so brisk that Jill hardly had time to think. About three o'clock she had a minute in the kitchen with Felix and told him that no matter what Greg got for the kids' dinner, to make up a separate take-out for Greg from the prime rib. Then things became so busy that she didn't see Greg when he came in, but Connie gave her a little thumbs-up sign when she asked if he'd got his meal.

They usually closed the Shack at eleven, or earlier if the last diners had finished and gone. Tonight Jill put up the closed sign at ten-forty, and went into the kitchen. She always helped with the clearing up when necessary. She had two student kitchen helpers, Herbie and Oliver, but today Herbie had called in sick, so they were shorthanded.

There had been a brief slow period right after nine, and she had been able to cash out the register and prepare the night deposit, which Felix always dropped off on his way home. Jill had started doing it herself, but Felix had decided that it wasn't safe for a woman to go near the bank's night deposit drop, and insisted on taking it over. Greg had agreed.

Felix, well past forty and overweight, always complaining about something, would have been helpless in a holdup, but it was good of him to volunteer.

"I'm no hero," he had told her. "I'll just hand over the money before I faint, but better me than you. It's not that I'm out of condition," he had added "I've never been *in* condition, but dangerous stuff is a man's work." She had been touched by his gesture. Complainer or not, Felix had a good heart.

But just as she finished filling the salt and pepper shakers there was a loud rapping at the front door.

"Good grief," Felix moaned. "Can't they read the sign?"

Jill hurried to the door to send whoever it was away, only to find that it was Laura. She opened the door quickly.

"Come in. If you've come to eat I'm afraid we're just closing up. I could fix you something...."

"I didn't come to eat," Laura said coldly. "I came to talk to you."

Jill's heart plummeted. Greg had told her! How could he?

"Come over here. We'll use this small corner table." Jill led the way. She wanted her mother-in-law as far from the kitchen door as possible if there was going to be an argument. "Can I get you something? A cup of tea?"

"No. Nothing, thanks." Laura seated herself and stared at the dark window beside her, looking at her reflection in the glass.

"Could you lower the blinds? It seems so public."

"Of course." Jill got up to do it and sat down again.

"Jill, I'm trying very hard not to be angry. I hardly know where to begin."

Jill felt a rise of her own anger and tried to quell it. This was Greg's mother and he loved her. "Am I to assume that Greg has talked to you about our discussion last night?"

"He didn't want to, but I got it out of him. I don't know if you know this or not, but my late brother, Jason, left Greg a small trust fund—about ten thousand dollars now. I was his executor. Greg asked me if there was any way he could get at the money now. Then of course he had to tell me why. I am appalled at your selfishness!"

"Laura," Jill said, knowing she was sounding grim, "you and I have always had our differences. I'm sorry you are upset, but this is between Greg and me, and we'll be the ones to work it out." She could feel herself flushing. *I won't lose my cool. I won't let her get to me.*

"Over my dead body. You are not going to burden Greg with all the family expense. That's not fair. You and he married with the understanding that you wanted a well-paying career. He was counting on it. If you want to waste yourself being a stay-at-home mommy and watching soap operas all day, that's your problem, and maybe you'd better get some counseling. I would think you'd have more self-respect. But I will *not* permit you to force Greg to work day and night to pay for it. I've found another day care place—more reliable than the one you had. I was going to tell you yesterday, but I was too busy.''

"We're not changing day care places," Jill said evenly. "Greg isn't going to press any charges. It was an accident. We agree on that. It—"

"Not press charges! Ridiculous! You have grounds for a civil suit! You could get a large settlement!"

"I doubt that. It's a smallish operation."

Laura almost visibly gritted her teeth. "From their *insurance company,* Jill. Where is your mind? They have to be insured to operate." A little white line had appeared around Laura's tight mouth.

"But Laura, the kids *like* the caregivers there. They'd be upset at a change. Unless they could stay at home."

"Nonsense! They're young. They'd forget."

Jill's hands tightened into fists under the table and she mentally counted to ten. How many times had Laura brushed aside something Greg wanted when he was little? What childhood treasures or relationships had he lost?

"I'm sorry you made the trip over here. At the risk of making you angrier than you already are, I consider this an intrusion. Greg is my husband and we will solve our own problems as best we can. We may give up the Shack, for now at least, so I can stay home and raise my kids and make a good home for my husband—which he hasn't got right now. We took on too much and we have to cut back. We're just working it out now. Greg said he would—"

"I know what Greg said he would do. You've always been able to twist him around your little finger."

Not lately, Laura. Not lately.

"Laura, please, lower your voice. We don't want the whole world to hear."

"I don't care who hears us. I will not let you do this

to Greg. I'm proud to say that I always pulled my own weight financially in my marriage. I was *never* a burden to my husband.'' Laura's eyes were bright with angry unshed tears.

Jill spoke, lowering her voice in the hope that Laura would, too.

''There are more ways to pull your own weight, as you call it, than bringing in money. Maybe I can make a better life for all of us. Maybe—''

''Nonsense! Utter nonsense! You were the one who wanted a career. And now you've found out that it's a lot of hard work and you want out. You want to freeload on Greg—with the three children *you* insisted on having.'' Laura was shaking with fury now.

''Please keep your voice down,'' Jill pleaded, knowing hopelessly that Laura's voice was carrying into the kitchen, loud and clear. There were no cleaning-up sounds from the kitchen now—just dead silence. The staff was obviously getting an earful.

''After all the work you put into this place—all the work you *and Greg* put into it—that you'd even think of selling out, for pennies on the dollar, is unbelievable! Do you realize—even *faintly*—how irresponsible that is? I will not have it, Jill! I will not! I'll talk some sense into Greg if it's the last thing I do.''

Jill was about to say something else, but Laura got up from the table and walked swiftly to the door. Jill closed her eyes and flinched as the door slammed. She sat at the table, listening intently as Laura's car door slammed and the car roared away.

Now, what was she going to tell the silent people in the kitchen, who must have heard every word? Well, she'd better face it. She got up from the table and walked into the Tacky Shack kitchen.

She paused at the doorway. The three people there were suddenly fiercely intent upon their work. Connie was bent low over the grill she was wiping clean. Felix was transferring legs of lamb from the freezer to the fridge. And Oliver, his big hands protected by the extra-large mitts she had ordered especially for him, was taking hot dishes out of the dishwasher to put on the shelves in neat stacks. Not one of them looked at her.

She couldn't speak for a moment.

How can I leave this?

She gazed around at her state-of-the-art kitchen, with all the first-class equipment she had bought. The shining metal hot table, the white porcelain salad sinks, the large restaurant-sized range top and massive oven, the lovely immaculate tile floor that somebody had already mopped. A lump rose in her throat. She had worked so hard.

Was Laura right?

"Okay, guys," she said when she could speak. "You must have heard the row. Shall we have a staff meeting and clear it all up?"

Felix shut the fridge door and sat down on a stool he kept handy. "Good idea. I'd welcome a sit-down. My feet are killing me."

Connie, not looking at her, went to the sink. "I'll be with you in a minute, when I wash the crud off."

And tall, lanky Oliver, who was washing dishes while he hoped for a basketball scholarship to college—any college—put his last stack of hot dishes away and took off his mitts.

"I'll hafta catch up tomorrow, if it's okay. I gotta date." He looked embarrassed and Jill wondered if he really did have a date. Oliver, at eighteen, was an oddly sensitive and perceptive boy.

"Fine, Ollie, go ahead," Felix told him. "Thanks for

doing Herbie's work as well as your own. I owe you. Take that sack of cinnamon rolls I saved for you. I know your mom likes them.''

As Oliver ducked out the back door Jill pulled over two stools and sat down on one while Connie, still drying her hands, sat down on the other one, the damp towel lying forgotten in her lap.

Jill cleared her throat. ''Well, in the first place this is all very premature. Greg and I have been…discussing the possibility of my giving up work…uh…for a while maybe, to stay home and raise our kids. Me being a…homemaker, instead of us both running our legs off while I do my Wonder Woman act as a working mother.'' She paused, not knowing quite how to go on. Connie was looking down at the towel in her lap, her face not visible. It was Felix who broke the silence.

''Your mother-in-law's comment about *selling* the Shack is what put me into cardiac arrest. Is that a possibility?''

''Greg and I were discussing it,'' Jill said cautiously, feeling faintly sick at the very idea of it. *Selling the Shack?* What had she set in motion? ''If…it actually happens—and it seems I've got a lot of opposition—and we did sell the Shack, well, I know that you and Connie want to own your own place, so, well, you'd get first refusal, of course.''

She owed them this. They'd been with her from the beginning. She'd gone through the restaurant management classes with Felix, an older student.

''And if you two wanted to buy me out I'd…I'd give you very generous terms. In fact,'' she added impulsively, ''if I let the Shack go, I wouldn't want anyone else to have it.'' She realized immediately how unbusinesslike this comment was, and flushed in embarrassment.

Felix, usually very undemonstrative, got up from his stool and lumbered over to her. He bent and kissed her on the forehead, muttering, "Thank you, love. That was a nice thing to say."

"You realize, of course, that this is all very preliminary. I mean, I wouldn't have mentioned it if Laura hadn't blown up and yelled."

Connie raised her head and looked straight at Jill, tossing the damp towel onto a nearby counter.

"I think you're a fool," she said distinctly.

Jill was stunned. She and Connie had been fast friends ever since Connie and Felix had married. Connie *couldn't* be looking at her this way, her dark eyes reflecting—what?

"Do you want to waste all your talent, waste your education? Just to be a *housewife?*"

Wanting to cry, Jill recognized the look Connie was giving her. Connie, dear, kind, Connie, with whom she had laughed and cried and worked until they were both ready to drop, was looking at her with clear, open *contempt.*

Chapter Three

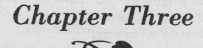

It was almost midnight before Jill drove into the garage. The door rose and the light went on as she drove in. Greg was good about rigging up convenience things. And since their garage was at the back of the lot, not attached to the house, she knew that the instant the garage door shut the floodlights would come on to light a path through the backyard to the door. They had bought an older home, and Greg had been renovating it during the past few years.

He met her at the back door, which surprised her. He was usually in bed asleep by the time she got home.

"What are you doing up?" she asked with a sudden lifting of her heart. He looked so terrific in the bright light. And he was smiling.

"I wanted to thank you for the prime rib. What a great idea. I had a rough day and it kind of made things right with my world." He bent to kiss her briefly, and shut the door. "I don't know why it never occurred to me that I could order something different from the kids' meal. Anyhow, thanks."

"You're welcome," she said, and before she could stop

herself added, "I know something about your rough day. Laura stopped by the Shack." She could see his retreat, his withdrawal, and wanted to bite her tongue.

"I'm sorry," he said distantly, and then, "I made some cappuccino. Do you want some? I know you like to unwind a bit."

"Thanks, yes." She made her tone warmly grateful.

They went into the kitchen. Someone, Greg obviously, had mopped the floor, because it wasn't sticky anymore.

"Did you clean up in here?"

"Yeah. I wanted to wait up for you—" He paused uncertainly. "So I decided to do some cleaning to fill the time."

They looked at each other for a long moment before Jill said carefully, "Don't worry about your mother. We didn't have a quarrel. I mean, not exactly. She's upset because I want to give up working and stay home. She...just stated her objection and then she left. She mentioned that you asked for money, some sort of trust?"

"Yeah. Sit down. I'll get the coffee." He got the little cappuccino pot and two small cups and joined her at the kitchen table.

"My uncle Jason—you didn't know him. He died before we got together. He was quite a bit older than Mother. He was a real nice guy, didn't have any kids of his own, and was fond of me. I remember he used to help me make model boats. Anyhow, his health began to fail in midlife and he had to take a very early retirement. He was about fifty, I think, and his retirement pay was pretty skimpy. But he did keep up one life insurance policy, the remains of which, after his last expenses were paid, comes to me. He tied it up in a trust, though. I don't get it until I'm fifty-five."

"Fifty-five! You're kidding!" Jill almost laughed aloud.

"No. He may have had the right idea, though. He was awfully hard up at the end, poor old guy. And too proud to take anything from Mother. He said in his will that it was harder to be poor when you were old than when you were young. So in case I ended up old and poor, I'd have a little nest egg. We could sure use the money now, but no dice."

Jill tried to concentrate on her coffee, very aware that Greg had said if "I" end up poor, not "we."

"Anyhow," he continued, "I did put in some time on a realistic review of our finances. I didn't have the Shack's books handy, so I used some top-of-the-head estimates there instead of hard figures." He was looking at her steadily, his well-shaped hand holding the small coffee cup just off the saucer. "If you're dead set on this, I can tell you that it's probably do-able. But just barely. Have you thought any more about it?" He lifted the cup and took a cautious sip and, finding it too hot, put the cup back down.

"I...I am dead set on it, as you call it," Jill said.

"Do I detect a hint of hesitation there?" Greg didn't miss much.

"Yes," she said frankly. "Sure I'm having second thoughts. I love that place. I built it. It's...it's cost me something personally to...think of giving it up." Despite her effort, there was a quaver in her voice. She cleared her throat. "I've been having this on-again, off-again argument with myself for weeks. The phone call from the police about Meggie did it, I guess. They said 'your little girl,' and...I didn't even know which little girl." She *wasn't* going to cry. "You said you had a rough day," she reminded him. "Was there anything else besides

Laura being upset? Or was that enough? I'm sorry. Scratch that last."

"Okay. It's scratched. Just the usual hassle at the office." But the tone of his voice told Jill he was worried about something. They hadn't had time to talk together privately for a long time, and she wasn't going to let the moment go.

"Come on, Greg. You sound worried."

"I guess I am. Not worried exactly, but…uneasy, perhaps. You know how it is. People jockeying for position in any company. Marv is retiring in less than a year, which opens up the VP slot. I have…or maybe I had…a good shot at it. But we got a new staff member today."

Jill's heart skipped a beat. Greg worked so hard, and he was good at his job. He wanted—expected—to advance. He *must* advance if she gave up the Shack.

"What kind of staff member? Some ball of fire from Harvard Business School? What are his credentials?"

He grinned halfheartedly. "*Her* credentials, Jill. And I don't know whether she is a ball of fire or not, but she…got the VIP treatment today when Marshall took her around to introduce her to the rest of us."

"Did you talk to Snipe the Snoop about it?" Jill asked. "He'll know all the details." Greg colored slightly, so she knew he had talked to Barry Snipe. Barry was the office manager and lived for office gossip. If anybody knew anything about the new hire it would be Barry Snipe. It had been impossible not to combine the name Snipe with snoop, and she thought Barry might have coined it himself.

"Yeah," Greg said too casually. "Old Barry was bubbling over with it. We usually hire from applications or do our own search, but Barry says the company paid a whopping fee to a headhunter firm to find this one. Her name is Felice Fletcher, incidentally. Barry says...'' He paused uncomfortably. "Barry says management, by which he means Marshall, intends to groom her for great things.''

"Is she pretty?'' Jill surprised herself by asking. *What a dumb thing to ask. Okay, so maybe I'm secretly jealous.* She could feel warmth rising in her face. Greg, having noticed, smiled smugly.

"Not pretty, exactly. More like beautiful, but...''

"But what?'' She couldn't help smiling in return, feeling a wave of happiness. It had been a while since she and Greg had bantered this casually. It must have been the prime rib.

"Beautiful in a kind of...well, *sleek* is the only word I can come up with. She's flawlessly blond, flawless skin. Flawless features. Flawless everything. And I think here I hit the snag. She's so flawless that a guy...well, a guy wouldn't know what to touch. I mean, a guy would just *know,* looking at her, that messing up her hair would be a capital offense, know what I mean? Messing up...your hair isn't...a capital offense.''

She saw the sudden flare of desire in his eyes, and her heart thudded in response. *Come back to me, Greg. Let it be like old times.*

"Do you really want coffee tonight?'' he asked, pushing aside his own cup, his eyes holding hers.

"No...not really,'' she answered, reaching out to him.

The next morning Jill had a few minutes alone after Greg and the kids left the house and she went over his review of their finances. It was sobering. He spent *that* much on the boat? Then farther down the page. Good grief! She spent *that* much at the hairdresser? That couldn't be right. On the other hand, maybe it was. Greg was, after all, a CPA. He paid all the charge card bills. And let's see, about three years ago she had stopped doing her own nails. And then there were the facials. She'd have to cut all that out. There was a lot she could trim off the expenses if she stayed home. A lot. Wasn't there?

She heard the mail drop through the slot Greg had put in the heavy old front door and, seeing her mother's handwriting, she tossed aside the financial statement and snatched up her mother's letter. She'd just take time to read it. Maybe she could even call Kate about it before she left for work. Their parents had waited so long for their grand tour of Europe and they were enjoying it so much. Mom loved to travel and wrote such wonderful letters about it. She wrote about once a week and divided the letters equally between the two daughters. One to Kate. One to Jill. One to Kate. One to Jill, knowing they would share.

Mom and Dad planned to be gone about a year, because they wanted to sojourn rather than visit, lingering two weeks here, three weeks there, getting to know the place. None of this it's-Tuesday-so-this-must-be-Belgium for Mom and Dad.

Jill ripped open the letter and scanned through it. They were in Germany...the Black Forest...food marvelous but fattening...Dad feeling a bit under the weather so they had had to miss one side trip....

Jill's brow creased in a slight frown. Dad under the weather? Dad, who hiked all the nature trails. Dad, who didn't need to see a doctor for years on end. The clock on the mantel gave its half-hour *bong* and Jill jumped. She had to get out of here.

She reached the Shack at the same time as Connie and Felix, and for some odd reason they all seemed a little embarrassed. They covered it up with laughter, making rather a big thing of getting the door open and starting on their day's work, but Jill was remembering Connie's cold, contemptuous *I think you're a fool.* And she knew Connie was remembering it, too. And Jill knew, somewhat sadly, that they would spend the day being overly gracious to each other, both trying to forget it.

Am I really a fool?

It was a fantastically good business day. *I must be a fool. This place is beginning to pay off so well. Maybe Greg is right. Maybe Laura is right. Maybe Connie is right.* Then the image of Meggie in the hospital bed pushed aside all else, even as she packed up the canvas bank bag at day's end for the night deposit drop at the bank and gave it to Felix. He took the bag, bouncing it up and down on his hand, and cleared his throat. He was going to ask about the Shack.

"Have you thought any more about the... changeover?" he asked diffidently.

"Yes," she answered steadily. "Greg worked out another financial statement. We...we're still working on it. We think, that is, he thinks, that it's do-able. Just barely. Give me a little more time. Have you and Connie thought about it?" she added as an afterthought.

His round face looked embarrassed and there was a sudden sheen of moisture in his brown eyes. "We've done nothing else," he said simply. "It would be a dream come true...that is, if you decide to go through with it. And—" He stopped, his face darkening.

"Don't be embarrassed, Felix, old buddy. This is a business deal. Speak up."

"Well, we did a little inquiring. Connie's cousin, Angel, was talking just the other day about investing. He's got some loose money. Connie was thinking that maybe he'd want to buy in…if we couldn't get all we needed from the bank. It's a thought,'' he added weakly, and Jill knew that her sudden—and silly—aversion to some outsider buying in had shown for a moment on her face. How unfair to Felix. If they wanted to buy her out, she had no business interfering in how they did it.

If she wanted to sell. She clung to that last thought. *If* she wanted to sell. She felt sick for a moment.

Greg was asleep when she got home and Jill took an hour to go over his review of their finances again. There *were* a lot of things she could cut out. It was encouraging. Somewhere she had read that two-thirds of the woman's income went into the family finances in a two-income family, the other third being used up in her work expenses. As she slashed this and that, she could well believe it. She began to get sleepy in the quiet house, and promised herself that she would go over it all again on Monday, day after tomorrow, which was her day off, when the Shack was closed.

''Mommy?''

She looked up and saw Megan in the hall doorway.

''Why aren't you in bed, punkin?'' she asked, holding out her arms. Meggie came running and Jill picked her up. She sat, half-asleep, rocking Megan, feeling a vast content engulf her. Megan, half-asleep also, was telling her something. Something about Ben crying.

''Why was Ben crying, Meggie? What was he crying about?''

'''Cause Daisy's gone.''

''Daisy's gone where?''

But Meggie only shook her sleepy head and cuddled closer. ''Di'nt come back,'' she muttered.

''Daisy didn't come back to day care?'' Jill asked, but Meggie didn't answer. Jill swallowed a bubble of laughter. Megan, their little oddball. Always asleep or awake at exactly the wrong time. She just never got it right. Then Jill was thinking of small Ben, crying for the day care Daisy, and knew she must make time to take Ben over to see Daisy. If she stayed at home she would *know* when one of the children cried. And why.

On Monday she met Greg downtown for lunch at a new coffee shop near his office. He had some papers for her. They had snatched time now and then to talk about the situation. Greg approved the cuts she had suggested in their budget, and the financial picture looked somewhat more promising. She got to the restaurant before Greg and took a table near the entrance so she could see him when he came in. When he did, she noticed his face looked strained and he hadn't gotten a haircut after she had reminded him, but she didn't mention it as he sat down, giving him a bright smile instead.

"You look tired, and it's only noon," she said. "Trouble at work?"

"Well, kind of, I guess. Mother's still pretty upset about us. She called me—she knows I don't like to take calls at the…" He paused, and Jill knew he regretted mentioning Laura, so she let it pass.

"How's your flawless blonde doing?" she asked to change the subject, and saw his mouth tighten.

"I'll forget you asked that. The lady's been on my back all morning." Greg's eyes glinted with rare anger. "I've managed to talk to both Felix and Connie," he said, changing the subject, "Their credit's okay. And they can get a good-sized chunk of money from Connie's cousin, Angel, so I think they can swing it."

Jill felt a sinking sensation in her midriff. *No, I don't want to give up my Shack.* She swallowed hard and managed to say, "Thanks, Greg. I'm sorry to put you to so much work." *I do want to give up my Shack. How else can I stay at home?* She hoped her inner conflict didn't show in her face, but Greg knew her well.

She had made opportunities to talk to the children about staying at home, not going to day care anymore, but with mixed results. Only Megan seemed to be happy about it. Day care was such a permanent part of their lives that Laurie and Ben were both wary of anything else.

"Stay at home? All the time?" Laurie had asked. "But what are we going to *do?* We don't have the right stuff here. We don't have anything to *climb* on." And Jill knew she was thinking of all the colorful state-of-the-art play equipment at the day care center.

Ben had received the news very soberly. "Will Daisy be here?" he had asked finally.

"Jill," Greg said levelly, "if you're having any second thoughts about this, for Pete's sake tell me. We've set up appointments with the lender for Felix and Connie."

"No. No, of course not. It's just that, well, any change is scary, but I've...decided. This is what I want. What I think will be best for all of us."

Greg gave a sigh that sounded like exasperation. "Okay, I've gone over everything again, the sale price, the debt, and after all bills, taxes and everything, we're getting a fairly solid chunk of money. Not nearly as much as we thought in the beginning, but something, anyhow. I'd suggest that we bank it and hold on to it for any emergency that might come up. Emergencies have a way of doing that."

"Oh, I agree," Jill said too quickly, giving up the idea of buying the coveted bright and colorful "stuff to climb on" for Greg to install in the backyard for the kids. That's what she'd have to do from now on—*cut out the impulse buying.* On the other hand, if she put it on a charge card, maybe—*cut it out, Jill.*

"Jill, come back from wherever you are. Take these papers home and look them over. And I think we'd better look at the menu, if we're going to eat." He handed her some papers and she folded them over and put them in her handbag, and picked up a menu.

"Another thing," Greg said, glancing down the line of offerings on the menu, "we're going to have to forget that we have credit cards. You do realize that, don't you?"

"Oh, yes, that's understood," she said meekly, her mind on the entrées, the content of the entrées and the price column next to them. She had already noted the coffee shop's furnishings, state of cleanliness and the waitress's attitude. *Forget it. I'm not in this business anymore.* She put the menu down suddenly, her appetite gone.

"I think I'll just have the soup and salad special," she managed to say.

Greg had only the soup and salad, too, and she bit back the impulse to urge him to eat something more. He looked thinner today, or drawn, or...something. She couldn't quite place it.

"What's-her-name, Miss Flawless. You said a while ago that she'd been on your back all morning. What did you mean?"

Greg put down his soupspoon. "Please, not while I'm eating," he said, grinning, which worried Jill even more. He was going to make a joke of it and she knew him well enough to know that it wasn't a joke.

"Seriously, is she going to be a problem?" she persisted.

"Not going to be. Is."

"She's not taking any of your big accounts, is she?"

Greg had moved up in the company in the several years he'd been there and was—or had been—thought by Carl Marshall, the owner, to be the "best." Maybe Marshall no longer thought so. *Nonsense*. Greg had had his choice of several jobs when he'd decided on Marshall's.

"No. Nothing like that." He paused, reluctant admiration showing in his eyes for a moment. "She doesn't need to. She brought in three big new accounts when she came on board. She's a real powerhouse. I've got to give her credit. No, it's just that with all this new work, we've got to expand our space for new hires. Part of another floor in the building will be available in about three months and I spent most of this morning on the phone negotiating with the building owner."

"But that's Barry Snipe's job. He's the office manager."

"Yeah, well. Miss Flawless doesn't think much of Barry. So I was pressed into service. Let's forget it, okay? This is good soup. This was only a one-time thing. I got what we needed, so that's that."

When lunch was finished and they parted at the coffeeshop door, Jill held up her face for a goodbye kiss, but Greg didn't notice. She watched him get into his car, feeling bereft. Then she went to her own minivan. They had decided to keep both his car and the minivan, expensive as it was to run two cars. If Greg made it into the vice presidency slot, he'd get a company car and they could sell his. In the meantime, with Laurie starting kindergarten in a few months, they had decided to keep the minivan.

On sudden impulse she decided to call the day care center and tell them she was going to pick up the children early. Then she'd take them over to see this Daisy. That would please Ben, at least. However, she made the mistake of calling to check her messages on her answering machine and found there were five urgent things she had to do if she was going to run the Shack until she sold it. Poor little Ben would have to wait a while.

She took care of what business she could from the phone booth, then drove home, stopping at the deli on the way. Monday-evening dinner was her responsibility. *This is the last of the expensive deli food. None of that now, Jill, old girl.* She'd better take a crash course from Kate on how to cook on the cheap.

At home she concentrated on clearing up accumulated paperwork for the Tacky Shack Café, a kind of bittersweet labor of love. About four o'clock she was finished, and she went into the big backyard and stood under their gigantic maple tree. The maple tree had been one reason they had finally decided on this house. It had been midsummer, just like today. She and Greg had stood together under its spreading branches, enjoying the shade and hearing the constant whisper of the breeze among the thousands of soaring leaves. She had been pregnant with Laurie.

"Our kids will love this," Greg had said, looking up into the vast greenness of it. "Maybe I'll build them a tree house. Kids love tree houses."

But the maple tree, when they got to know it, showed them its bad side.

"Well, nothing's perfect," Greg said as they spent hours raking fallen leaves every autumn. "I grew up in an apartment, so how was I to know? Anyway, they turn a pretty color, if we want to look on the bright side."

And Laurie still had small scars on her left arm where metal pins had been removed after her broken arm had healed. She had managed to climb up into the tree, but couldn't climb down and had fallen.

Jill stood under it now, listening as they had that first

day to the faint and constant whispering of the leaves. *Oh, dear God, let me be doing the right thing.* Her sudden instinctive prayer halted and she was embarrassed. *I'm sorry, God, I should have asked You first maybe, but please, let this be right.*

Back inside her home she was seized with an urgency to *clean.* Let this be the beginning. She hurried to the closet where the cleaning things were kept, took out the vacuum cleaner and worked as if possessed.

When Greg came home with the children from day care, the living-room and dining-room furniture gleamed dustless and polished, with the faint lemony scent of furniture polish still in the air.

"Boy, what a transformation," Greg said, looking around. "You've got it looking like a model home." He put Megan down.

"And we've got roast ham for dinner, sweet potatoes and the most beautiful-looking salad you've ever seen. And we can have that other rhubarb pie. I took it out of the freezer."

"Oh, this is wonderful," Greg said, grinning.

Jill's heart lifted. This was the way it would always be now. Everything in order. Everything right. It was going to work out fine.

"Mommy," Ben said, "where's my blocks?" He was looking around the immaculate living room, a puzzled frown on his small face. "I have my blocks *here.*" He indicated the corner of the living-room carpet.

"Ben, sweetheart, I put them in your toy box. You know that nice toy box Grandmother gave you for Christmas."

"My blocks in the *toy box?*" Ben said in disbelief, and both Jill and Greg started to laugh.

"Wow," Greg said, "Toys in the toy box. What's the

world coming to? You've got your work cut out for you, Jill.''

It was the best evening they had had for a long time, and Jill reveled in it. They resolved two minor crises during dinner. Ben was persuaded that it was okay to keep his toys in the toy box, and if he did Santa would remember. And Laurie was ecstatic when Greg promised her he would hang two swings from the maple tree, and think about building a playhouse.

In the days that followed, Jill held on to the memory of that perfect evening. Business was such a grind of niggling little details. The bank was working its cautious way through the sale of the Tacky Shack Café from one owner to another.

Felix seemed torn between a kind of panic at becoming an owner and fear that she'd change her mind at the last minute. Connie vacillated between being embarrassingly humble and stridently testy.

"Look," Jill said in exasperation one afternoon, "it's a done deal, Connie. Don't sweat it. Felix isn't going to be cheated out of entrepreneurship. It's the bank. Banks are slow. S-l-o-w is one way to spell bank." And Connie had gone all humble again.

"I'm sorry, Jill." She was almost crying. "It's just that this has been Felix's dream for so long and...and..."

Then suddenly Jill knew that Felix, overweight, complaining, middle-aged Felix, had a wife who loved him to distraction. Well, who could understand the odd ways of the human heart?

"And I don't want anything to mess it up," Connie had finished. It came out then, in a rain of tears, that Felix and her cousin, Angel, didn't get along very well. Felix was a passionate cook. When the recipe called for butter, Felix would die before substituting anything else. That was one reason the Shack was so successful. The food was excellent. Now it seemed that Angel wanted to cut corners to increase the margin of profit even more, and Felix was having none of it.

No way, Jill thought. *I'll just put a stop to that.* Then she recalled that it wasn't her fight anymore.

The bank, with glacial slowness, finally closed the deal and they all sat around in the bank's office, smiling and congratulating one another and signing a multitude of forms. She hoped Greg understood them all, as she lost track of things, wondering for the thousandth time if she was making a mistake. And, of course, there were some unexpected costs, so there wasn't as much left over as Greg and she had expected, but at last it was over.

They even got to meet Connie's cousin, Angel, briefly, because he had to sign his share of documents. He was a lean, nervous man, and excused himself as soon as he could. Connie explained him in one rather testy comment.

"Angel never has any time. He's working two jobs. He wants to be a millionaire before he's thirty."

Even with Angel's money, Felix was short a few thousand, and Jill had agreed to take a promissory note on which Felix would make monthly payments. She was determined to put these right into their emergency fund.

Greg had taken the morning off work, and they finished at the bank just before noon. Jill, feeling a mixture of excitement and fear plus regret at giving up her business, wanted desperately some time alone, but this was not to be. It appeared that Felix, euphoric and beaming with goodwill, had stayed up half the night preparing a grand luncheon, which they were all to enjoy over at the Tacky Shack Café. Oliver and Herbie, he told them, were even now waiting to serve it to them.

Oh, no, I can't go back, Jill thought in panic, and Greg,

sensing her emotion, took hold of her hand, holding it tightly, giving her the courage to paste on a big smile and pretend enthusiasm.

"Felix! What a wonderful idea! What a lovely gesture."

Somehow she got through it, determined not to spoil Felix's sheer joy at being host, trying not to notice when Greg twice sneaked a look at his watch, knowing he wouldn't let Felix down, either, but that he was desperate to get back to his job, which was now their only livelihood.

The lavish luncheon finally ended about four o'clock, and they were able to leave after prolonged farewells and promises to keep in close touch.

After Jill dropped Greg off at his office it was almost time to pick up the children from day care. It was their last day. She found that the day care manager had given the Rhys children a little going-away party. There had been games and prizes, ice cream and cake, and farewell songs. The kids were elated at having been the center of attention and clambered into the minivan joyfully. Nobody would want much dinner tonight. Jill headed the minivan toward home, feeling slightly sick.

This is it, Jill, old girl. Sink or swim.

Tuesday morning at eight-thirty, half an hour after Greg had left for work, the toilet in the children's bathroom ran over, flooding out into the hallway carpet because Ben had tried to "fix it" by flushing it again and again. Jill worked for a frantic sweating thirty minutes with their trusty plunger, hoping to drag up one of Megan's cuddle toys. What the plunger did drag up defeated her, and she called Greg at the office, something she had promised herself she would not do in her new homemaker role. But she had also promised Greg that she wouldn't spend any of their emergency fund without talking it over with him first. When he answered he sounded in a hurry, so she didn't mince words.

"The maple tree has struck again, Greg. We've got our first emergency. The kids' bathroom toilet is stopped up and all I can get up with the plunger is tree roots."

She heard him mutter something. Then he said aloud, "Okay. That's what the emergency fund is for. You'll have to call a plumber and we'll hope for the best."

At seven o'clock that evening, under the benign-looking maple tree, she and Greg were standing by the trench being dug across the backyard from the house to the alley. The tree's strong roots had simply crushed their way into the outlet pipe connecting their house with the city sewer system.

"How much do you think it will be?" Greg asked.

The plumber shook his head, wiping sweat off his face. "I'll have to figure out your estimate, but it won't be cheap."

Jill wanted to cry. This was certainly not a good start. Sobered by this big expense, they went back into the house after the plumber had covered the trench with boards and put up his yellow flickering warning lights.

"What are we doing for bathroom facilities?" Greg asked.

"Next door," Jill said tiredly. "I never really got acquainted with her before. Her name's Mrs. Hopkins. She's offered her downstairs bathroom. When you want to shower, I'll show you. I've already bathed and fed the kids." She sat down at the kitchen table. They could hear the children squabbling in Ben's room. The TV was on too loud.

It had been a chaotic day. Greg had worked late at the

office. She looked at him blankly for a moment, standing uncertainly in the kitchen doorway. She was so tired she couldn't think straight.

"I'm sorry," she said quickly. "You haven't had any dinner, have you? Neither have I, come to think of it." She had wanted nothing so much as to get the children fed and ready for bed, and wanted now only to fall into bed herself.

"Forget it," Greg said, "It's okay. You've had a rough day." He sounded remote, as if to distance himself from the confusion. "I think I'll go down to the boat for a while. I'll pick up some fish and chips down at the marina. I have some reports to read through."

Oh, Greg, please don't go. "Okay, thanks," she said through stiff lips. "Things will be better tomorrow." But he didn't hear. He was already out the back door.

Chapter Four

By September Jill had come to the realization that stay-at-home mommies worked their heads off and never *finished* anything. Her respect for day care workers rose. In late July she had finally taken Ben to visit Daisy, and benefited from it. Daisy had given her some helpful hints on keeping children amused and busy. Reassured that the Rhys family wasn't going to press charges for the van incident with Megan, she was pathetically grateful, although she wasn't sure she'd ever go back into day care work. She mentioned that she might work with the elderly, but hadn't decided. She herself was beyond middle age and had gone back into the workplace after not having worked for years. She didn't volunteer why, and Jill didn't ask.

"Children are too much responsibility," she had said, stroking Megan's dark hair, and Jill silently agreed, looking at her three. These three small human beings might succeed or fail in life depending on how she, Jill, handled their childhood. It was a sobering thought.

"They've only got one childhood. Give them enough

to play with,'' Daisy had said, and Jill thought again about some play equipment for the backyard.

Then, heedless of repercussions, she had plunged ahead and bought what she thought they needed. A sandbox, slide and climbing bars. They all came in large boxes of unassembled pieces with little plastic bags of nuts, bolts and screws that only Greg would be able to cope with. He was furious, and it led to an ugly quarrel with him after the children were in bed.

''We had *agreed* not to charge,'' he reminded her. Like Laura, when he was deeply angry, there was a little white area around his mouth.

''But Greg, it was on *sale. Half price.* I couldn't pass it up.''

''We can't *afford* it, Jill. Not unless we use Felix's monthly payment,'' he retorted. ''And we decided not to do that. That money was going into our reserve fund—which, I might remind you, isn't as big as it was by a long shot due to the plumbing bill.'' They were getting ready for bed and he was sliding his muscular arms into the sleeves of his pajama top.

''But the kids already know the stuff is here,'' she said helplessly.

''I'm not sending it back, Jill. I wouldn't do that to the kids. They don't understand about money, but you can't just spend on impulse. Ever again. We had a deal, and you didn't keep your end of it.''

''You don't have to stay home all day with three whining children who have nothing to do,'' she snapped, stung by his criticism.

He didn't say a word, just turned and looked at her steadily, and she could feel her face flaming in embarrassment. ''I'm sorry,'' she faltered. ''I know staying at home was my idea, but...but...''

"I'll put the stuff together this weekend," he said coldly, buttoning his pajama top. "I can't do it any evening, because I've got to put in some overtime. But *don't*, I repeat *don't*, blow any more money without checking with me first."

"I won't. I promise," she said humbly, hoping the quarrel hadn't wakened Meggie.

After they were in bed she tried to keep some conversation going. They shouldn't end the day in anger.

"Why do you have to do so much overtime? Isn't Miss Flawless doing her share?"

"Miss Flawless is doing more than her share," Greg answered and, after a moment, added, "What ever happened to that navy blue suit I had?" He paused, waiting, and Jill's heart plummeted.

"The navy blue? Oh, Greg, I gave it to Goodwill months ago. You almost never wore it, so…"

"Okay, it doesn't matter." He turned away from her to face the wall.

"You didn't like it much," she murmured.

"It's okay. Forget it," he muttered. "Good night."

The *good night* meant keep quiet. He wanted to sleep, but she didn't. She knew that he lay quietly beside her, thinking his own thoughts, shutting her out. Well, she deserved it. She should never have spent so much money. Not after the plumbing bill. Not after she had promised. But he needed a couple of new suits. Did she dare mention it? He mustn't look shabby at work. He must be feeling shabby, or he wouldn't have asked about the navy suit. She had always bought his clothes for him, and the navy blue had been her one failure.

Greg worked almost all day Saturday at his office, but spent most of Sunday putting together the play equipment. It was all in wild happy colors. The children were enchanted with the vivid purple of the sandbox, the red-and-yellow slide and the multicolored climbing bars. He had even brought thin, tough rope from the marina and bought two slabs of wood for swing seats, so he could hang side-by-side swings from the biggest branch of the maple tree, commenting that the tree could start earning its keep.

They painted the wooden swing seats during the long summer twilight evening, after the children were asleep.

"This place is beginning to look like Kiddyville," Greg said, looking around at the bright play equipment, wiping his paint-stained hands on a rag.

"Yes, it is. I really appreciate this, Greg. And I'm sorry..."

"Forget it, Jill. It's history." He spoke politely but with an edge. "You don't need to grovel just because we had a fight."

An awkward silence fell. It was a beautiful night. The sunset was magnificent. She looked at him in the failing daylight, filled with longing so deep she couldn't speak. *This man is the love of my life. Oh, thank you, God. What would I have done if I hadn't found him? Thank you. Thank you.* A sudden impromptu prayer always filled her with a kind of serenity. God was, after all, not so very far away if you just asked.

"Let's sit out here a while in the cool," Greg said, sitting down on one of the lawn chairs. "These could sure use another coat of paint, too," he added as she joined him. "You know, I was talking to Barry Snipe today. Barry always looks good. He's a sharp dresser. And he told me today that he buys most of his clothes—that's suits, topcoats, all but his shirts—from some thrift shop. Would you believe it?"

Thrift shop.

Jill froze, her serenity shattered.

"Oh, Greg, no! You can't do that!" And suddenly she was crying desperately. *My husband must not wear secondhand clothing. Oh, dear God, what have I done? I should have kept working.* She got up to run into the house, but Greg caught her.

"Hey, come on. It's no big deal. Garments are garments. Cloth is cloth. Didn't Kate tell us that she goes to thrift shops all the time?" He was holding her loosely.

"But for the kids," she gasped. "I think she meant just stuff for the kids to play in. I don't...I don't want you to wear somebody's *castoffs.*"

He put his arms more closely about her, holding her close, murmuring comforting words into her hair. "Yeah, but just suppose the previous owner is some rich guy who has tailor-mades out of thousand-dollar-a-yard cloth and just happens to be my exact size, what then?"

"Don't joke about it! Please!"

"Okay, if you feel like that," he said quietly. "We'll forget it. I can make do with what I have for the time."

"But you shouldn't have to make do. I told you months ago that you needed some new office suits. Why didn't we get them then? Can't we get them now? We could use the rest of Felix's payment. Please, can't we do that?"

He strained to see her tear-wet face in the failing light. "This really matters to you, doesn't it?"

"It *matters!*" she said fervently.

He shrugged. "Okay, let's see what you can get for me with what's left of the payment."

"Next month we'll put the payment away in the reserve fund. I promise."

She knew that trying to shop with three children in tow was the slowest possible way to do it, so she took the time to drive across Seattle to leave them with Kate while she shopped for Greg's suits.

Suit.

She hadn't done this for a while, and she discovered that prices had gone up alarmingly. She settled for one good suit, of a gray she thought might be a close match for his eyes, and waited during the lunch hour for the alterations—she knew his measurements by heart. Then she went victoriously back to Kate's to pick up the children.

Kate and all the children admired Greg's new suit and Kate made her a belated lunch of a peanut-butter-and-jelly sandwich and some fresh apricots from her backyard tree.

"I'm reading between the lines here, but things aren't going too well, are they?" Kate asked during the lunch.

Jill's guard came up immediately. "Well, it takes a little getting used to. It's such a drastic change from what I've been...used to." Suddenly the delicious apricot didn't seem as good as it had, and she put down the un-eaten half.

"You've been at it almost three months now, haven't you?" Kate said, picking up the plate and putting it into the sink. "You should be settling into it pretty soon." She came back and sat down opposite Jill.

"Actually, I think I'll make it okay," Jill finally said, "But I had no idea that I couldn't just jump in and...and...*do it*. It's odd, but when I was away working all day, sometimes I just...what can I say...just *yearned* to be with my children. If maybe Laurie had a skinned knee. Or maybe I was remembering Ben being so sweet. Or something. Now..."

"And now," Kate said reasonably, "you have them twenty-four hours a day, and they drive you up the wall. Join the club." They both had to laugh.

"Sometimes I just *die* for someone to *talk to*... someone *grown up*."

"I wondered why you were calling me so often these days. Believe me, we've never been so close before," Kate said, her voice warm with understanding. "Can you talk to Greg about it?" She let it rest there, having seen something in Jill's face that stopped her.

"Look, I've got an idea," she said hurriedly. "That gray suit just pleads for a silk tie, a really good one, and I have just the thing. Follow me!"

"You've got what?" Jill asked, surprised, and after a quick look into the backyard at the children playing there she followed Kate into her bedroom.

"Yes, it's one of Claude's." She turned back to look at Jill, half embarrassed, half defiant. "After...after Claude died I...couldn't get rid of all his things right away. I know that was dumb, but I just...couldn't." Even now, five years later, there was for a moment sharp grief in her eyes. "So I hung on to just this one tie." She led Jill over to the chest of drawers and opened one, rummaging beneath a stack of clean worn underwear, and pulled out a thin tissue-wrapped parcel. Taking it over to the bed, she unwrapped it carefully, revealing a silk tie in several muted shades of blue, burgundy and gray.

"This was the most expensive tie Claude ever had. He never actually wore it. He was...saving it for something special." She handed it to Jill.

Jill took it almost reverently. "But you kept it all these years. Are you sure you want to..."

"Yes, of course. I can handle it now...life goes on. And it'll look great with Greg's new suit."

"Do you mind if I tell Greg?"

"No. By all means tell him. I want him to treat that tie with respect."

"Thank you," Jill said, knowing it was not enough. *Oh, thank you, God, for Kate.*

She and Kate waited on the back step another half hour while the children finished some complicated game they had devised. The game organizer was a child Jill had not seen before.

"Who's the fair-haired kid?" she asked. "Isn't he older than the others?"

"Yes," Kate answered, sounding fond. "That's Raymond McAllister from next door." She indicated the larger house to the left of hers. "The McAllisters are divorced, and Raymond lives with his father, Ian, and a series of live-in housekeepers. The last housekeeper but one that Ian hired was a real dragon. Raymond was afraid of her. I found him one night hiding under this back step, afraid to go home. He hadn't had any dinner. The housekeeper kept calling him and getting madder and madder. I've kind of taken him in. Needless to say, Ian got a new housekeeper as soon as he got back from a business trip."

"It doesn't bother him to play with younger kids?"

"Doesn't seem to. He's eleven, I think, but a very young eleven. And he's such a lonely, solitary little kid. I encourage him to come over here."

How typical of Kate, Jill thought, getting up, as the game seemed to be finishing with all the children falling down on the ground and lying there as if frozen.

"Come on, kids," Jill said. "We have to beat the traffic going home."

The following Thursday Jill called Kate three times before she finally got an answer.

"Where have you been?" Jill asked. "You're usually home mornings."

"Right." Kate sounded winded. "But that was before

my washer went kaput. For the last time. It's absolutely
dead. So I take the heavy stuff over to Mom's house to
use her washer and dryer. I know the neighbors are watching out for the house while Mom and Dad are gone, but
it's good to have someone in and out. So that's what I'm
doing now. The little stuff I just wash in the tub on the
back porch.''

"By *hand!*''

Kate laughed. "Of course by hand. Women have
washed by hand for centuries. I'll survive.''

It was on the tip of Jill's tongue to say, "I'll get you
a new washer,'' but she bit it back. She couldn't. There
was no way now that she could help out Kate financially
anymore. The idea stunned her. She felt a moment of
frustrated anger. *But I've always had my own money.* And
oddly, she felt angry at Greg, knowing it was unfair.

"Jill? Are you still there? If you're thinking what I
think you're thinking, forget it. I'm doing fine. Don't
worry about it. I'll figure something out. There's a place
over in Ballard that has rebuilt washers and dryers. I'm
going to check it out. Now, don't worry, Jill.''

But Jill did worry. Never had she felt so helpless, so
frustrated. She was impatient with the children and short
with Greg that evening when he reminded her of his quarterly company dinner, which they would have to attend.
They'd have to get a sitter for that evening. She didn't
want to go to the company dinner. She didn't want to get
a sitter. Maybe she'd just drive the kids across town and
leave them with Kate. But if she did, Ben would get upset.
He didn't want to sleep anywhere but in his own bed, and
if he was this set in his ways at four years old, what would
he be at fifty? She was barely able to be civil to Greg
during dinner and, perversely, was angry when he left for
the marina shortly afterward.

Sitting alone in the living room, after the children were down for the night, Jill brooded. *I can't go on like this. I have to have my own money. I have to be somebody. They all were right. I'm wasting myself.*

What would happen if she took enough money out of the bank to buy Kate a *brand-new* washer? Not some rebuilt relic. She was startled out of her angry fantasy by the phone ringing, and she dived for it before it could wake Meggie.

"Hello?" she said in a guarded tone.

"Hi. It's me, Felix. Why are you talking in such a low voice?"

"I don't want Megan to wake up. I just got the kids down for the night."

"Oh, well, I see. How're you doing?"

"Felix, don't ask. This is not a good time. How are you doing?" It was good to hear Felix's voice. She missed him, missed them all. A silence stretched out at the other end of the line. "Felix? You did call me, you know. Why don't you say something? Is something wrong?"

"Uh...not really. Is Greg there?"

"Of course not. He's down at his stupid boat. Where else?"

"Can I...come and see you for a little while?" He sounded very tentative. How odd. They'd been friends for a long time.

"Of course you can. When did you want to come?" That would be nice, seeing Felix again. She had deliberately avoiding going to, or near, the Shack, for her own reasons.

"Now. Uh...I'll be right there. I'm out front. I'm calling on the car phone." And it was only moments until she heard his heavy tread on the front steps. She flung open the door and put her arms around him. "Felix. It's so good to see you. What can I get you? Do you want some coffee?"

"No, really I'm about coffeed out. I've been..." He paused, and his large dark eyes seemed to have tears in them.

"Felix, is anything wrong with Connie? The children?" she asked anxiously.

"Oh, no." He sat down on the couch and leaned back with a shaky sigh. "They're all fine, it's just... Did anybody ever tell you that running a restaurant is a tough job?"

In spite of herself she felt a small thrill of satisfaction. *Now* they knew how hard she had worked, how much she had contributed to the Tacky Shack's success. "What's wrong, exactly?"

"Ah, I knew you'd be right on target. *Exactly* what's wrong I can't tell you. It seems to be a million things I can't really put my finger on. I guess part of it is Angel. He's always on my back about 'profit margin.' And then Connie had a fight with the new hostess and fired her. And Oliver quit—did you know Oliver has picked up a good basketball scholarship? Well, he has, so he quit and Angel doesn't want me to replace him. He says we don't need two kitchen helpers. Jill, I can't seem to *manage* and *cook* at the same time." He looked as if he were about to cry. "And that's not the worst of it."

"What could be worse than that?" she asked, patting his plump hand.

"Even with all the work, and the hassle I...the profits just aren't adding up the way they did when you were in charge. I'm going to need some...uh...time on this month's payment to you folks."

Jill's heart sank. "But you paid the bank, didn't you? They could foreclose. We wouldn't."

"I know. That's what makes me feel so rotten. Jill, you're the best friend I ever had...." He stopped, because he couldn't seem to continue without breaking down. "I don't want to stiff my best friend, but..."

"How...late do you think you will be?" Jill asked, feeling a hollow pit in her stomach. This was the payment she had promised Greg would go right into the reserve fund.

Felix's face became a dull mottled red. "Jill, I don't think I can actually make the payment this month. I'll try to make it up as soon as I can. We've got four parties booked, and..."

"Okay," she said steadily. "If that's it, then that's it." She was filled with dread at having to tell Greg. "See if you can do better next month."

"It's just a temporary setback," Felix said, almost pleadingly, but Jill wondered sickly if it was. Maybe Felix and Connie couldn't make it as owners. Maybe the restaurant would fail, go broke, out of business. The very idea made her want to scream.

Not if I were there.

It took all her self-control to assure Felix that it was okay, and to try to encourage him a little. He looked so beaten, so defeated. *He mustn't fail.*

She spent the next hour discussing the Shack's problems and giving advice. *Terrific,* she thought. *I'm managing a restaurant once removed, and not getting a dime for it.*

When Greg came home about midnight she was still sitting hunched over in the chair, her head in her hands. She looked up at him. The living room was dimly lit with one lamp but the porch light was still on behind him, which made a kind of halo of his blond hair. He came in.

"Why do I get the feeling that if I say one word you'll

snap my head off?'' He reached over and turned off the porch light. ''Did something happen while I was gone to make you feel worse than you felt when I left?''

''Yes,'' she said dully. ''And I may as well give it to you straight. Felix has to skip this month's payment.''

''Well, that's giving it to me straight, all right.'' He sat down on the couch where Felix had sat. ''What's his problem?''

''Money problems,'' she snapped, hating herself.

''I think I had already guessed that.'' His voice held a sarcastic edge that was becoming more familiar. Greg never used to be sarcastic. ''And since we're in the pits, I may as well tell you something I held back from telling you at dinner. The insurance company raised the car insurance premiums.''

''*Why* did they raise the premium?'' Jill fairly shouted.

''Jill, calm down. They don't tell you why. They just send the bill.''

''Mommy?''

Jill looked over and saw Megan standing in the doorway to the living room, and wanted to scream at her. ''Will you do something about Meggie?'' she asked Greg tightly, gripping her hands into fists.

''Sure,'' Greg said, getting up. ''Look on the bright side. At least she's got her nightgown on. You don't have to go looking for it.''

''Don't be funny!''

Greg ignored that and picked up Megan. ''What do you want, Meggie? Want me to read you a story?''

''*Green Eggs and Ham,*'' Megan answered promptly.

''I never would have guessed. Good old Dr. Seuss. I don't know if you know this or not, Jill, but I don't read that story. I recite it while Meggie turns the pages. I know it by heart.''

"Tell me about it. You think I don't read the stupid thing to her?"

"Let's just say that our youngest is developing great listening skills."

"Well, I wish she'd listen to something else," Jill said sullenly, but Greg was already gone.

She thought about Kate again. She'd rarely seen her sister lose her patience with her children. And why did Kate have to be so *cheerful* about being permanently hard up? Why didn't she find some part-time job to increase her income? Angry tears seeped out of Jill's tightly shut eyes. *This is awful. This isn't the way I planned it. What am I going to do?*

At breakfast Greg was still in his cool, remote mode. Well, she guessed she deserved it. After he had gone and she had shooed the children into the backyard to play, she continued to sit at the uncleared kitchen table. *This is it, Jill, old girl, You made your bed. Now lie in it.* And that didn't seem like such a bad idea. She would not, repeat not, turn on the TV and watch the mindless spill-your-guts TV talk shows, or soap operas. *Never.* Laura had stopped by several times during the day, ostensibly to see the children, but Jill was sure she was checking up.

She got up from the kitchen table, feeling tired, and went into the bedroom and lay down on the still-unmade bed, running her hand over the side where Greg had slept. *How can I be tired? I've only been up a couple of hours.* For a while she idly watched the ceiling. *Okay, Jill, the ceiling isn't going to do a single interesting thing. Get up. You have chores to do. You are a charwoman now. You are a baby-sitter. Go char and sit. That's your career.*

She sat up with an effort. Greg had left the closet door open again. You would think that a CPA could remember to shut the closet door. And what was she going to wear to Greg's office party? Greg's firm always had very dress-up affairs. *Nothing new, Jill. You can bet your discarded checkbook on that.* She'd better have Greg's tux cleaned. *Oh, these important decisions. For this I went to college. For this I beat my brains out learning.*

She went to the closet and began pushing garments this way and that. Something she hadn't worn to the dinner before. Let's see. Ah. She snatched out the ivory satin evening suit, actually a slim sheath dress with a short jacket with little pearls on the lapels. And when the jacket was off it was just a lovely shimmering sheath with spaghetti straps. *You have such beautiful shoulders, Jill,* Greg had said so many times, running little rows of kisses along them. She paused, half smiling. And the sheath was so short. Great. Greg always said she had such terrific legs.

It might be kind of fun. She hadn't been dressed up, really dressed up, for weeks. She'd worn T-shirts or cotton tops over her oldest, raggediest jeans. She stripped them off and tossed them onto the bed. If she'd lost weight with all the physical work she'd been doing maybe it wouldn't fit right. She started sliding into the sheath, but something was wrong. The ivory satin stopped at her waist and would go no farther. She'd *put on* weight! She struggled out of the sheath and ran into the bathroom to get on the scale. *Eight* pounds. Oh, no! And every ounce of it on her hips. Impossible!

And why is that, Jill? Could it be the snack crackers? The peanut butter sandwiches in the middle of the afternoon because you are bored? Is that it, Jill? But you can't possibly be bored, not a dedicated homemaker like you. Because you chose this life.

She sat down on the side of the tub, still holding the crumpled ivory sheath. *What am I going to wear?* Near panic, she rushed back into the bedroom and tried on everything in her side of the closet. It wouldn't matter if she had worn it to the last office party, if only she could just get it on. How much time did she have? How long did it take to lose eight pounds if you didn't eat at all?

She pulled out something in watermelon pink. She looked good in warm colors. It went on easily. Too easily. It was the one maternity dress she hadn't given away after her pregnancy with Megan.

She stood before the mirror, looking at herself. She needed her hair styled, or at least cut. It looked long and shaggy. Unkempt. And she would *not* pull it back and hold it with a rubber band, as Kate did. *Never.* She peered closer, examining her skin. There was a sound behind her, and she heard Ben.

"Mommy?"

She whirled around. *"What?"*

Ben stood just inside the door, holding something out to her, blinking in surprise. "I made you something," he said hesitantly, holding out a tight little bunch of dandelions, tied together with a string. Laurie was right behind him.

"Ben, dandelions are weeds. Don't you know the difference between a weed and a flower?"

"Never mind," Jill said carefully. "Thank you, Ben. They're beautiful." She reached out and took them. "Let's not quibble, Laurie. A yellow flower is a yellow flower. Come on, I'll put them in water. I have just the thing." The two followed her into the kitchen, where she took down a small juice glass for the dandelions, her throat aching because Ben looked confused and uneasy, not sure what he had done wrong.

She made a great business of pushing aside the dirty

breakfast dishes and putting the tiny arrangement in the exact center of the table, admiring it extravagantly.

"Thank you, Ben. That was very nice of you to get Mommy this. You're a good boy. I'm very lucky to have you."

"I got it for you because you're—" he paused, struggling for a moment "—because you're not glad today."

No, I am not glad today. Out of the mouths of babes.

"Well, I'm glad now. That's just what I needed." And she was rewarded by Ben's sudden sunny smile, which lit his whole little face.

"Okay, then," he said, heading for the door. "I'm gonna go swing awhile." And he was gone, slamming the door behind him.

Laurie was looking at her with a puzzled expression. "Why are you dressed like that, Mommy? You were dressed regular before. When we ate."

"I was just trying on some clothes, to decide what to wear to Daddy's office party. Now, why don't you go outside with Ben, sweetheart, and let Mommy get into the day."

"Well, okay," Laurie said, still looking slightly worried.

When she had followed Ben out, Jill stood at the kitchen window for a moment, watching them. Meggie in the sandbox, which she loved, soberly filling her little bucket with sand, patting it down, and then carefully dumping it out again in some little game of her own devising. Both Ben and Laurie were swinging from the maple tree. *Beautiful children.*

There was the sudden whirring buzz of the doorbell. *Terrific.* She ran pell-mell into the bedroom and struggled back into her jeans as the buzz came again. Now she recognized these old jeans. She had worn them in her freshman year at college while she was feasting on burgers and fries and chocolate shakes. B.G. Before she had met Greg and taken an interest in her appearance, beginning a relentless weight-loss plan.

The doorbell rang a third time.

Chapter Five

"Coming!" Jill called as she buttoned her blouse and got to the front door to open it. The man, who had started to leave, turned back and smiled.

"Hi. I'm Brian Bailey." He held out his hand. He was of medium height, fortyish, with a somewhat tanned, outdoorsy look. "And you have to be Jill Rhys. I was prompted to call by my friend and colleague, Cyrus Ledbetter, your sister Kate's pastor."

"Uh, yes. Come in." Oh, why had Kate done this? She and Greg *had* a church affiliation, even if they seldom attended anymore, and she had never heard of this Brian Bailey. Their pastor was named...what? For a moment she couldn't recall, then she did. "We're not the most regular churchgoers, I'm afraid, but our pastor is William Gibbs."

"I know. I'm his successor. He's retired. About six months ago, I think."

Jill felt herself flushing. Had it been that long? "I didn't know. As I said, we...we are kind of irregular about getting out Sunday mornings. Please sit down."

"Thanks," he said. "I know it's a bit early for a call." He glanced at his watch. "But I figured ten o'clock was okay and I wanted to check in with you."

Ten o'clock. Good grief, and nothing done yet. The breakfast dishes, all the housework and then dinner to fix, plus the thousand interruptions by the children, which now made up her days.

"When Cyrus mentioned you to me I looked into the church membership roster and there you and Greg were, and the children. How're they doing?"

"Oh, fine. They're out in back now playing." Kate really shouldn't have sicced the clergy onto her. She had enough to cope with.

Pastor Bailey leaned forward, his elbows on his knees, and looked at her. He had nice eyes. Kind. "I don't mean to intrude, which is what I sense that I'm doing, but Cyrus said you had tackled something new for you, this stay-at-home-mom business. We've got three young mothers in the parish in the same fix, so I know it has its problems."

Jill felt herself stiffen. *I'm okay. I don't need help. I can do it.* "It has taken some getting used to," she conceded coolly, "but actually I'm doing pretty well. Everything new has its challenges." She hoped she didn't sound too cold. He was only trying to help.

"How true. I just wanted to let you know that our young moms have formed a support group. They meet once a week, talk, share experiences, trade off babysitting." He ended on a questioning note, obviously expecting her to be interested. He was being kind, trying to offer help, but the idea horrified her. What did they do? Crochet? Knit? Trade granny's recipes? Discuss potty training? Watch soap operas together? No, thanks.

"Well, it's certainly nice of you to mention it. If I...if I feel I need that kind of...of support group, I'll call you.

Or maybe just the church office.'' A support group, indeed. That was the last thing she needed.

He stood up, perhaps sensing how unwelcome he was. ''Any chance of you and Greg stopping in some Sunday morning? We're in the same place.'' He smiled again. He did have a nice smile. ''And next Sunday we start the fall Sunday school classes for the children.''

''Yes, there's a good chance,'' Jill said. ''We were talking about it just the other day. When we were both working it just didn't seem possible. And I used to work Sundays, too. But now I'm not.''

''Good. Keep it in mind,'' he said cheerfully. ''We've got a really great fall program in place for the kids.''

After she had seen him out, she leaned tiredly against the front door. No, she wouldn't call Kate and tell her off. No point in getting into an argument. Kate had meant well.

Maybe they ought to get back to church, though. And enrolling the children in the Sunday school classes was a good idea. It would give them something else to be interested in. No, scratch that. There were better reasons than that to send kids to Sunday school. She heard the back door slam and the sound of small feet running. She could tell it was Laurie. Now what?

''Mommy! Come quick! Ben's bleeding!''

Jill leapt into action, rushing toward the back, meeting Ben coming in the back door, holding a cut finger in the palm of his other hand.

''Stay outside, Ben!'' Laurie shouted. ''Don't bleed on the floor! Bleed outside!''

''No, Laurie. It's all right. Come here, Ben.'' Jill picked him up and headed for the bathroom medicine cabinet.

It was a rough day, but by the time Greg got home the house was fairly presentable and she had prepared a fairly good dinner. True, the condition of the house wasn't up to Kate's or their mother's standards, and the food wasn't as good as Felix's, but she had done it all, and she was exhausted.

Greg had called, saying he would be late again, so she had fed the children, and waited to eat with him. She was ravenously hungry but, considering the eight pounds, was determined not to snack. Seven times today she had absentmindedly opened the cupboard where she kept the snacks, and seven times she had remembered in time and shut the door. Staying at home all day was a trap, one of many traps.

Greg appeared preoccupied during the meal, and it seemed impossible to hold his attention for very long.

"Sorry? What did you say?" he asked, suddenly looking up.

"I said I got a letter from Mom today. They are in Brussels. Dad's not feeling too well and isn't really comfortable going to foreign doctors."

"Brussels. That's nice," he said absently. Then a moment later he realized what she had said. "Your dad's not well? That doesn't sound like Ralph."

"No, it doesn't. Mom seemed worried but trying to cover it up."

"Have you talked to Kate about it?"

"Uh, no, not yet." She paused, wondering if she should tell him about the pastor's visit, then decided to.

"I was a little miffed with Kate. She talked to her pastor about me...um...about me getting used to staying home. He sent over *our* church pastor, a new man named Brian Bailey." Then she told him about the support group for young stay-at-home moms. For a moment she thought she had lost his attention again, but he gave her a wintry smile.

"Who's Brian Bailey? Isn't our pastor named Gibbs?" And when she told him that Reverend Gibbs had been retired for the past six months he looked embarrassed.

"And he suggested a support group for you?" he asked with just a hint of sarcasm. "It might be a good idea, if you need such a group for what you do. Ask him if he has a support group for hassled husbands."

She put down her fork. "Are you a hassled husband?" she asked directly.

He looked embarrassed again. "Don't pay any attention to me," he said finally. "It's been a rough day."

"My day hasn't been exactly fun and games," she said tightly. And the rest of the meal was eaten in chilly silence. Later, as they were going to bed, she had second thoughts about getting angry. He looked tired, worn, strained. Maybe his day had been rougher than hers.

"Look, Greg," she said, "I'm sorry I snapped your head off at dinner. Are you having trouble at the office? Tell me. We used to be able to talk things out."

"No point in burdening you with my troubles," he said after a moment. "Nothing you can do about it." But he sounded less irritated.

"Well, what is it? At least I can sympathize."

He gave her one of his now-rare smiles. "I've passed the big three-oh and I figured this company was my permanent life career. I mean, I've been moving up in the company. I like the job. I've liked this work. I've…"

"Don't you like your job now?" She felt a small qualm of fear. *The bills. And I don't have money anymore.*

"Sure, but I've always been… Well, I was always second in charge, Marshall's right hand—his number one, he used to call me."

"And he doesn't now?" Jill's mouth was suddenly dry.

Greg shrugged. "He seems to be completely enamored of Felice."

"Felice?" For a moment Jill didn't recognize the name.

"Yeah. Miss Flawless. Felice Fletcher. And I must say," he added, "I can't fault her for anything. She's doing a spectacular job. Would it…" He sat on the edge of the bed, bent over, looking somehow defeated. "Would it bother you a lot if I…if I *don't* move up to the VP slot when Marv retires?"

A dozen ideas collided in her mind. They didn't have enough money. Felix's payments were shaky. Somehow they must save for the kids' college.

I mustn't pressure him.

"No. Not really," she heard herself saying. "It wouldn't bother me if you don't move up to be VP. We're doing okay. And we'll be doing better as I get the hang of managing the household money better. Don't worry about it. Ease up. Maybe it's just because she's…so good-looking." She got into bed and waited until he did before she reached out to switch off the light.

"She's that, all right," Greg said, turning to face the wall. "She's a real knockout."

Jill had been reaching out to him in the darkness, but stayed her hand. *Knockout?* One thing she had never had to worry about was Greg's commitment to their marriage. As perceptive as he was, he had to be aware of how attractive he was to women on the prowl, but his faithfulness and loyalty had never wavered. His intense loyalty to his mother, Laura, had been an inconvenience all during their marriage, but the flip side was that his loyalty also extended to her and the children.

Was that going to change? Was the flawless, beautiful, accomplished Felice going to find a chink in his armor?

It took Jill a long time to find sleep, and she was just beginning to doze when he turned restlessly and she knew he hadn't been asleep, either.

"Will I meet her at this upcoming office dinner?"

"Sure, she'll be sitting right at the head table. She's scheduled to speak on possible areas of company expansion."

She had to ask it. "Will you be speaking again this time? You always have."

"No," he said stonily, "I won't be speaking this time. We...won't be at the head table. We'll be sitting at one of the round tables with the rest of the staff." He paused. "Which will make it easier to dance when the music starts, if we want to look on the bright side."

"Right," she said, feeling so sorry for him that her heart ached, but mixed in with the ache was a new strange anger. Why couldn't he be more forceful? More competitive? How could he just let some new staff member move in on his prospects of promotion? He should think of the children, their future. Resolutely she pushed the thoughts aside and, after a long time, realized that she was silently praying. It made her feel a little better, and she finally went to sleep, knowing vaguely that Greg still lay tense and wakeful beside her.

Kate called the following day, and Jill felt a twinge of guilt because she hadn't called Kate as soon as she had received their mother's letter, although she was no longer irritated about Pastor Bailey stopping by.

"Have you heard from Mom?" Kate asked. "It's about time." Trust Kate to get right to the point. "She writes so on time and it's your turn to get the letter."

"Yes. I'm sorry I didn't call you yesterday. She did write."

"And how're they doing?" There was an undertone of worry in Kate's voice.

"Not good, she says. Wait a minute, I'll get the letter and read it to you. Let me turn off the kettle." Jill turned off the heat under the teakettle and searched a few minutes until she found the letter. She'd have to get better organized.

"Kate? You there?"

"Yes. What do you have the teakettle on for in the middle of the afternoon? Are you giving a tea or something?" She was laughing.

Jill laughed, too. "You're almost right. I'm making another jug of iced tea. Iced tea is a lot cheaper than a six-pack of cola. I'm learning to economize, because I drink a lot of it. I…Kate, I look awful. I've put on eight pounds. And I can't get into that ivory sheath I wanted to wear to the office party Greg's boss gives every quarter."

"What's tea got to do with it?"

"Well, tea is no-cal if I don't use real sugar. And I've cut out snacks completely and I'm always hungry. Okay, that's my secret life. Let me read Mom's letter." Jill read it, and Kate was silent for a long moment.

"Kate?"

"That's not like Dad. Dad is always so sort of trouble free." Her voice was unsteady and Jill remembered that Kate had always been Daddy's girl. "Did you answer the letter?"

"Yes. I sent it to the next stop on their itinerary. I told her to push Dad into seeing a doctor, whether he wanted to or not."

"Good. Maybe he's just bored with all the travel. You know, Mom is always the one who wanted to go to the faraway places, and now she's getting to. Maybe they're overdoing it."

The sisters were silent for a moment, then Kate spoke, somewhat hesitantly.

"Look, Jill, I did something that maybe you won't like, and I don't want you to take offence at it. You may get a call from your new pastor."

"I already have," Jill responded, half-laughing. "He came by yesterday and pitched the church's support group for mommies at home. I was offended, but I got over it."

"What offended you? The fact that I'm interfering in your life, or the fact that he came to see you?"

"Both. Plus the idea of *support group*. I hardly need that. I'm not trying to kick a drug habit. I don't know if it's luck or brains or what, but I've managed to make a fair success of my life so far. If I can start and run my own restaurant I certainly don't need other little stay-at-home mommies to tell me how to raise my children."

"Raising children is, of course, very simple. A cretin can do it." Kate's voice held a familiar warning note. "That's why there is no juvenile delinquency in this country. That's why every child is a perfect child and grows into a perfect adult. Is that what you're saying?"

"Uh…no, of course not," Jill said, suddenly embarrassed. "I guess I sounded pretty conceited. I'm sure—"

"Conceited is an understatement. Listening to you talk about your trials the other day I realized that you don't have any plan at all, any *schedule*. You simply shoo the kids outside in the morning and hope for the best. Kids need structure. Guidance. You don't have any overall plan for keeping them busy, do you?"

"Ah, I got that play set, swings, slide and—"

"And what are you doing for yourself?"

"Myself? What do you mean?"

"Jill, I know you're supposed to be the brainy sister, but are you just letting *yourself* go?"

"I just told you I've put on eight pounds, which I'm working at taking off," Jill said tightly.

"Not that," Kate said patiently. "Your mind. Your *brain*. Have you read a single book since you quit work? When the kids grow up and leave, will you have kept up with Greg? He's out in the world every day, keeping up with things. Will you be able to have an intelligent conversation with him when you are both, say, fifty, and the kids have left the nest? Or will you be one of those whiney, always-sick women, whose life is suddenly empty? You've seen those older couples eating in restaurants together, not looking at each other, not saying a word. Each isolated, living in a separate world."

Jill had a sudden recollection that Kate always had some project she was working on, or some course she was taking. She made constant use of the public library and free events in the city. She brought her attention back to what Kate was saying.

"And the other day you were saying that you might go back into business when the kids are grown, but will you even want to? Will you have lost all your self-confidence? I don't mean to rain on your parade, but we've always been honest with each other, and you've been doing this for about three months now and..." She let it rest there.

"And I guess I'm making kind of a mess of it," Jill said in a small voice, feeling suddenly hopeless.

"Look, Jill, why don't you come over today? Let's talk it out. You're so bright and I think, just maybe, you've gone into this with a kind of...well, I'll go ahead and say it, with a kind of contempt for it, as if anybody can do it. And raising kids and also continuing your own growth is not that easy. It's not fair to your kids, or to Greg, to sacrifice yourself when you're doing it. Raising kids doesn't *have* to be a sacrifice. Women can do anything they want today, and raising the kids is a *calling*, just like any other career. Can you?''

"Can I what?"

"Come over today."

"Oh, I don't know," Jill said despondently. Kate so rarely sounded off that it still had shock value, and she felt very subdued.

"Bring the ivory sheath. Maybe I can let out the seams and you can wear it after all."

That decided it. She packed up the kids and a jar of mayonnaise, which Kate was out of, and they spent the day at Kate's. There wasn't enough fabric in the sheath to let out the seams, but they had a long talk and Jill came home in midafternoon feeling subdued but encouraged and knowing one thing. She *would* look into the support group. The members were going, or had gone, through the same confusion she herself had been experiencing. She also had a packet of folders and schedules. The city offered a great variety of free or very inexpensive events for children and parents. She had been willing enough to serve a long apprenticeship of study and work before venturing into the restaurant business, and there was no reason she couldn't do the same with this mothering business.

She had resented Connie's and others' criticisms of her decision to stay at home, had been angered at their condescending attitudes, at the accusations that she was "wasting" herself. Now she realized that she had been doing the same thing. She had felt she was stepping down to stay at home, abdicating her responsibility to do more important work. *What could be more important than shaping your children's lives and training them up in the way they should go?* As much as she loved Kate, she had always faintly despised what she saw as Kate's lack of ambition, Kate's willingness to get along on so little money, or, as their late grandmother used to say, "live on the ragged edge of nothing." Now she realized for the first time that Kate saw what she was doing as a *calling*, just as important as founding and operating a business. Kate took as much trouble in planning her schedule for her children and herself as she herself had ever taken in planning her work in making the Tacky Shack Café a successful business.

Kate had said at first, "You just don't get it, do you? You haven't a clue."

Well, she had a clue now. In a special kind of way as she listened to Kate lecture, her epiphany came and she "got it." Kate, widowed, with very little money, had made a good life for herself and her children. She wasn't sacrificing anything. She was taking deep satisfaction in what she was doing now and had slowly come to terms with Claude's death. Jill knew one thing with great clarity. From now on she would do better. Much better.

Carl Marshall, head of the firm where Greg worked, paid for four expensive office parties every year, due to his conviction that it kept him in touch with his staff on a personal level and was good for staff morale. These were keyed into the changing seasons, and were usually held in a posh hotel. This would be the autumn party. It would start with an excellent dinner in a large private dining room with the tables circling a small dance floor. After dinner, selected key employees made speeches about subjects currently important to the company, and when this was over, a small group of musicians started to play dance music and those inclined danced for an hour or so. The rest lingered at tables until it was time to go, which was usually about eleven.

Jill had settled for a sleeveless pale green dress with an A-line skirt, which she dressed up a bit with a gold-toned metal belt Mom had given her last Christmas, and with the jade earrings that had been her first-anniversary present from Greg. She had splurged a bit getting her hair styled, as it had grown so long and shaggy. She felt pretty good about herself until she saw Miss Flawless, also in pale green.

The only word to describe Felice Fletcher was *elegant,* Jill thought. Or maybe *totally poised,* she added mentally as Carl Marshall introduced Felice to the assorted wives of staff. Or maybe *super intelligent,* Jill added again as Felice Fletcher made her speech about opportunities for firm expansion.

The lady had done her homework.

Jill was miserably conscious of Greg sitting next to her at one of the round tables for six that surrounded the dance floor. He ate scarcely anything, but kept up a steady stream of banter with their tablemates during the meal and between speeches. He was handling himself very well. He was such a private person that he wouldn't let any of them know how badly he felt at being sidelined. She tried to keep up her end of the table talk. A galling moment occurred when Felice thanked Greg with somewhat overdone graciousness for all his help during her settling-in period at the company.

''The transition from my other work into the work here at Marshall's would have been much more difficult without the help of Greg. He single-handedly put my office together for me. I'd say that Greg is the office *authority* on where everything is, from paper clips on up.'' This got a murmur of laughter, even if it made Greg seem like an underling. ''Stand up, Greg, and take a bow.'' Jill's throat ached, but she had to admire Greg's poise as he stood up, smiling, and gave a good-natured little wave.

As soon as the speeches were finished and the music started, Felice came straight over to their table. The men dutifully stood at her arrival. One couple left to start dancing, and Felice slid into a vacant chair next to Jill.

"I'm so fascinated by your courage, Jill," she said, smiling brilliantly. Jill wondered where she had ever seen such a sincere blue gaze before. Felice's eyes were as lovely as everything else about her. "I can't imagine giving up your *career* for the sake of the children. I know Greg must be so proud of you."

"I didn't necessarily give it up," Jill said stiffly. "I've only put it on hold. I intend to go back to work later...when it's more convenient." She was aware of Greg's intent gaze, which told her nothing, as he had that closed, remote look he sometimes assumed. He seemed to be waiting for something, expecting something. At that moment Myrna Marshall, Carl Marshall's wife, approached the table. She was a solid, heavyset woman who made no pretense about being middle-aged. Her salt-and-pepper hair looked frowsy, and she had eaten off what lipstick she had worn on her small, petulant mouth.

"Jill, dear, how good to see you," she said, resting her stubby hand on Jill's shoulder. Jill welcomed the interruption, and Felice rose gracefully from her chair.

"Sit here, Myrna," Felice said, smiling, while Myrna, stone-faced, sat down heavily. Felice turned and placed her perfectly manicured hand on Greg's arm.

"Jill, if you and Myrna are going to catch up on homemaker talk I'm going to steal Greg for a dance." She gave a throaty laugh.

"Be my guest," Jill said, feeling a ridiculous surge of pure jealousy. *Do your best, lady. I don't need to worry about Greg.* She turned deliberately and gave Myrna Marshall her complete attention. The combo had started an oldie for slow dancing.

"I wanted to talk to you, dear," Myrna was saying. "I couldn't help but hear what Felice said, and I agree. It takes pure guts to stay home and raise the children in today's world. I did it, and I've never regretted it. You did the right thing."

Pleased at the praise, Jill relaxed slightly, but she remained aware of Felice and Greg dancing together.

Jill forced herself to pay attention to Myrna, trying to remember about her children. Oh, yes, the Marshalls had two daughters, both attending university now.

"How are the girls doing at college?" she asked.

"Quite well. I miss them, of course. We're quite a close family. But it's just as well they've gone, as my health isn't what it was."

"Oh, I'm sorry to hear that," Jill said with real concern.

"Yes, I seem to have a lot of stress. I've had to go into therapy, but it doesn't seem to help much. I've just changed therapists, so that might be the answer. Then, of course, I have this ongoing weight problem, and my internist keeps at me to lose a few pounds. I think part of it may be that I just *know* that the *house* is getting on my nerves."

"The house?" Jill asked blankly.

"Yes. I spent months redecorating everything last year, and it all cost a mint, of course, but I just can't seem to *live* with it now. And Carl is no help at all. He could live in a cave or a mansion and not notice the difference."

Jill's attention had wandered back to the dance floor, but there were more couples dancing now and she couldn't see Felice and Greg. She wanted desperately to escape from Myrna, and saw the approach of Carl Marshall and Barry Snipe with relief.

"There's my girl," Carl said jovially, taking Myrna's arm. "I always have the first dance with her," he added as she stood with an effort and an expression of slight— what? Boredom? Yes, Myrna was bored. Jill knew instinctively that Carl was embarrassed by Myrna, and she went cold. *I must never be like Myrna. Greg must never be embarrassed by me.* She turned a wide smile to Barry Snipe.

"Are you going to ask me to dance?" she asked. She had always liked Barry. He was past middle age, tall with a stoop and a forward-thrust head, slightly thin on top. He had lived at home with his mother until her death seven years before and had had a series of fiancées, but relationships never seemed to work out for him. *I think they get tired of his nit-picking,* Greg had said. *I don't think he's ever paid a check in his life without adding it up again in front of the waiter. And he's a lousy tipper.*

"You bet," Barry said. "That's what I came over here for."

She got up with some relief and started dancing with him, at the same time looking for Greg and Felice and trying not to be too obvious about it.

"They're over there. Want me to dance you over?" Barry asked cheerfully, and she had to laugh. Now she saw that Felice and Greg had sat down at another table and were talking with the group there. She was slightly relieved and ashamed of herself at the same time.

"Wanna know the scoop on Miss Flawless?" Barry asked.

"Is that what you call her in the office?" she asked, suddenly recalling that Barry knew all and told all at Marshall and Associates.

"Yep. I think it was Greg who named her, and he sure called it right. The lady never makes a mistake."

Just then she saw Greg and Felice get up, leave the table and start dancing again.

"She'll make her first mistake if she doesn't stay away from my husband," Jill said. She meant it as a joke, but it sounded quite grim. This delighted Barry, and he gave a yelp of laughter.

"She certainly likes Greg," he said. "Did he tell you he had to fix up her office for her? My job, really, but I guess she thought Greg was the best man for the job."

"I thought we were joking," Jill replied, startled. "Is she really that obvious?"

"You bet," Barry said. "And poor Greg, he's such a straight arrow he didn't even catch on for a while. He was just annoyed because she was taking too much of his time. The whole office has been watching it."

Jill drew back. "You've got to be kidding. Didn't she know he's married with children?"

"Oh, come on, Jill. For some women that's just an added challenge." He saw that she was getting upset and was instantly contrite. "But not to worry. You know Greg, true-blue."

"I'm not worried," Jill said, wishing she weren't, because for the first time in her marriage she felt…unsure. She looked at Greg and Felice over Barry's shoulder. He was *so* good-looking. And they were laughing together about something, sharing a joke.

"Look, don't pay any attention to me," Barry was muttering. "You know ol' Barry. Snipe the Snoop. I live on gossip and…well…maybe sometimes I exaggerate a little, just to keep things moving."

Jill forced herself to laugh, but the idea clung in her mind. Barry danced her over to Greg and Felice.

"How about a trade-off," he said to Greg. "Lemme have one dance with Felice, okay?" And amid some banter and laughter the trade-off was made and Jill went into Greg's arms. The feeling was so familiar, so good. She tightened her arm on his shoulder, but the slow song ended and the combo moved on to another faster number. Jill and Greg separated, dancing face-to-face but apart. She watched his expression. He was half smiling, and looked as if he might be enjoying this part of the evening.

About eleven the party began to break up on schedule. Carl and Myrna looked tired, so people began drifting over to thank them and leave.

Jill was picking up her handbag from the table where she had left it when Felice came over again.

"That was nice, wasn't it?" Felice was smiling. *Perfect teeth, of course. What else?* "I really enjoyed it. Carl's very generous about entertaining the staff."

"Yeah," Greg answered, "and we'll have another one just before Christmas. Do you have a way home?"

"Oh, yes, I came in my own car. Are you going to be working on your boat this weekend?" she asked, and before Greg answered Felice turned to Jill. "I *love* your boat, Jill. I guess everyone in Seattle has a boat. I'm beginning to love this place."

"When did you see our boat?" Jill blurted before she could stop herself.

"Oh, let me see. I guess it was last week sometime. Wasn't it, Greg? I just happened to be down at that marina and there was Greg putting some kind of varnish on the floor. I guess I mean the deck, don't I? I was fascinated. And to think he built it himself." She gave him a glance of admiration. "Well, I've got to go. It was so *fun* meeting you, Jill." She gave them a cheery little wave and left, calling over her shoulder, "See you, Greg."

Chapter Six

"I detest that woman," Jill said as soon as they were in the car in the underground garage.

"Felice?" Greg said, easing the car into the line leaving the garage. "You're not alone. She's not the best-loved person at Marshall's, either."

"What was she doing down at the boat? Barry said she was after *you,* to put it bluntly. Is she?"

"Oh, come on, Jill," he said, glancing over at her. "Don't pay any attention to Barry. His hobby is making mountains out of molehills."

"*She* said she was down at the boat."

They had reached the garage exit and Greg concentrated on getting out into the line of nighttime traffic. "You wouldn't think there'd be this many people downtown at night. When do they sleep?"

"Don't change the subject," she snapped. "*Why* did she come down to the boat?"

He laughed, sounding pleased. "For Pete's sake. You're jealous. I don't believe it. To answer your question, she said she just happened to come down to that marina and just happened to see me there putting sealant on the deck. She's new to Seattle and she goes exploring on her time off.''

''And you *believe* she just *happened* along?'' Jill asked tightly.

He sighed. ''No, of course not. If she had any significant other, she's left him back East somewhere. My guess is that she's just looking for a little…companionship.''

''And she targeted you.'' Jill could feel her anger mounting.

Greg stopped at a red light and flipped on the turn signal. ''Jill, forget it. What's got into you? She's not the first female who's found me—what can I say?—appealing. And she won't be the last. Some women are attracted to any guy who doesn't have two heads, just for practice. This kind of thing has never bothered you before. It shouldn't bother you now.''

''Well, it does bother me!''

The light changed and he turned. ''What do you expect me to do? I work with the woman. I'm handling it the best way I can. Forget it.''

''I will not forget it.'' She swallowed, because she had an intense wish to cry. No, not cry. Bawl. Howl.

''*How* are you handling it?'' she finally asked when she felt she could speak calmly, but her voice wasn't as calm as she wanted it to be.

''How?'' He laughed again. ''Oh, come on. The usual ploys, I guess. I pretend I don't get it. I change the subject. I talk about my kids. I talk about my wife. I rub the lady's nose in how solid my marriage is.''

Jill thought about this for several blocks, then she said, ''How solid is it?''

He was quiet for some time and she thought he hadn't

heard, but finally he answered. "Maybe it would be more solid if your disposition ever improves."

"My *disposition*," she snapped. *"What's wrong with my disposition?"*

"You don't really want me to answer that." Now Greg was becoming angry, too.

"Yes! Answer it!"

"For one thing, you're becoming a world-class complainer. Every day is a rough day for you. Our kids are driving you crazy. You're bored out of your skull and you take it out on me. My job isn't exactly a piece of cake these days. And you gripe constantly about how much time I spend down on the boat. If you would come with me. If we could actually *sail somewhere* on the boat. If you would work at becoming a better sailor..."

"I can't help it if I get motion sickness! I can't even ride in the back seat of a car! I don't do it on purpose!"

"And since we seem to be reviewing grievances, have we cut my mother completely out of our lives? The kids are her only grandchildren, you know. We used to have her over to dinner once in a while."

"Oh, great. I suppose Laura is complaining to you. Well, for your information, she's stopped by a few times to see the kids, okay? She hasn't much use for me these days. And she never fails to get in a dig about what a burden a nonworking wife is to a husband. Am I too much of a burden, Greg?"

"This is ridiculous," Greg said shortly, and they drove the rest of the way home in a smoldering silence, with Jill acutely aware that he hadn't answered the question.

When they got home, for Daisy's benefit they put the best face they could on the fact that they had been quarreling. Jill had hired Daisy to baby-sit because the children didn't like it when she and Greg went off together and they all liked their old day care worker. Greg paid her and drove her home, which gave Jill enough reprieve to cool down, and by the time Greg returned she was in bed pretending to sleep.

It was two o'clock in the morning when she realized with deep sadness that this was the first time in their marriage that they hadn't kissed each other good-night. Somehow her life was unraveling, and by the time she finally drifted into sleep she was convinced she was causing it.

Sleep, when it finally came, was deep and drugging. She was aware of Greg trying to wake her for some time before she could bring herself into wakefulness.

"Hey. Wake up," he was saying. "I've got to be off."

"What? What?" She groped her way out of what seemed like a dark fog. "What's the matter?" She couldn't even seem to think clearly.

"I have to go to work," he was saying patiently. "And I don't want to leave the kids here with you still asleep."

"What time is it?" she gasped, pushing aside the covers.

"Almost eight-thirty. You were sleeping so deeply I didn't want to wake you, so I let you sleep as long as possible. The kids are up and I gave them breakfast, but they aren't dressed yet." He was standing beside the bed, dressed for work in his gray suit with the silk tie Kate had contributed. *Oh, Greg, why do you have to be so drop-dead gorgeous? Why can't you be a nice homely man like my dad?*

"I'm sorry." She scrambled out of bed, staggering a little, trying to regain her balance. He steadied her.

"That's okay. I happened to wake up early for once. Are you really awake?"

"Yes. Yes, I'm awake. And thank you. Thank you." She noticed that all three children were standing just inside the bedroom door in their nightclothes, observing her soberly.

"Are you sick, Mommy?" Laurie asked in an uncertain tone.

"No. Not at all. It's just that we were out late last night and I overslept a little. I'm fine. Really," she added at Laurie's doubtful look. Then Ben spoke up.

"Mommy, do you think you'll feel glad today?"

"Yes. Yes, of course. It's going to be a good day." But even as she said it she was filled with a slow dread. *Another endless day for stay-at-home Mommy.*

"Well, okay, then. I'll get going. If I need to work late I'll call and warn you," Greg said.

"Thanks." She tried to sound brisk and in charge, feeling a deep sense of shame. Children were sensitive. They were aware of her mood swings, especially Ben, who was very perceptive. His scrubby little bunch of dandelions was still on the kitchen table. She couldn't bring herself to throw it out yet.

By midmorning she had made up her mind to call Pastor Bailey about the support group. She could at least look into it. If it proved to be a dead end, she'd try Kate's system of adding some interest to life by taking a course in something.

When she called the church office the secretary put her right through to the pastor, and for a moment she didn't know what to say.

"I, uh, this is Jill Rhys. You called to see me the other day and you spoke about a support group for..."

"Right. Do you think you want to explore that idea?" His cheerful tone gave no indication that he remembered her rebuff.

"Yes. I...have to...do *something.*" Her voice broke

and she was acutely embarrassed. She cleared her throat to cover it.

"Are you busy this afternoon, Jill? It's okay if I call you Jill, isn't it? We're a pretty informal group around here." His voice had changed slightly. She hadn't fooled him. Reading between the lines and picking up on nuances of the human dilemma was, after all, his work.

"Yes." Ridiculously, she wanted to cry, she was so grateful for his unspoken understanding.

"I'll tell you what," he was saying easily. "Why don't I stop in to see you again, say, this afternoon. Would that be okay? When do you put the little ones down for a nap?"

Relief flooded her. *Maybe this kind man can help me.* For the first time she could admit to herself that she needed help.

"I give them lunch at noon sharp. Then, even with all the stalling tactics, I manage to get them sleeping by about one-thirty or two."

His ready laugh came over the line. "I know all about the stalling tactics. Fortunately my two are way past nap time. My son's away at seminary and my daughter is in college. Why don't I stop by about two, then?"

"Yes. Yes, please. That will be fine." Hanging up the phone, Jill leaned against the kitchen wall. Good. That was done. And so his son was away at seminary. That spoke well for him as a parent. The PKs—preacher's kids—often went off in the opposite direction from the father. She'd heard that somewhere. If the boy wanted to follow in his father's footsteps, well, then… Suddenly she felt a lot better.

For Pastor Bailey's visit she changed from denim cutoffs and T-shirt into her best summer dress of light blue. She was glad she had had her hair styled for Greg's office party. After this she would keep it cut, at least, for Greg's sake.

As it approached two o'clock she waited near the door so he wouldn't need to ring the bell and risk waking Megan. And when she heard his step on the porch she opened the door.

"Hi," he said, keeping his voice low. "All clear? No patter of little feet?"

"Not so far," she said, smiling and crossing her fingers as he came into the room. Jill indicated the two chairs flanking the now empty fireplace, and they sat down. He got right to the point.

"Good. All the way over I was trying to recall positive things about this particular group. Let's see. They're all fairly young. There are three of them in this group, and they'd welcome a fourth who has also left a career, as they all have. There's Daphne Ingersoll. Incidentally, she lives just a few blocks down on this street. Maybe you know her?"

"I...don't think so. We don't know many neighbors. We know the elderly lady who lives next door. That's Mrs. Hopkins. Because she lent us her downstairs bathroom when we had our plumbing torn up. But that's about it."

"Well, Daphne used to be a loan officer at Seafirst Bank. Then there is Isabelle Ridley. She has a master's degree in fine arts. Used to work in one of the museums restoring old paintings and keeping them in good repair. Then there is Marijane—now, that's all one word. She's had to spend a lot of her life telling people how to spell her name. Last name is McAuliffe. She is a credentialed teacher, and she now teaches primary grades in our Sunday school. She didn't have the nerve to refuse when I asked her to, because in the public school system she taught primary grades. Now that she's in it, she loves it. So that worked out okay. I thought it would when I asked her. Sometimes my hunches pay off. Sometimes they blow up in my face.''

"I...my..." Jill's throat seemed to close, and as she looked at Brian Bailey's kindly rugged face her eyes filled with tears.

"Something blow up in your face recently?" he asked gently. "Is it something you want to talk about?"

"Yes, I..." The words came tumbling out. She told him about the Tacky Shack Café, how hard she had worked to make it a success. About the increasing worry about how she was caring for the children. How she couldn't seem to make it work out. How her anger and secret resentment were building up, and she knew that was wrong. Then she found herself telling him about her strained relationship with Greg, how he seemed to be slipping away from her. About his present insecurity over his job. She even poured out her heart about her mother-in-law, Laura.

"You see," she finally admitted, "I'm the one who is failing. Maybe I made the wrong decision. Maybe this is something I *can't* do well enough to do it. But it's too late to go back. I can't...undo it. And I can't seem to make this work." Her voice dwindled away into nothing and she balled up the several tissues now damp in her hand, which Pastor Bailey had been handing to her one at a time. She went to toss them into the wastebasket behind a chair in a corner and came back to her chair by the fireplace. *Oh, please say you can help me.* "Do you always come to see people with a packet of tissues?" she asked.

"Supplying tissues is part of my job description," he said easily.

"I'm sorry. I didn't mean to..."

"This is my work, Jill. Sometimes I'm privileged to help people. And don't ever apologize for letting another person see into your heart for a moment. We all keep too many walls around ourselves. Why don't we pray about this?"

"Yes, please," she said tiredly, bowing her head. She was aware that he was standing, and she felt his hands lightly on her head. He prayed in a low and thoughtful voice, as if he were having a conversation with God. Jill felt a kind of tranquillity pervade her, easing away the worry, the tensions, the anger, the hopelessness. When he said, "Amen," she said it, too. "Thank you," she added as he sat down again. "It does help, doesn't it?"

"Always, Jill. Always. Never question that. God is *there.*" Then he surprised her, starting where she had finished. "About your mother-in-law. Laura, isn't it? You've got a lot of unresolved anger about her."

"I'm afraid she's got a lot of unresolved anger toward me, too. She's never forgiven me for taking Greg away from her. I didn't. He's still her son. He loves her, is loyal to her, but—"

"Of course, and as Greg's helpmate you've probably tried to love her, too, and been rebuffed."

"Oh, I've been rebuffed, all right." Jill heard the grimness in her own voice. "Somebody once told me everyone should be completely honest with three people—their lawyer, their doctor and their pastor. So to be completely honest, I've never even tried to *like* Laura, let alone love her. Some things are just not possible."

He grinned. "Since I'm a pastor, allow me to give you my second-favorite Bible quote. '*All* things are possible with God.' You say Greg loves her. Maybe you can, too— sometime in the future, not today. Think about it." He paused for a moment. "My French is very rusty, so I won't try it on you, but the French have a saying that fits nicely here. 'To understand is to forgive.' Sometimes if we can understand someone, know where they are coming from, forgiveness begins. And after forgiveness often comes love."

"Well," Jill said, "because you're being so kind, I'll give it a try, but no promises. By the way, you mentioned your second-favorite Bible quote. What's the favorite?"

"'God is love,'" he said simply, and the conviction in his voice reached Jill. "It's a good quote to meditate on when you're doing something routine that doesn't require any thought. I do it while I'm cutting the grass or something like that. But let's move on. How long have you been staying at home?"

"Let's see. About three months now. Maybe I haven't really given it a good try yet."

"I was thinking the same thing. I wouldn't give up until you've done it at least a year. Keep in mind that you could fail. It's not for every woman now, you know."

"I thought…" She was surprised.

"No. You mentioned your friend, Connie. She seems to be quite happy and successful as a working mother. Some women are. Some aren't. You have to find your own place, what is right for your family."

"I suppose so, but when I was working I wanted to be here, with my children."

"And maybe that was the right decision, and this is just a period of adjustment. Give the support group a try. And don't take it to heart when dedicated career women ridicule you for what you are doing. Women have been short-changed for centuries. Then, finally, women's turn came. Women found they could be whatever they wanted to be. The door was finally open."

"That's all I ever heard when I was in school."

"Yes, and the choice for women was so new that once the door did open women got the idea that they *had to* go through it. That women *must* fulfill themselves with a career outside the home. They forgot there are many ways for people to fulfill themselves. Now there is a growing trend for women doing what you have done, *choosing* to bypass a career outside the home, or at least putting it on hold for a time. They're finally getting the idea they can go through the door or *not*—that either way is a valid choice for a woman. So don't let others put you down for 'wasting' your education. You're not. I would urge you also to get to know Greg's co-worker, this Felice Fletcher. She sounds like a troubled woman to me. Try to get behind the mask—we all occasionally wear a mask. Get to know her, if you can."

"You mean to know her is to love her?" Jill asked, smiling. She felt so at ease with him now. "I rather doubt that, Pastor Bailey." And they both laughed.

"Okay, one thing at a time. But promise me you'll give it a try."

"Okay," Jill said with a grin, "but again, no promises."

They talked for an hour or so more until Jill looked over and saw Megan standing in the doorway to the living room.

"I woke up," she announced unnecessarily.

Pastor Bailey left shortly afterward. Jill closed the door behind him feeling enormously better, and determined that they were going to church again, starting this Sunday, because she wanted her children to begin the fall Sunday school session with the other children. She was eager to talk to Greg about it. Her euphoria lasted until Greg phoned at about five to tell her he was working late.

"Don't wait dinner for me, Jill. I'll grab a burger or some fish and chips down at the marina. And I'll be late getting home, so don't wait up."

"Oh, you're going to work at the boat?"

"Yes."

"Greg, I really think you could postpone work on the boat until weekends..."

"Jill, I can't. I'm meeting someone. I mean, I've got an appointment down there. I...look..." Jill heard the clicking sound that meant he had another call. "I have to go. I'll talk to you later."

She hung up the phone, frowning. Meeting someone? But he had changed that to "an appointment." Who could he have an appointment with down at the marina except somebody else in the boat crowd? At first she had tried to enjoy the boat with him, had taken the Dramamine for the motion sickness and stuck it out. But after Laurie's birth she had given up. At first he had been very disappointed, but lately he hadn't seemed to mind. Occasionally he took the children with him, but had stopped asking her. She sat down slowly. *Why* didn't he mind anymore that she didn't join him on the boat? It was an ugly idea and she tried to push it away.

Later, she had a long conversation with Daphne Ingersoll of the mom support group. There had been that lucky instant rapport between them that sometimes happens between strangers. They had gone to the same college and knew some of the same people. Jill had hung up the phone knowing she had made a new friend. It was a good feeling. She was looking forward to being part of the group. For one thing, it would cut down on what they had to pay for baby-sitting on the rare occasions when she and Greg went out together now. The women in the group traded off baby-sitting now and then. Daphne had even offered. She had an infant daughter she called Posey. Jill wasn't sure if that was the baby's real name or just a nickname, but she looked forward to meeting Daphne and the others.

Daphne had said...what had Daphne said?

"My husband is an airline engineer and he has to travel a lot. The company is always sending him to far-off corners of the world to figure out why one of their planes crashed. So any time you want me to baby-sit, I'll be glad to if Gary is off into the blue yonder, which he is at the moment. Posey can sleep through anything. I'll just pack her up in her carrier and come on over. Have baby, will travel."

All the time Jill was preparing the evening meal she thought about it. Have baby, will travel. All she had to do was call Daphne, her new friend.

"Look, Daphne, I'm sorry to call you so soon about this, but I've got an errand to do. Could you come over for, say, about an hour? The children will be in bed asleep, so..."

Did she dare just *show up* at the boat?

Just park the van. Walk down along the marina, past all the long mooring docks stretching out into the water with hundreds of boats berthed alongside, until she got to the one where Greg kept the *Far Horizon*.

"Hi, Greg. I just thought I'd stop by."

But if Felice was actually there, what would she do? Did she really want to know?

"Mommy, you're not eating. Don't you like it?" Laurie asked. "I'd rather have spaghetti myself, but meat loaf's okay."

"Meat loaf is good," Ben said, his mouth full. "Daddy likes meat loaf."

"I guess I'm just not hungry tonight," Jill said weakly,

wishing it was eight o'clock, wishing they were in bed and asleep, then immediately feeling a familiar sense of shame. She was being ridiculous. Of course she wouldn't—couldn't—go. For one thing, Greg would be furious, and rightly so. She was not going to behave like a jealous wife, although actually she was a jealous wife. More shame.

It was almost nine-thirty before she surrendered and called Daphne, and it was ten-thirty as she walked down the marina past the lines of moorage docks stretched out like long fingers across the dark water. As the tide was out, the sailboats were riding low, the boats rising and falling with the constant movement of the water. It was a beautiful end-of-summer night. And there was the *Far Horizon,* riding gracefully with lights on in the cabin. The short curtains were drawn, so she couldn't see in. She paused on the edge of the dock, wishing she had worn a jacket. There was a chill in the air, the beginning of autumn, her favorite season, when the maple tree's leaves turned red. She had changed her high-heeled shoes for flats, so it was easy to jump down lightly onto the deck.

"Greg?" she called, standing there, suddenly wishing she hadn't come. The door to the cabin opened and Greg came partway up the steps.

"Jill? What's the matter? Is something wrong with the kids?"

"No. I...I just wanted to..." She stopped, unable to continue as she saw a deep flush mount into his face, and his eyes narrowed as he realized immediately why she was there.

"I don't believe this," he said softly.

She couldn't speak, and wanted to sink through the deck. *Oh, why did I do this?*

"Well, now that you're here, come on down." He gestured to the cabin below.

"No. No, it's all r-right," she stammered. "It doesn't matter."

"Oh, but it *does* matter." He came all the way up the steps to stand before her, talking quietly so that no one else could hear. "You came down here to check up on me. We'll pass over the fact that it's a despicable thing to do. But now that you're here you're going to see it through."

"No, uh, no. I'll just...uh...skip it. I really shouldn't—"

He reached out and took her arm. "No, we won't skip it. I'll give you a choice. You can either walk down the steps into that cabin with some dignity, or I can carry you down. Which is it?"

She swallowed hard, her mouth dry.

"Who's...who's down there?"

"All right, I'll carry you."

"No," she gasped. "No, it's okay, I'm coming." Hating herself for creating the situation in the first place, she started down the steps, with Greg close behind. He reached over her shoulder to push open the door, which had swung shut, and revealed the lighted cabin. She got a quick glimpse of the sleeping bunks now folded neatly into padded benches for seating, the chairs and, at the far end, the galley and eating table, which was spread with papers.

"Felix! What are you doing here?" she gasped. "And Angel!" Felix and Connie's cousin, Angel, both stood up. They had been seated at the table. There was another chair pushed aside where Greg must have been sitting.

"Greg is bailing us out," Felix said, a sound of relief

in his voice. He had always considered Greg some sort of financial genius.

Angel spoke up. "Greg's going to do the books for the Shack," he said, his thin, hawklike face intent as always. Jill wondered fleetingly if she had ever seen him smile.

Then Greg spoke in a deceptively quiet voice. "Felix has too much to do. He's decided to farm out the Tacky Shack's accounting."

Angel shook his head. "Jill, you can't imagine the mess Felix makes of the accounts. He really screwed up the quarterly State Business and Occupations tax. I'm a desperate man. I can't do it myself, even if I knew how. I'm working two jobs, so I told him to get Greg. Pay him anything, but get him. And I'm paying this out of my own pocket. It's worth it to stop worrying and get some sleep."

"I don't want to overwork Greg," Felix was saying placatingly to Jill, "but you know how it is with me and figures."

"But Felix, I explained it all to you."

"Yeah, sure. In one ear and out the other. I did try to remember everything, but…I guess I'm a chef, not a bookkeeper. It's better this way. And Greg says he can use the extra money now that you're…I mean, now that there's only the one income…. Are you angry?" He looked hangdog, like a spaniel that had been kicked.

"No, of course not. It's fine," she said quickly. Both men were now realizing that something was wrong and were becoming embarrassed. Greg rescued the situation as best he could.

"Okay, we're finished here, and I've written an explanation for the foul-up. But Felix, you *have* to send it express to get it there ASAP. First thing in the morning, without fail. Okay?"

"Give it to me," Angel said. "I'll get it off at the crack

of dawn.'' And Greg handed him the brown manila envelope into which he had slipped a thin stack of filled-out forms and a cover letter. An odd little silence fell, which Felix finally broke.

"Well, then, that's that," he said very briskly. "Let's go, Angel."

"I'll see you guys out," Greg said, mounting the steps behind them. "And don't worry, Angel, I've set up an arrangement with Connie. She'll know what to do now. It's a simple matter of…" The cabin door swung shut and Jill couldn't hear any more. She had made a fool of herself. And what a rotten thing to do to Greg. Straight-arrow, true-blue Greg. He would never forgive her. She couldn't look at him coming down the steps into the cabin again.

"Would you mind telling me where you stashed our kids?"

"I-I've met one of the women in the, uh, mom group. She only lives down the street a ways. And she's… uh…baby-sitting. The kids are in bed asleep. They don't even know I'm gone." She forced herself to look at him. He didn't look angry anymore, only tired. "Greg, I'm so sorry."

"Forget it. Come on, let's go. I'm through here." He began to sort and straighten the remaining papers and put them into a flat zippered case.

"Greg, I had no idea you were…I mean, I…"

"I told you I was working." He zipped the case shut.

"I didn't know you meant…I thought you meant on the boat, getting it—I mean her—ready for winter. And you said you were…meeting someone." Her voice faded away.

"I can't do this kind of work at home, Jill. The kids are too noisy. It's fairly quiet out here at night. But it's okay that the kids are noisy. I don't *care* about that. Kids are supposed to make noise. I was determined when I had kids of my own that nobody would ever shush them, never make them be quiet if they didn't want to. I can remember—'' He stopped himself, and she knew one more thing about his childhood. Sometimes what Greg didn't say was as revealing as what he did say. "Come on." He went about turning off lights and locking up. She followed him, her heart aching.

In silence he helped her up onto the dock, as the boat was riding lower now, and walked her over to her van. He was opening the van door when she could stand the silence no longer. She turned to him.

"You're entitled to yell. Tell me off. I was wrong and I know it. And I'm—''

"Okay, you're sorry," he said remotely. "Let it go. You don't have to grovel. It doesn't matter. What's done is done. You can't undo it. But know this. I've *never* cheated on you, Jill. And it would never have occurred to me that you'd question that. When I took my marriage vows I meant to keep them, and I have." He paused, and the faraway look came back as he stared for a long moment out over the dark moving water. There was a half-moon and it made the surface of the water gleam in shining, ever-moving patches here and there. "And I always will," he added slowly.

Feeling sick, she got into the van and he shut the door. Her hands were shaking as she inserted the ignition key. She felt as if she had taken a blow and was reeling from it. Suddenly she had understood. He would be faithful, fulfilling his commitment, going through the motions, whether he loved her or not. Because he had taken the vows. He'd got himself into a trap, but he'd stick it out, because that was the deal.

He drove his car carefully behind her all the way home, and pulled in to the garage beside her, and once in the house she introduced him to her new friend, Daphne, and he was smiling, pleasant, polite. *Greg, going through the motions.* Daphne, a bit chubby, with flyaway blond hair, rolled up her knitting and picked up the carrier with Posey still sleeping placidly in it.

"This was very good of you, Daphne," Greg was saying. "What do I owe you?"

"Oh, nothing," she said in surprise. "Jill will do it for me some time. We trade off now and then. We'll all be so glad to have Jill in the group."

"Well, it's after eleven. I'll walk you home. Here, let me take that." He reached for the baby's carrier and took it. To Greg, politeness was bred into the center of his bones, regardless of the situation, regardless of how he felt. Had the lonely, quiet child become the lonely, quiet man? Putting aside his own feelings and making all the right motions. What was he feeling now? This moment? Was he angry, hurt, humiliated... *trapped?* Just marking time in quiet desperation? Apart. Greg was apart. Outside looking in. Living in his private place. The place she could not enter.

She made herself smile and wave at Daphne from the porch, then went back inside. But it had been so good in the beginning, so much love, so much laughter. Where had all the love and laughter gone?

She was still sitting on the couch when Greg returned.

"You still up?" he asked politely. "I thought you would be in bed. It's getting pretty late." He was going to let it go. Act as if nothing had happened. As if she hadn't spied on him, and embarrassed him in front of Felix and Angel. Was he so burned out with their marriage that he really didn't care enough to quarrel? Well, so be it, she thought helplessly.

"I...wanted to ask you something, if you don't mind." She spoke diffidently. It was like speaking to a stranger, someone she had just met.

"Ask away," he said, pulling his tie loose and starting to unbutton one shirt cuff.

"Are you...have you taken on any other accounts to work on?"

"A couple."

"Do we...do we need the money that badly?"

He looked at her thoughtfully for a moment, with that unreadable expression that shut her out. "We're not broke, if that's what you're afraid of, but a little extra money doesn't hurt. Is that it?"

"Yes," she said almost formally. "Thank you."

"Okay, then. It's late. I'm beat. I'm going to hit the sack. Good night."

"Good night, Greg."

She held back the tears until he was out of the room.

Chapter Seven

The next morning Jill and the children lingered over the breakfast table, all caught up in her somber mood. Greg, pleading work, had left without breakfast.

"I'll pick up a Danish, and there's always coffee at the office," he said on leaving.

"Daddy should eat with us," Laurie commented sourly, stirring around her cereal. "I don't want that toast," she added, pushing aside her toast plate.

"You asked for toast," Jill said, trying to keep the annoyance out of her voice. It was her fault the children were uneasy. She couldn't seem to hide her moods from them. Children were aware of much more than she had imagined them to be. Ben sat with his head down, stolidly eating his cereal.

"You put on the wrong jam," Laurie complained. "I wanted yellow. You put red."

"There isn't any more apricot jam," Jill said patiently. "It's on the list for the next time we go to the store." She indicated the list held to the refrigerator door with a magnet shaped like a strawberry. Another endless mommy day was beginning, and beginning badly. And this was the day the other three members of the support group were coming. She had made the arrangements with Daphne the day before on the phone. For a moment she was tempted to call and cancel it, or at least put it off. *Look, Daphne, this is a bad time for me. When I asked you to baby-sit for me last night, I did it to go spy on my husband and he was furious. Now he…*

No, she couldn't do that, not after Daphne had so kindly come to baby-sit. Anyhow, this had to be the day for the get-acquainted meeting because it was the only day the women could come without their children. Isabelle Ridley's mother-in-law was visiting and had offered to baby-sit for the group while they talked with their prospective new member. Daphne had explained that.

"Look kids, can you hurry it up a bit? Mommy has some people coming later, and I've got to get the house in order."

Ben looked up from his empty cereal bowl. "Who's coming?" he asked, frowning in faint alarm. Ben had spent the whole four years of his life so far establishing small routines for himself. Whenever any of these routines were disturbed he didn't like it. But instead of flying into a temper tantrum as Laurie might have, he retreated into a kind of pained acceptance, which was harder for his parents to bear. Greg had said more than once, "This kid has the makings of a world-class martyr. We're going to have to do something about it." But neither had ever figured out what. There were always more urgent things to deal with, and of the three Ben was the most tractable.

"Just three nice women from church. They're coming to see me today. This afternoon. At two." Two o'clock, and it was already after nine, and there was so much to do. She quelled a sudden panicky impatience. Children should be allowed to eat at their own pace.

"Would you like to start Sunday school next Sunday?" she asked them.

This got a good response from Laurie, who had started eating her toast with the red jam on it, and Megan was receptive.

"Is it fun?" Megan asked.

"Yes," Laurie answered decisively. "There's pictures to color and stories and you get a gold star stuck on the chart if you come." She turned to Ben. "You remember, Ben. A long time ago we went. You got some gold stars and so did I."

Ben was looking at her soberly. "I don't remember that," he said finally, pushing aside his cereal bowl. "I'm going outside."

"After you brush your teeth," Jill reminded him.

He gave her a look of weary patience. "I always brush my teeth," he said, and headed for the children's bathroom. Of course. Ben always brushed his teeth. It was one of his sacred routines. She should never have reminded him. It was confusing sometimes, remembering how different each child was from the other two. But Ben's departure made both girls want to finish up, regardless of Mommy's unglad mood, and get into the day.

Somehow she got through the long morning, with Greg always in the back of her mind. The children played outside, the children came in with questions and problems, the children came in for lunch and the children went to sleep for their naps. And somehow in the intervals she got the house presentable and a casserole ready for the oven and salad ingredients washed and ready to put together for the evening meal. When it was two o'clock she was at the door waiting in order to avoid the noise of the doorbell.

The three women came in together and kept their voices low without being asked to.

"Well, I'm Daphne, as you know from last night. I'm a former loan officer at Seafirst Bank. And this is Isabelle Ridley, Master of Fine Arts, former restorer of fine paintings. And this is Marijane McAuliffe, former primary school teacher. And you?"

Jill picked up on the half-humorous, half-rueful mood and responded, "I'm Jill Bennett Rhys, former restaurant owner. Come on in. Sit down and make yourselves comfortable." All of them seemed to be in their mid-thirties, probably having waited a while to start their families. Isabelle Ridley was a pretty woman who had kept herself up. Her dark hair was well styled and she was slim, unlike Daphne, who was a little plump. Marijane McAuliffe would never put on weight, being spare and lean to the point of thinness. There was an all-over beigeness about her—light brown hair, tanned, somewhat weathered skin and a look of near middle age—but her smile was so genuine it warmed the heart and made it impossible not to smile back.

"I brought you the literature from FEMALE," she said. "You can look it over when we go. This is a kind of get-acquainted meeting, I guess. Pastor Bailey seemed to think you'd like us and fit in."

"I hope so." Jill reached for the pack of leaflets the other woman was handing her. Then she saw that the top leaflet was headed FEMALE. "I have some soft drinks and, of course, coffee," she offered.

All three voices asked for coffee, and Daphne laughed. "True Seattle-ites all. Coffee all around. I'll help. Let me get it for you. I investigated your kitchen last night when

I was warming Posey's bottle, and you can glance over that stuff Marijane just gave you.''

"Okay. Thanks. What is FEMALE?" Jill asked.

"Its an acronym for Formerly Employed Mothers At Loose Ends." Marijane laughed. "Actually, that was the original name. They changed it after it got so successful. Now it's Formerly Employed Mothers At the Leading Edge. I think it's both. Sometimes I'm leading edge and sometimes I'm very loose ends."

"I urge you to join. We all urge you," Isabelle said. "The monthly newsletter is worth its weight in gold."

"You said 'successful,'" Jill prompted, hearing in the back of her mind Daphne opening and shutting cupboard doors in the kitchen. She felt a rising sense of kinship with these women.

"Oh, it is," Isabelle said enthusiastically. "Once it got started, it took off like a rocket. You have no idea how many women have opted to put career on hold to raise the kids. And I think every woman who did it thought she was unique, totally alone."

"Not so." Marijane was shaking her head. "Literally thousands of women are doing the same thing we are."

Jill frowned. "Is it some kind of backlash against women's liberation? I don't think I'm being conceited about it, but I was doing a heck of a lot better job of running my restaurant than the man I sold it to, much as I like him."

"Not exactly a backlash," Daphne replied, coming in with the coffee tray. The cups rattled faintly as she set it down on the coffee table when Jill pushed aside the magazines to make space.

"Yeah," Marijane said. "When women first put their shoes on and came out of the kitchen and proved they were as smart as men in the work world, everybody assumed that was *it*. Women would have careers. Fine. That's what all women should do."

"Then," Isabelle said, "it was slow in coming, and not everybody has got it yet, but some of us figured out that if you didn't actually *want* a career more than you wanted to raise the kids, you didn't have to. And the sky wouldn't fall. You could work outside the home or not. What a concept!"

"Without being accused of not fulfilling yourself," Daphne said tartly, beginning to fill the cups and hand them around. "Milk and sugar on the tray, Marijane," she added.

"I've had that experience," Jill said quietly. "And from one of my best friends."

"Oh, it's always a best friend," Isabelle said warmly. "They think they are helping you get back on track. When you aren't *off* track. You're *on* track. Doing what you want to do."

"As if wanting to raise your own kids is some kind of lapse," Daphne muttered, sitting down.

"And you can have it both ways," Isabelle continued.

"How do you mean?" Jill asked.

"I haven't given up my career," Isabelle answered. "I've just put it on hold until my twins are out of high school and off to college. I was good at my job," she said simply, "and I still am. I make it my business to keep up on what's happening in the art world. When *I want to* I'll go back to work. Of course," she added, "my field is ideal for short assignments and part-time work. The restoration of worn, faded, dirty or damaged paintings isn't your usual nine to five."

"And in the meantime," Marijane said, "we group together to keep the motherhood thing from becoming just a boring, mind-numbing interval of wiping noses and cleaning up messes and trying to stretch the family budget.''

"I'm grappling with that now," Jill said, somewhat grimly.

"But it can be a very rewarding period," Isabelle said quietly. "Until Rick and I produced these two little identical girls I had no idea that twins were any different from other kids. But there are subtle differences. I'm boning up now on twinship, on what it means to be half of a pair of people. We're learning that they have this special relationship that neither Rick nor I nor anybody else can enter. It's fascinating. You've got three little stairsteps, haven't you?''

Jill smiled. "Laurie's five. Ben's four. And Megan's almost three. And they are all so…different. My sister, Kate, tells me that I'm looking at this as a kind of job to do. She thinks I should enjoy it more. I thought when I was working that I *wanted* to stay home with them. I thought…''

"It takes a while," Daphne said gently. "I…had some basic training…with my little boy, Johnny, but…" She paused. "We lost Johnny," she added, and Jill felt a wave of pity. So Posey, who had slept so placidly in her carrier last night, was a second child. *What would it mean to lose a child?* There was an odd silence. Nobody spoke for a long moment. There wasn't anything to say. They were all mothers. Nothing needed to be said. The sense of kinship deepened. Isabelle leaned forward and refilled Daphne's cup, an empty little gesture, but something, a little reaching out. Jill was touched. These were good women, kind and caring, sensitive to one another. How wise Pastor Bailey had been to lead her in this direction. In a swift little act of love Jill leaned forward and kissed Daphne on the cheek.

"Mommy?"

"This is Megan, my youngest," Jill said, getting up to bring Meggie in. Megan must have heard the voices, because she had tried to dress herself. Her dress was on but unbuttoned and one of her socks was inside out, but she had tried. Jill felt a silly rush of pride. She sat back down, holding Megan, who seemed to be drifting in and out of sleep.

Rocking Meggie gently back and forth, Jill continued to listen to her new friends, and felt much more hopeful than she had. They filled in the other details about FEMALE, which was now worldwide and had over a hundred local chapters, one in Seattle where they all attended meetings whenever they could.

"We've moved beyond just support now," Isabelle said. "The organization is into advocacy very effectively. There's a continuing campaign going on to make business more aware of the changing American family. Business and government are getting the message about job sharing and flextime for those of us who want to work only part-time."

"Then," Marijane added, "for those women who have got to work, and don't have the choice, there's a big push on to persuade companies into on-site day care. The world is changing."

The time fairly flew. They discussed the day-to-day, hour-to-hour problems of raising children. Jill poured out her worries about Laurie, who was their most fractious child, and got what she thought was some good advice. The women left after three-thirty, and Jill couldn't resist hugging them. She hadn't felt so upbeat for weeks. It was going to work. It was going to be good. All good. She couldn't wait to tell Greg. He would certainly be interested in this, if only because of his devotion to the kids.

But at five-thirty Greg called that he'd be late again.

"I have to go over some stuff. This is office stuff. Here at Marshall's. I won't be down at the boat," he was careful to add, and Jill felt her face grow warm.

"I wasn't going to visit the marina again, Greg," she said defensively.

"Well, I thought I'd better mention it. Just in case. I wouldn't want you wandering around down there alone at night. Too many weirdos around."

"Thanks for your concern," she answered tartly. "Since you won't be home, I think I'll take this casserole over to Kate's, and the kids and I will have dinner over there. I have a lot to tell her. My support group came over today and we had a great visit." She wanted desperately for him to ask about it, and held her breath for his answer.

"Oh, good. I'm glad it went well. I don't know really when I'll be there. Expect me when you see me."

"Where will you eat?" she couldn't resist asking. Maybe he'd want her to fix him something when he came home.

"Eat? Oh, here. Felice said she'd send out for something when we get hungry. Look, I've got to go. Tell Kate hello for me."

Jill hung up the phone with a sick feeling in the pit of her stomach. Felice had said she'd send out for something? Who *else* was working down there tonight? Was it just the two of them? Angry at herself, she pushed aside the idea. Greg would be faithful. Greg would go through the motions. Hurriedly she started to dial Kate's number, but had to make two attempts to get it right. Finally the phone gave four rings and Kate's answering machine came on. Why didn't Kate renew her messages once in a while? It would have taken only a minute to say where she was going. Well, it wouldn't be far. She'd be home for dinner. They never could afford to eat out. Sometimes when she'd had the Shack... Well, that was history.

She would go on over there. Kate would probably be back by the time she and the kids arrived, considering the cross-town traffic. She wanted to tell Kate about the support group, what great people they were.

"Come on, kids," she called. "We're going over to Auntie Kate's for dinner." She knew she was trying to recapture the upbeat mood she had had earlier, and listened to the children's whoops of delight with some lightening of her spirit. They all liked going over to Kate's and playing with their cousins.

However, when she drove her minivan into Kate's driveway, she realized that Kate's old Chevy wasn't there, the open garage door revealing a vast emptiness. Kate must have the cleanest garage on the planet. Well, they had each other's keys. She'd just go in and wait.

"Hi."

Jill glanced over and saw the same fair-haired boy who had been playing in Kate's backyard the last time she'd come.

"Hi," she answered. "Your name's Raymond, isn't it?"

"Yeah. Raymond. Hi, guys," he added to the children in the back seat. When the greetings died down Jill started over.

"You remember me. I'm Mrs. Graham's sister. She doesn't seem to be at home."

"Yeah, well, she's gone," Raymond said, whistling through his teeth.

"I can see that." Jill tried to keep from sounding impatient. "Do you happen to know where she went?"

"Yeah."

"Well, where!"

"Uh, she went over to Mrs. Bennett's house to do her big wash. You know, the sheets and heavy stuff. Like that. I wanted to go, too, but Mrs. Cody wouldn't let me."

"I see. Mrs. Cody is your housekeeper, isn't she?"

"Not mine," he said quickly. "My dad's." His voice was sullen and he scowled at the ground.

"Well, I think I'll go on over there," Jill said, starting the van and putting the gearshift into Reverse.

"Any chance I can go with you?" The scowl was gone, replaced by a very winning smile as he placed a grubby hand on the car door. "Mrs. Cody's at the store."

"Sorry. Afraid not," Jill said, smiling to soften it. Kate was right. He was a doleful little waif. She felt sorry for him. "But we'll be coming back here for dinner," she added. He was really a rather beautiful child, in a fair-skinned, delicate way.

"Yeah, well," he said, turning away and slouching off.

Laurie leaned out the back window. "Maybe you can eat with us, Raymond," she called to his retreating back, but he didn't answer.

"Mommy," Laurie said, "is Gramma Beth back?"

"No, not yet. I wish she were. I miss them. It's just that Aunt Kate is over there using the washing machine. Now, settle down and put your seat belt back on."

It wasn't right, Kate having to lug her laundry over to Mom's to wash. Maybe she should open the subject again of some sort of job. Part-time, maybe, if the support group was right about the job-sharing thing, flextime and all the other innovations. Soon Joy would be in kindergarten half days. Kate was going to have to do something, no matter how well she had made peace with her lot. Somewhere college costs loomed ahead for her two children.

Their parents' house was only a ten-minute drive from Kate's, so they arrived quickly. Driving the van into the long driveway of Mom's big old two-story house always brought a wave of nostalgia. Dad had bought the house before Kate had been born, so she and Kate had never lived anywhere else. They had expected a large family because Mom was a hard-core mother and wanted several children, but that hadn't happened. The long driveway was partly covered by a white arbor, heavy with Concord grapes. Large bunches of the purple fruit hung down heavily everywhere she looked. She felt a sudden lifting of her spirit and gave her trademark three beeps on the van's horn. This brought both Joy and Tommy out through the gate, and her three scrambled out of the van.

"Hi," Kate said, sticking her head out the side door. "Come on in. I'll be with you in a sec. I have to put this load into the dryer."

"Now, you kids don't waste the grapes, and watch out for bees," Jill cautioned. "And keep track of Meggie." She went up the two steps to the side door that led into the sunroom, which was actually rather shady due to the grape arbor. Kate always made grape jam and jelly for the whole family from Dad's arbor.

"Sit down. I'll be right in," Kate called from the back, and Jill selected one of the sagging white wicker chairs, which had been there since before she was born. The cushions really needed replacing, she thought for the thousandth time. Kate joined her in a minute, sinking into another of the chairs. She looked tired and there was a sheen of sweat over her round face.

"How come you're here this late?" she asked.

"Greg had to work tonight and I thought I'd bring over my kids and my casserole and we could all eat together. I want to talk to you, anyhow. That support group came over today and I feel so hopeful. They are such great people, and we're all in the same boat." She launched into a recital of the afternoon. Before she wound down the rest of the clothes were dry and they went onto the back porch to fold the laundry together, as they had years ago when both had been teenagers required to do their share of housework—only now it was fun and not a chore. When all the folded laundry was loaded neatly into the two plastic baskets, both sisters took a break in the sun-room again to talk a while. An odd little silence fell be-tween them.

"Do you have something on your mind?" Kate asked quietly after a while. Jill was the sister most likely to go off on some impulsive tangent, later regret it and confide in Kate.

She grinned ruefully. "Is it that obvious?"

"Well, I thought last time there might be some prob-lem, but you kind of clammed up. It's Greg, isn't it?"

Jill nodded, and resumed when she thought her voice would be steady. "Some of it I brought on myself. He's been working his head off at the company. And things aren't going too well there. He's got this hotshot female who's turning everybody's head. He may not...he may not get the promotion we both expected when Marv Hig-gins retires."

"She's that good?"

Jill nodded. "And then I met her the other night at the quarterly company dinner and, to quote my husband, she's a knockout."

"Ah, too bad. Brains plus beauty. But you don't have to worry about Greg," Kate said in her most comforting tone. Jill was aware that her hands were clenched and she carefully relaxed them, looking down at them. Her nails looked awful. When had she last done her nails? Felice's were probably flawless.

"But it isn't the same, Kate," she blurted out. "It's not

Get 3 Books FREE!

Get All 3

*W*e'd like to send you three free books to introduce you to *Love Inspired*. Your three books have a combined cover price of $13.50, but they are yours free! We'll even send you a wonderful thank-you gift—the elegant jewelry box shown below.

free!   **free!**   **free!**

Love Inspired

Faithfully Your
Lois Richer

God's miracle
can lead to
unexpected l

Love Inspired

THE *RISK*
OF LOVING
JANE PEART

A fateful encounter...
a chance to love again.

Love Inspired

The
Wedding Quilt
Lenora Worth

An unexpected stranger.
A wedding worth
waiting for...

Each of your free *Love Inspired* novels is filled with joy, faith and true Christian values. Th stories will lift your spirits and gladden your heart! There's no cost. No risk. No obligation to buy anything, ever.

Steeple Hill

SPECIAL FREE GIFT!

We'll send you this elegant heart-shaped jewelry box, absolutely FREE, just for giving *Love Inspired* a try! Don't miss out—mail the reply card today!

© 1997 STEEPLE HILL

Books FREE!

DETACH AND MAIL CARD TODAY!

HURRY! Return this card promptly to get 3 FREE books and a FREE gift!

YES, send me the three free *Love Inspired* novels, as explained on the back. I understand that I am under no obligation to purchase anything further. **Also send my free jewelry box!**

Affix peel-off
3 FREE BOOKS
sticker here.

Name	
Address	Apt.
City	
State	Zip

103 IDL CFAH
(U-LI-1-01/98)

PRINTED IN U.S.A.

Steeple Hill Reader Service™—Here's How it Works:

Accepting free books places you under no obligation to buy anything. You may keep the books and gift and return the shipping statement marked "cancel." If you do not cancel, about a month later we will send you 3 additional novels and bill you just $3.19 each, plus 25¢ delivery per book and applicable sales tax, if any.* That's the complete price, and — compared to cover prices of $4.50 each — quite a bargain! You may cancel at any time, but if you choose to continue, every month we'll send you 3 more books, which you may either purchase at the discount price...or return to us and cancel your subscription.

*Terms and prices subject to change without notice. Sales tax applicable in N.Y.

nearly the same. I don't think…I don't think that Greg would ever make love to me if I didn't prompt him. He…we…we used to be friends. We had jokes. We had such fun. We laughed and kidded around. But it's all different now. We talk, but it's as if he feels some sort of…duty to me. He told me down at the marina, just last night, he said—I'll never forget it—he said, 'When I took my vows I meant to keep them, and I have.' And he got that look he gets lately, as if he wished he could be a thousand miles away from me. You know, it was as if…as if…he'd stick it out just because he had to, but there was no joy in it for him anymore. I thought…I believed…that we had a good marriage. It was hectic, sure, with three kids and both of us working, but I thought…'' She stopped herself. She couldn't say it, not even to Kate. She couldn't admit that she felt Greg didn't love her anymore. Not to Kate. Not to anyone.

''Oh, Jill.'' Kate was beside her chair, her arms around Jill, hugging her. ''Maybe it's just that the honeymoon is over. Finally. You and Greg had the longest honeymoon period of any couple I've ever known. Maybe it's just that real-life marriage is happening now. Marriage isn't all hearts and flowers.'' She sat back on her haunches to look up at Jill, worry showing in her round little face.

''Maybe you're right,'' Jill said, not really believing it.

''You said a while ago he was having trouble at work. That can really get a man down. Maybe he's got a lot more on his mind that he's telling you.''

''I suppose so.'' It was comforting to be little sister again, and have Kate's loyalty and concern, so genuine, so obvious. ''It'll be okay, I guess. Greg will stick to the marriage, I know that. He's Mr. Integrity, but his heart isn't in it anymore, and that's what hurts.''

''You don't know that for sure. Marriage, just the *dai-*

liness of it, isn't the honeymoon. At some point that's finished and the real marriage starts. Marriage is the long haul in relationships, Jill. And somewhere along the way it changes from hearts and flowers, the excitement of a new and different relationship with someone, to the steady, day-to-day togetherness, the mutual dependency, the giving and taking, the blended habits of being part of two people. I think in Greg you got a real prize. Maybe he's not as romantic as he was in the beginning, but consider that some of the shine may be off for him, too. To you, the hearts and flowers are gone, but the toilet seat's still up. Maybe he's getting little doses of reality from you, too, that drive him up the wall."

Jill had to laugh. "I know. I probably have a dozen things, habits, that irritate him. But he certainly has his share. I don't think he's ever shut a closet door in his life. A large part of my marriage has been shutting doors after him!"

Kate laughed, too. "When Claude used to be stressed out he wouldn't sit still. He'd have to pace around—here, there, all over. If I was trying to talk to him I'd get a crick in my neck keeping him in sight. Then when he was really stressed he'd start cracking his knuckles. It drove me up the wall."

"Greg grinds his teeth in his sleep. I told the dentist and he said to wake him up when he did it. That goes over like a lead balloon. Yes, I guess the honeymoon is over when everybody starts to nit-pick."

Kate stood up. "Come on, let's go over to my place and have dinner. You round up the kids and I'll put the laundry in my car."

Jill suddenly remembered that she hadn't told Kate about her trip to the marina and Kate hadn't thought to ask why she'd been down there, where she seldom went.

She was glad. She didn't want even Kate to know what a fool she'd been.

They managed to get the laundry and the children back to Kate's house. All the children chose to ride in the back of the van with Jill, and there was more than the usual amount of giggling, but Jill was getting used to that and tuned it out.

The evening went well, although Kate was still unreceptive to the idea of supplementing her income by part-time work.

"Stop worrying about it, Jill. I thought we settled that," she said when dinner was over and she was putting the dishes into the dishwasher. It was old, and Jill worried that it would go the way the washer had. "I'm okay. Really."

The long twilights of summer were gone and it had been full dark by seven. Now at eight, the children's usual bedtime, Jill called hers in from the backyard where they were still playing some game that included the two flash-lights Kate kept and another apparently supplied by Raymond. Her children piled into the back of the van laughing and giggling. Jill felt good about it, driving home. Maybe she wasn't doing such a great job, but she would improve. And the kids seemed happy for the most part. She'd get into the planned games and structured activities as soon as she could. Ben would love that to the bottom of his little organized soul. Jill's mind was filled with plans. Maybe she was a kind of failure as a wife, but she could be a good mother. When she drove the van into the garage she saw that Greg's car was there.

"Daddy's here," Ben announced, and all three children scrambled out of the van into the backyard just as the floodlight came on and Greg was at the back door.

"Hi," Jill said. "I'm sorry we didn't make it home before you did. Did you get something to eat?"

"Oh, yes, we had deli sandwiches sent in," he said, holding the back door open so they could all go into the back porch and then the kitchen.

"Come on, kids, it's way past bedtime," Jill said, and went in to run the first tub of bathwater as the children greeted Greg exuberantly, all talking at once telling him about the evening. Finally, two hours later, all was quiet and Jill, feeling somewhat drained, went into the living room.

"You know," Greg said, putting down the newspaper, "there's one benefit I get from your staying home now."

"There is?" she asked warily.

"Yes. With you at home, you do it all. I love my kids, but having to feed them, bathe them and read the bedtime stories got to be a real drag after a long day at the office."

It was a tiny olive branch, a little gesture, and Jill felt a lump in her throat. "I'm glad" was all she could say as he raised the newspaper to resume reading it. Greg was good and decent and he would stay the course. And...and...she would have to settle for that with the best grace she could, and make it as easy for him as possible. He was, after all, the sole provider now, which must be a heavy responsibility. What was he worried about? His job security? His advancement? Should she ask him? Should she try to draw him out? He was so adept at withdrawing into himself and shutting others out when he wanted to.

There came a very distinct sound from the empty kitchen. Someone had just shut the refrigerator door. Greg had heard, too, and put the paper down. They looked at each other questioningly, then both got up and went to the kitchen, pushing open the swing door. The light was on and both Laurie and Ben were there. Startled, the children stared blankly at their parents.

"What are you doing in here?" Jill asked, although it was obvious. Laurie was making a sandwich on the kitchen table. She was doing a rather good job of it. She had laid out two slices of bread and was spreading one slice with chunky peanut butter. The jam jar stood open beside the peanut butter jar. Ben stood beside her, holding against his stomach the gallon milk jug, which was about half-full. Laurie was in her pink nightgown, and Ben was in his Barney pajamas but had added his red sweater.

"I'm making a sandwich," Laurie said unnecessarily.

"We can see that, sweetie," Greg said. "Are you hungry? Ben, why don't you get rid of that load?" He reached over to take the milk jug, but Ben gripped it more tightly and looked anxiously at Laurie.

"What's up, you kids?" Jill asked. "If you're hungry—"

"We're not hungry," Ben said.

Laurie gave a gusty sigh. "We just thought we'd, uh, make this sandwich and maybe go out in the backyard."

"But Laurie," Jill said, "you can't have a backyard picnic at—" She looked at the wall clock. "It's after ten o'clock. You can't have a picnic this late."

Greg had walked over to the kitchen window to glance out. He turned.

"Jill, I think there's someone in our garage. I saw a light moving around. I'll check it out."

"No! Greg! It could be a prowler. I'll call nine one one." She reached for the wall phone.

"No! Mommy, no!" Laurie said anxiously, slamming the sticky knife down onto the table. "It's not a prowler! You've ruined everything! It's Raymond. He has to run away and...and he doesn't know where. So he's...and he's hungry. He has nothing to eat out there.'' Laurie was angry, almost crying.

Frowning, Ben added, ''It isn't right to have nothing to eat when you get hungry.''

Chapter Eight

"Who's Raymond?" Greg asked blankly.

"Oh, dear," Jill said in dismay. "He's the little boy who lives next door to Kate. He's sort of…" She didn't know how to phrase it in front of the children. "His parents are divorced," she said finally, "and he lives with his father."

"His mommy walked out," Laurie said bluntly.

"Poor kid," Greg said. "I'll go bring him in."

"Daddy, you can't," Laurie protested. "He's hiding."

"Well, sweetheart, he's not hiding now, because you just blew his cover." He turned to Jill. "Better call his home. His father's probably frantic."

"He isn't there," Ben said. "He goes away a lot."

"Well, call Kate," Greg said, going out the back door. "Maybe she knows something. Maybe they're out looking for him."

Jill dialed Kate's number, but got her answering machine. She left an urgent message, telling Kate that Raymond was safe and with them. Greg wasn't gone more than five minutes before he came back with Raymond, who looked hangdog and frightened. On his thin face were traces of wiped-away tears that tore at Jill's heart. He must have cried, all alone in the van in the dark garage.

"I made you a sandwich," Laurie said angrily. "But they didn't let me bring it out."

Raymond gave her a weak smile.

"Sit down, Raymond," Greg said kindly. "Or do you want to wash your face and clean up a bit first?"

"I wanna go to the bathroom," he said dolefully.

"Okay. This way." Greg's hand was on Raymond's shoulder and he led the boy out of the kitchen.

"I think he should have a hot meal," Jill said distractedly. "Where *was* Raymond? I didn't see him."

"You weren't supposed to see him," Laurie said sullenly. "That was our plan. He was way back in the van. And he said he wanted peanut butter and jelly."

"He likes hot chocolate," Ben offered, and added, "I'll put this back now," referring to the gallon milk jug, "now that he's in." Jill opened the refrigerator door and helped him. Then she took it out, deciding to make a big pot of hot chocolate they could all share. It was a small enough gesture, but better than letting the lonely boy eat alone. She also cut him a generous slice of gold cake with caramel frosting, which was courtesy of Felix. At least once a week Felix sent Herbie over with some sort of treat for them. All the activity in the kitchen brought Megan in, so they were all gathered around the kitchen table, making sure Raymond got enough to eat and sharing what was left of Felix's cake, when the phone rang. Greg reached over and plucked the receiver off the wall.

"Hello?" Then there was a long pause and he mouthed to Jill, "His father's home now." Then Greg spoke again. "Yes, he's fine. He's sitting here in our kitchen with us eating a kind of late supper.... Well, it looks as if he stowed away in the back of my wife's van when she was visiting her sister, Kate, your next-door neighbor. Apparently the kids were all in on it.... Yeah.... I'll be glad to run him home, Mr. McAllister, as soon as he's finished.... No, not at all.... Well, if that's what...okay. Sure. No problem. Talk to you later." He hung up, turning to Raymond.

"Your dad's back from his trip and he was frantic looking for you. But don't worry. He's not mad, just relieved." He turned to Jill. "He's coming over to pick Raymond up and take him home." Just then the phone rang again and it was Kate. Greg handed it to Jill. Kate sounded exhausted.

"Jill, I'm so glad he's okay. Ian's here with me. We've been out scouring the neighborhood. We were about to call the police when we got back and got your message. Didn't you *know* he was in the van?"

"No. How could I? He was hiding way in back."

"Well, the kids were in on it. I've given Tommy and Joy a good talking-to, and I'm not finished! They're grounded! No TV for three days! And that's final!" Jill could hear groans of protest in the background, and it occurred to her for the first time that she'd better talk to Laurie and Ben, too. What they had done was wrong and they should understand that.

She hung up the phone thoughtfully. She and Greg were both too lenient. Was it because they loved their children more than Kate did hers, or was it because it was the easiest way? She remembered her own parents and the house rules. She recalled them as kind but firm. Sometimes very firm, but with love. Being too lenient didn't really prepare children for the world, because the world is not lenient. She should talk with Greg about this...if she could talk to Greg.

She watched him for a moment, loving him so much it hurt. She'd have a hard time convincing him that children shouldn't be spoiled rotten. Was this his personal private backlash from his own childhood experiences? To want his children to run wild? She recalled the wistful expression in his eyes the night he had told her about his late uncle. *He used to help me make model boats.* How much of her *time* had Laura given him when he needed her time?

How much time was she herself giving Laurie and Ben and Meggie? Kate had said, *You can't just shoo them out the door.* It was a sobering thought.

She was still remembering some of the good advice she had heard earlier from the support group when Kate's neighbor Ian McAllister arrived to pick up Raymond.

Raymond, now well fed, was increasingly nervous, and stood up when he heard his father on the porch. Greg went to the door.

"Hi, I'm Greg Rhys." He held out his hand. Ian McAllister was another tall, fair-haired man. Most old Seattle families had at least a few Scandinavian ancestors somewhere. His eyes were on his son. "Come in," Greg was saying. "Jill, this is Raymond's dad. And this is our brood, Laurie and Ben and Megan."

The introductions finished, McAllister thanked them fervently and turned to his son. "Why, Ray?" His voice broke and his nice eyes filmed over with tears.

"I can't stand that Mrs. Cody," Raymond said desperately. "She's...a lousy cook. I *hate* the stuff she cooks. And...she..." He started to cry, great gulping sobs, and ran to his father's outspread arms. McAllister grabbed him and held him tightly.

Laurie spoke up. "Mrs. Cody punches him. She punches his back when he won't sit up straight at the table. And she thumps him on top of the head with her thimble. It hurts.''

Ben said, ''She sews things.''

''Dad, sometimes I...sometimes I...just don't *feel* like sitting up straight.'' The rest was lost in a mumble into his father's broad shoulder.

It took another half hour of mingled apologies and thanks from McAllister and assurances from Greg and Jill before McAllister left with Raymond.

''I'm tired,'' Ben announced, taking off his sweater. ''I'm going to bed now.''

''We're all tired,'' Jill conceded, looking at her watch. She knew she should talk to the children, but it was too late now. She'd have to do it tomorrow. As she herded the children toward their bedrooms, she wondered if she really would. She must start doing better.

After she put the children to bed again, she went back into the kitchen to clear up the mess. She was rinsing cups and putting them into the dishwasher when Greg came in.

''You need any help?'' He was still dressed, but had pulled off his tie.

''No. Everything's under control. Thanks.''

''That poor miserable little kid. I can't get him out of my mind.'' He came to stand beside her at the sink, looking out into the dark yard. He turned to her. ''Jill, our kids are happy, aren't they?'' There was something like a sigh in his voice.

''Yes, of course,'' she said in surprise. ''At least, I think so. I try. We both try.''

''Yes,'' he said remotely, as if his mind were elsewhere, in some place she couldn't follow. ''Sometimes I...worry about Laurie,'' he added slowly. ''She's so...discontented.''

Jill closed the dishwasher. ''Yes, I know. She's a little

fusspot. I was talking about it to the support group.'' She felt a sudden warm feeling of confidence. ''Isabelle, one of the group, has twin girls just a bit older than Laurie. She says Laurie's a bright child and she's ready for some responsibility. She wants to be part of the family, wants to help, but doesn't know how. I'm trying to figure out how I can involve her somehow.''

Greg looked at her thoughtfully. ''That could be why she bosses the other kids around so much,'' he said. ''I guess they're growing up.'' He glanced at the clock. ''We'd better hit the sack.''

For the next few weeks Jill tried to focus on the children, the image of miserable little Raymond always in the back of her mind. Her children would never wander disconsolately around, lonely and lost. They must belong, have roots, be *connected*.

Isabelle helped her make a chart for each child like the ones she had for her twins. Jill held a meeting around the kitchen table with the children. Both Laurie and Ben were very interested, wanting to be involved. Meggie went along, although she wasn't quite sure what was going on. She made an effort, wanting to be part of it.

Jill taught Laurie and Ben to make their own beds. Megan was too small for that, so she was delegated to Pick Things Up and Put Them Away. She worked quite consistently at this, although she sometimes put them away in interesting places, and expected to be often admired for her efforts.

Ben's other task was to take the house trash baskets out and empty them in the big can at the end of the yard by the alley. For two days he did this faithfully, carrying each basket out whether it had very much in it or not. Then on his own he made an efficiency move. He decided that if the basket didn't have much in it, he could empty the contents into another basket and make fewer trips out to the big can.

"Way to go, Ben," Greg said when Ben explained this to his father.

Laurie's most responsible task was to clip grocery coupons from the Sunday paper and from the coupon books that arrived in the family mailbox. She couldn't read much yet, but going by the illustrations, she made very few mistakes. Jill, who hadn't had time to clip coupons, used these to cut down the grocery bill. She always gave Laurie the store receipts and Laurie circled the amount after Coupons Tendered, gloating over how much money she was saving. She kept the slips in a special box she had decorated in crayon with dollar signs. Sometimes Jill's little helpers were more trouble than they were worth, but she knew they were learning, and they were involved in the family.

They started going to church again on Sundays, and Jill found herself more deeply affected than she had anticipated, feeling something very like love for the church itself, although she knew that the church was the people, not the building. It wasn't a large church, and it was somewhat old. The brown-shingle siding needed staining, but there was a round, clear-glass window over the altar through which the congregation could see the sky, passing cloud formations, sunlight or rain coming down. Jill thought looking off into the sky itself was better than any stained-glass pictures. None of the other windows were stained glass, either, but a kind of speckled amber. The wooden pews were slick from many years of polishing, the padding on the kneelers was becoming frayed and some of the pages in the hymnals were loose, but there was a simplicity about it that appealed to Jill. It was as if the church itself was saying these are material things, they don't matter too much.

She noticed that Greg seemed to take some deep satisfaction from coming back. Sometimes he knelt in silent prayer longer than she did. What did Greg pray about? What did he take to God? And she prayed for Greg. *Please help my husband. Please help Greg with whatever it is that's troubling him. Show me how to help, God. I want to be a good wife.* How odd. She had never thought about being a "good wife" before.

The children loved the Sunday school classes. They showed off the gold attendance stars. They saved the leaflets of Bible stories. They seemed to be thriving on the careful structure Jill was adding to their lives, which were just beginning. Pastor Bailey had said one day, *Train up a child in the way he should go, and even when he is old he will not depart from it.* It stuck in her mind. How had Laura "trained up" Greg? He loved her, was loyal to her. She tried to be more friendly to Laura, but the wall remained between them. She tried to talk to Laura about what she was doing with the children, but Laura seemed impatient. It almost came to another quarrel.

"You seem to be obsessed with the children, the children, the children. Perhaps you should think a little about Greg. You're not doing much to help Greg," Laura said, gathering up her things to leave. She had been over to lunch, and it had not been a success. She wasn't really interested in Laurie's coupon collecting, or Ben's trash basket work.

After she had gone, Jill made rather a production of talking about how valuable what they were doing was to the family. And she felt in her heart she was right. Some day Ben would be a man, and maybe learning to be faithful in taking out the trash would help him faithfully perform something far more important. Laurie would be a woman, and maybe learning to manage the coupon search would help her cope. She tried hard at the mothering thing, and tried not to notice how much time Greg was spending down at the boat. She tried not to long for the excitement of running the Tacky Shack Café. *Stick with the program, Jill.*

Somehow, almost without notice, the whole of September was gone and there was a brisk chill of coming winter in the autumn air. The leaves on the maple tree in the backyard turned flaming red, and the tree started tossing them off in a kind of giddy abandon, especially when the wind was blowing capriciously this way and that as Seattle winds often did.

"Look, Mommy," Ben said excitedly. "Our tree is dancing." And it almost seemed it was. Jill and the children, bundled against the weather in sweaters and knitted caps, stood around watching the tree move this way and that in the wind, its branches often groaning as the leaves flew about.

"Look at the swings," Laurie shouted as the two empty swings swayed back and forth and sideways. Jill could hear in her mind Greg's voice—*Jill, our kids are happy, aren't they?* And now, at this one moment, she could answer yes. She sent up a silent *Thank you.*

"When is Christmas?" Megan asked suddenly as they were going back into the house for lunch.

"Oh, Meggie, Christmas is a long way off yet. It's only October. Come on, now, we've got hot tomato soup for lunch and grilled cheese sandwiches, your favorites."

October had always been a friendly month. Some of the best things in her life had happened to her in October. And good things were happening now. She had managed to lose a few pounds. Kate had found a used washer at an unbelievably good bargain price, Felix had paid his October payment and part of his delinquency, and there were nine exquisite bronze chrysanthemums in bloom. She would use them to decorate the table on Sunday when Laura was coming to dinner.

When the children were down for their naps Jill felt a wave of love for her home, this house that she and Greg had chosen as their place. She had a sudden urge to *clean.* Really clean. Like mopping the kitchen and bathroom floors and putting on a new coating of that plastic stuff. Like washing the windows. Like using that vacuum-cleaner attachment she hadn't yet used in seven years, which sucked all the dust off the ceilings. *Cool it, Jill. It's already two o'clock, and fixing dinner looms ahead.* She checked in the fridge and was happy to see a goodly supply of leftovers. Using leftovers creatively was a standing joke with the group, but she had picked up a few good ideas. Food was food, and not to be wasted.

Ah, there was enough leftover ham to chop up and put in a seasoned white sauce to spread over split hot biscuits. And she had finally got the hang of making biscuits without a mix. Much cheaper. She had plenty of greens for a salad, and some acorn squash, courtesy of Kate, to bake. So what's for dessert? Maybe she could bake some apples along with the squash. So dinner was taken care of.

She would do one big housekeeping job. Most of the house was fairly presentable, so what to do? *Windows.* She would do the windows.

She stopped doing windows a couple of times during the afternoon, once when the children got up from their naps and once to take a call from Kate, whose turn it was to receive Mom's letter. Kate read it to her.

"I'm worried," Kate said flatly.

"Why? Dad must be okay. Mom didn't say anything this time about him not being okay."

"Yes, but they skipped that side trip. Didn't you pick up on that? It isn't like Mom to skip *any* side trip. That's been their M.O. all along. At least Mom's. She wanted to see the far-off places, and she's seeing the far-off places."

It cast a pall on the rest of Jill's afternoon, and she went back reluctantly to complete the window washing. She shouldn't have taken on such a big job so late in the day, but she finally finished it, her muscles aching. She took a quick shower, put on fresh jeans and T-shirt and went into the kitchen. She ached, but the windows were shining. *Today the windows, tomorrow the ceilings with that vacuum thing.* She was just about to chop up the leftover ham when the phone rang. It was Greg, and he sounded strained, tense.

"Hi, Jill. Is it okay if I bring Marv home to dinner with me tonight? You can put another cup of water in the soup, can't you? It's only Marv, and he can take potluck." There was an undertone of worry in his voice, although he was trying to keep his tone light, and she got the impression someone else had come into his office. There was the sound of talking in the background, some laughter.

"Sure," she said, "that'll be fun. I haven't seen Marv since the last office party. Bring him along." *Chopped ham leftovers.*

"Okay...uh...just a sec." The phone was muffled and the indistinct sound of voices came through. Then after what seemed like an overlong pause Greg was back on the line. "Can we add one more? Felice wants to come." Now there was definitely strain in his voice. *Felice?*

With some disbelief she heard herself saying brightly, "Sure, by all means. The more the merrier." *Forget the chopped ham.* When she hung up the phone her hands were trembling. What in the world was going on! Greg *never* did things like this. He was too hooked on being Mr. Polite. He'd die before he inconvenienced anyone. When she put the ham back into the fridge her hands were steady again. She could figure out part of it. He and Marv had been good friends since day one of Greg's employment at Marshall's. Obviously they wanted to talk about something, but not in the office. But Felice?

Okay, Greg was in a bind. Good Wife would bail him out. Or die in the attempt. She went back to the phone and dialed the familiar number of the Tacky Shack Café. It was five o'clock—the dinner rush hadn't quite arrived yet.

"Connie? This is Jill. I love you dearly, but I haven't time to chat. Can you put Felix on?"

"Pronto!" There was laughter in Connie's voice, and almost immediately Felix answered on the kitchen phone and Jill heard the frantic bustling sounds of a restaurant kitchen, giving her a moment of intense nostalgia.

"Felix? Jill. I have an emergency. Greg is bringing two people home from the office for dinner and I only have some leftovers." She waited for his reaction, knowing what it would be.

"No! You can't!" He fairly shouted.

"VIPs," she added.

"Leave it to me. I'll send Herbie over with everything you need. Turn on your oven in thirty minutes."

Relief flooded through her. Good old Felix. "Wait a minute! Felix, if you're thinking something exotic, don't! Because this has to look—"

"Please! I'm not a fool. This will be your perfect home-cooked meal. Something you yourself just whipped up with your own dear little wifey hands. Herbie will be there in forty minutes. Will that do it?"

"Perfect. Felix, I owe you." She hung up, leaning against the kitchen wall for a moment. Why was Greg doing this?

She felt a sense of inward shaking. Greg wanted Marv's job so badly when Marv retired, and this smacked of office politics. The phone rang suddenly right by her ear and she jumped. It was Greg again, keeping his voice low.

"Jill, I'm sorry about this, but I kind of got trapped."

"I guessed that. But it's okay. No problem," she assured him. "What's going on, or can you tell me?"

"Not right at the moment. You sure this is okay?"

"Absolutely. You just keep your cool and don't worry. It's going to be a lovely evening."

"Thanks. I have to go now." He sounded tired, and it touched her heart. He shouldn't sound tired all the time; he was only thirty-two.

The clock seemed to be moving too fast. It was now five-ten. She called Laurie and Ben and they came running.

"Listen, kids, we have a surprise evening ahead. Daddy is bringing company for dinner." She hurried on in the face of Ben's sudden look of distrust. "Two people he works with. You haven't met them. There's a very pretty woman named Felice Fletcher, and there's Marv Higgins. And I've…uh…arranged a nice dinner. Now you can help me. Laurie, I want you to go out and get three, no more, just three of those bronze chrysanthemums we talked about this morning. Cut them off with one-inch stems. No more. Very short. Ben, you go out and pick up some of those red leaves on the ground. Okay?"

"I'll get the ruler off the desk," Laurie said, leaving the room running.

"We know Marv," Ben said slowly. "We saw Marv at that picnic Daddy took us to before."

"Oh, that's right, darling. I forgot the company picnic in June. Well, run out now and get Mommy some red leaves. Just the perfect ones, now." And Ben followed Laurie out back.

Jill got the step stool and took down the wide shallow dish she seldom used and, yes, she saw that she still had four of the little floating candles. She would float them with the three bronze chrysanthemums as a centerpiece. Then she started taking down the bone china with the gold rims which Mom and Dad had given them for their wedding.

About forty minutes of frantic activity followed. The centerpiece was lovely and the table set. Meggie worked hard at picking things up in the living room until it looked very tidy. Ben's red leaf harvest was lovely.

"Ben, take the leaves into the entry hall. That chest with the big brass candlestick, well, I want you to arrange the leaves in a wavy line on top of the chest to show them off. Can you do that for me?"

"Sure."

While Ben was busy at this task Jill dressed the two girls in their best. Laura had bought each child a really nice outfit when told that they were entering the fall Sunday school class. Meggie looked delightful in her dark plaid challis and Laurie radiant in the teal-colored sheer wool with an Irish lace collar. *Beautiful children.*

In changing her own clothes, Jill chose her rust-colored jersey, with a longish swishy skirt and a heavy plain gold necklace. It was a good combination for autumn.

There was a brief struggle with Ben when she took his brown suit from the closet. Laura had got him long pants, the first he had ever had, and he was very proud of them.

"Oh, no, Mommy," he protested when she took the suit off the hanger. "That's my Sunday school suit."

"Oh, Ben," she said desperately, "don't argue about this. Sure, you wear it to Sunday school because it's your best. And…uh…you want to look your best in God's house, but you can wear it for any important occasion."

"I ca-an?" he asked doubtfully.

"Yes, absolutely. Look at it this way. Daddy wants you to look your best tonight so he can be proud of you. That means you have to wear the best you have, and this is it. Don't you see?"

"Ye-es, I guess so," he said reluctantly, and let her help him with his shirt buttons and his yellow power tie that Greg had got him. She looked at him all dressed up. *What a darling child.*

Thinking it was almost time for Herbie, she rushed into the kitchen, only to find him already there, having come in the back door with his first load of containers.

"Hi," he said, his broad face breaking into a grin. "Big deal tonight, huh?" He was taking foil-wrapped dishes and trays and fitting them neatly into her warm oven.

On a hunch she said, "Wait a minute, Herbie. Let's put the stuff into my own pans—just in case any of my guests pop into the kitchen to help me. What am I serving, by the way?"

"Roast beef, the best. You can cut it with a fork. And Felix already sliced it for you. Here, lemme hold that. And those seasoned potato wedges with the skins on. And there's something he calls a vegetable medley with I'm not sure what, but there's some chopped broccoli in it. And this—" he indicated a bowl "—is artichoke and endive salad, so you better get it into the fridge. And here's the dressing for it. I'll loosen the cap for you." They worked side by side getting everything put away in the right containers.

"This can stay at room temp," he said. "Felix sent

those very soft brownies, and put this in the freezer part. It's some mocha ice cream for on top. I guess that's it. No, wait. I left a bag in the van.''

He ducked out the back door and came back with two bottles. She took them and looked at the labels printed in French. She knew nothing about wine, but she trusted Felix.

"This one," Herbie said, "this light-colored stuff is like what it says here, aperitif. This is before dinner to increase the appetite. And this red wine is for with the meal.''

"But Herbie, the Shack doesn't have a liquor license.''

"I know. Felix had me stop and buy this. He said you and Greg know nothing about liquor but your company might, so he figured he'd better handle it. Okay, I think that's it. I gotta go. I guess he told you Angel wouldn't let him replace Oliver when he left, so I got the whole kitchen to do.'' And amid profuse thanks he hurried out the back door and she heard the Shack's van roar out of the driveway.

She took the wineglasses out of the cupboard and gave them a quick wash, then set up the coffeemaker, timing it for eight, which she thought would be close enough. It was now almost six. She stood at the sink and took a deep breath. *Please, God, let this be right for Greg, whatever it is.*

Then she took a slow walk through the dining room. The table was exquisite. She would light the floating candles just before they sat down. She walked through the living room. Laurie was sitting on the couch looking like a little princess, leafing through a magazine. Ben, with an odd childish dignity in his brown suit and yellow tie, was beside her, fitting two construction blocks together and snapping them apart.

"I'll put 'em in my pocket when they come," he said without looking up.

Meggie, with her dark plaid dress still pristine, stood at the front window with the curtain pushed back.

"I'm watching," she said. "I'll tell you when they come. And I'm hungry."

"Well, it'll be a little while yet. You're all being so good, and I love you for it. Daddy will be proud of you." She went through the very attractive living room into the front entry hall. She and Greg *did* have a very nice house, she thought as she looked down at Ben's arrangement of red leaves on the polished chest. *Martha Stewart, eat your heart out.*

She was still in the front hall when she heard Greg's car come into the driveway and two other cars stop in front, at the same time that Meggie called out.

"They're here, Mommy!" All the children ran into the front hall. Jill opened the door, the children clustered eagerly around her, as Marv Higgins and Felice Fletcher came up the front steps of the large wooden porch. Greg was slower, having put his car in the garage. The wind had picked up again and swirled fallen leaves around the porch.

"Come in," Jill said. "Come in out of that wind. It certainly feels like winter is on the way. I'm so glad you could come."

Marv, always a kindly man, reached over to hug her. "Sure does," he said. "I don't think Felice has ever seen your kids." He started to introduce them as Greg came up the steps.

The wind ruffled Greg's fair hair and he was brushing it down as he followed them into the front hall.

"It was so good of you to ask me, too," Felice said, but her beautiful eyes didn't match her smile. "I must say, Jill, you made a picture, standing in the doorway with all your little brood about you. Something for a Mother's Day card for sure. And your children are just delightful." She reached down and ruffled Ben's hair, something he hated, and quick as a squirrel he darted away, smoothing down his hair as he went. *Right on, Ben.*

Jill herded them all into the living room in a kind of laughing all-talking-at-once confusion, while Greg took coats and put them in the hall closet. Somehow or other it was all sorted out and they were sitting down in the comfortable chairs and couch. The children, suppressing their excitement at having company, were behaving like angels.

"We were sorry to come on such short notice," Felice was saying, the smile still in place. "And I sort of invited myself." She assumed a look of diffident apology.

"No problem," Jill said brightly. "I'm just so glad you could come, too. It rounds out the group so well." *Meaning we're two couples, lady. You and Marv and Greg and me.*

"Something smells awfully good, Jill," Marv said.

"Roast beef," she said easily. "I think everybody likes that, so it was a safe choice." She ignored Greg's faint look of surprise.

"It's almost chilly enough for a fire," he said.

"Oh, why didn't I think of that? Greg, why don't you build one? There's plenty of wood out in back, and we can light it after dinner."

It made a nice little break. Both men went out to get the wood while she got the little wineglasses on a tray to serve the aperitif. There was a lot of joking and laughter as the men arranged the kindling and small logs, ready to be ignited later. She had an awkward moment when Marv sipped his drink.

"Jill, this is delicious. Better than I had in Paris last year. What is it?"

"I have no idea," she said after a moment. "I know nothing about liquor. I always have to depend on somebody else to tell me. *Whenever possible tell the truth.*

Greg helped her out. "Liquor store dealers usually know what to recommend." They shared a little secret glance. It was almost like old times. Jill began to relax. They all seemed to be having a good time.

Meggie suddenly stood up. "I'm going to the bathroom and I'm hungry now." It made everyone laugh, and Jill decided it was time to do something in the kitchen. By the time she had transferred the chilled salad to the small chilled salad plates and started taking them into the dining room, Greg was getting everyone to the table. He found the risers for the children's chairs so they sat high enough. She should have thought of that. Maybe they should entertain more often so she could better get the hang of it.

"Mommy," Ben said in a stage whisper, "you forgot to light the candles."

"Let me do that for you," Felice said quickly, and Jill handed her the small book of matches she had left on the sideboard. The dining-room lights were on dim, and she watched as Felice bent over to light the small candles floating on the water, making a lovely picture.

"Greg, didn't Jill do a great job with this table?" Felice

asked, forcing Greg to look at her. Then for a long moment Felice looked at Greg, her eyes wide and luminous. A look of total adoration, Jill thought grimly. Greg was no fool. He couldn't help but get the message. Then Felice was laughing and shaking out the tiny match flame.

"The table looks beautiful, Jill," Greg said smoothly. "You certainly haven't lost your touch."

Marv quickly echoed the compliment, but Jill took no pleasure in it, only uneasiness. Somehow she managed to keep up her end of the table conversation. Marv helped. He seemed to be enjoying himself, and she was glad of that. She could escape now and then, to take out plates or get the next course, waving aside Felice's offer to help. When it was time for dessert Felice insisted and followed her into the kitchen.

"I love your house," she said. "It's an older place, isn't it?"

"Yes, Greg and I bought it soon after we married. We wanted only the one house, so we got a big one. Then we wouldn't have to move up as our family increased." *See, lady, he's very married.*

Felice wasn't helping as Jill put a soft brownie on each small dessert plate and a scoop of mocha ice cream on top. She was roaming around the kitchen, restless as a cat in a strange room. She touched things, her beautiful nails clicking lightly on the sinkboard, the polished wood of a cupboard door.

"Greg put in these cupboards," Jill said. "He loves working with wood."

"I know," Felice said almost absently. "He built the boat. He's such a fabulous person." She turned and looked at Jill with something like envy. Surely not. It couldn't be envy.

"Why don't you start serving these?" Jill asked, just to get her out of the kitchen.

The remainder of the dinner progressed smoothly, with everyone commenting on how good everything had been. By the time they were finished, the children were nodding and Jill excused herself to put them to bed. *No baths tonight, kids. No time.*

"Greg," she said, picking up Megan, who was yawning widely, "can you bring the coffee into the living room? It's all set up and ready on the kitchen table. Just shut the dining-room door. Tell everyone good-night, Laurie, Ben."

While she was getting the children into bed Jill could hear talk and laughter from the living room, the clink of coffee cups. After she kissed Ben good-night and tucked him in, she was swept by a wave of exhaustion. If only she could crawl into bed beside him. She let herself linger another moment. There was no hurry, as they were deep in office talk, the way fellow workers did when they socialized. She gave herself another minute and then smoothed her hair and checked her makeup and joined them in the living room. *Okay, Good Wife, do your thing.*

Greg had the fire going in the fireplace, and they all seemed to be enjoying it. She got herself a cup of coffee and started sipping it. Maybe it would help her stay awake. Then she remembered the mess in the dining room. After the one cup to fortify herself, she took a twenty-minute break to at least get the dishes into the dishwasher and put away the leftovers. Dear Felix. He had solved the leftover problem for at least a week.

When she went back into the living room she went around refilling cups. They were deep in office talk again and she had an unpleasant feeling of isolation. *I'm out of it,* she thought in panic. *These people are the workers, the professionals, the doers. I clean up the leftover food. I put the dishes in the dishwasher. I fill the coffee cups. I'm nothing.*

It was, oddly enough, Felice who tried to include her. "That was such a lovely dinner. How in the world do you manage everything?"

"I'm learning as I go. I'm getting used to it," Jill said without thinking, and Marv, good old Marv, interposed.

"Jill was a heck of a successful entrepreneur before she opted for housewifery and motherhood," he said. "She had a very successful restaurant business. Do you find you miss the work life, Jill?"

"At first, terribly," Jill admitted. "It's just a matter of getting used to new routines, I guess."

"She does a terrific job," Greg said loyally, but she felt they were making an effort to include her and it embarrassed her.

They left about eleven-thirty, Greg turning on the porch light and seeing them out. She stood at the door, waving and smiling. When he came back she was shivering in front of the dying fire. The October wind had been chilling.

Greg stood in the doorway to the living room, looking at her somberly for a long moment. Then he came in slowly and sat down as she did. They were facing each other in the big chairs flanking the fireplace.

"What was all that about?" she asked. Her fatigue sounded in her voice.

"You sound beat."

She grinned. "I didn't cook that meal, so don't give me too much sympathy."

"Oh, I knew that." Greg gave a tired smile. "That was pure Felix. I knew it at the first bite of those potatoes." He leaned forward with his head down and she couldn't see his face. "First, I'd better thank you. You sure came through like a champion, even if Felix did do the actual cooking. As to what it was all about..." He looked up and she saw embarrassment, apology, defeat in his fine eyes, and she had to look away to the dying embers in the fireplace. And he said, "I'm not sure you want to know."

Chapter Nine

"Maybe not," she said, speaking gently, carefully. Their relationship was so fragile these days. "Let's just say I need to know...since I'm not really pulling my weight these days."

"Don't say that. Other wives stay at home. I should be man enough to take care of my own family. And I can...but we may need to tighten our belts as time goes on." He paused for a long time, again with his head down, as if he couldn't look at her. "I'm fairly sure now that I'm not going to get Marv's job when he goes," he said finally.

"But *why?*" she asked before she could stop herself "You've been led to expect it. Marv has...you've said Marv was grooming you for that for the last two years."

"Marv," he said, his voice hardening. "Sure, I'm Marv's choice, and he's made that clear to Marshall, but...it is Marshall's choice. Marv can only recommend."

Jill felt a pervasive dread. So it was real. Greg was at a dead end at the firm. She had pretended to herself it wasn't going to happen. "And you really think Marshall will choose *Felice?* How can he? She's so new."

He looked up. "She's very good. She's brought in substantial new business. She will bring more, and...she wants to stay here in Seattle." He seemed about to add something else, but didn't.

Surprised at the flintlike tone of her own voice, Jill said calmly, "She wants to stay here because of you?"

He shrugged. "Probably. I'm sorry about that. I didn't initiate it. That was partly what this deal tonight was all about. Marv was in my office. He's worried, disappointed that I'll be passed over. He wanted to come over tonight to discuss it here. Then Felice just happened to pop into my office. She just happens to do that a lot. She heard me setting it up with you. I think she wanted to get a look at the perfect home life I'm always touting. There was nothing I could do about it."

"I had guessed it might be something like that."

"I can get with Marv later, but I think I already know what he wanted to say. I got it from Barry this afternoon. I don't know how Barry does it, but he seems to know everything in advance. Anyhow, if Marv could, he'd put off his retirement a couple of years. Felice wants to advance. Now. She's impatient. It's like she's running some sort of race. If she had to wait for advancement at Marshall's she'd probably move on. But Marv has to retire on schedule. He's got the beginnings of emphysema—you know he quit smoking a few months ago. He's moving to his brother's place somewhere in Wyoming. Wide open spaces. Clean air."

"Oh, I'm so sorry," she said softly, wanting to cry.

"Yeah, that really hit me hard, too. Marv has been such a good friend. What's so *frustrating*—" He got up suddenly. His strong hands gripped the edge of the mantel, and he faced the dying fire, his back to her. "What's so frustrating is that *Felice* has got another job offer. I don't know where Barry gets this stuff. He says it's a terrific offer, somewhere in the Midwest, Cincinnati or some place. And she could take it. She's free as a bird. She's got nobody here to hold her. She could take off to the moon if she wanted...." He stopped.

And you're stuck here, anchored by three children and a wife who doesn't work. The unspoken words hung between them. She felt numb, her mouth gone dry. She made herself speak calmly. "Look, if you are at a dead end here at Marshall's why don't you update your résumé and look elsewhere? And if you can't relocate here in Seattle, which is a thriving, business-oriented city, you could go elsewhere. I'm...not anchored in Seattle. We, the kids and I...could move. Families relocate all the time as...as the family provider moves up in his career." She knew her face was hot with humiliation. Never had she felt so *beholden,* so worthless, so excess baggage.

He turned, shamefaced, apologetic. "Jill, I didn't mean it to come out like that. I don't want to leave here. Our families are here. Kate...your parents. And my mother was born here, lived here all her life. She would never leave. This is home."

"Well, then, maybe you can look around here, some other company...."

"I guess so," he said, but without enthusiasm. She had a swift mental image of him just after he'd got his degree. The recruiters had been on campus. He'd had three job offers, good ones. He'd been so enthusiastic, ambitious, alive...young. But he was still young.

"You're only thirty-two, Greg," she reminded him softly. "People change jobs all the time, moving up. Why don't you just think about it a while? Keep it in mind?"

It sounded halfhearted but she didn't know how far to go. He mustn't think she was pushing him, that she was critical.

He turned, not moving the way he usually did, but slowly, tiredly. "What about that mess in the dining room?"

"I cleared it. Everything's in the dishwasher."

"Then we'd better hit the sack. I'm bushed."

She wanted to reach out, touch him, hold him, comfort him, and she hurried to the children's rooms to check on them. Megan looked like a sleeping angel and Laurie had gone to sleep on top of one of her dolls. It couldn't be comfortable. Jill eased the doll out from under her and set it up by the head of the bed. Ben had kicked off his covers, and she put them back.

When she slipped into bed beside Greg he was sleeping deeply, looking more exhausted than she had ever seen him, and she found herself praying, for Greg, for all of them, and also for Marv. This surprised her a little, as she hadn't been thinking of Marv at all. As she drifted into sleep she regretted she had forgotten to tell Greg that Laura was coming to dinner Sunday. *I'm trying, Greg. I love you. I'm even trying to love Laura, too, but that's pretty hard going.*

The group meeting that week was fun. All the children were there and in and out of the house, as the women were working on costumes for Halloween. All the children were of a similar age, and Jill had learned early that her kids liked the group meetings as much as she did because it meant more kids to play with. Ben had established another routine—he wouldn't have missed a meeting. It was now part of his personal little world. Jill told them the story of the unexpected dinner guests and Felix's magnificent rescue. They were just starting to listen to a story from Marijane when the phone rang. Jill took it in the kitchen because there was no phone in the dining room where they were working around the big table.

"This is Mrs. Hopkins," the obviously elderly voice said, and it took Jill a moment to place it. Oh, yes, Mrs. Hopkins next door, who had lent her downstairs bathroom when the plumber had replaced the sewer pipe that the maple tree's roots had crushed.

"Oh, yes, how are you, Mrs. Hopkins? I'm afraid I don't get out much...." Jill began an excuse.

"I know. You're pretty much tied down with the children. I hear them playing out back. They sound so young, so full of life. I love listening to them. I wondered if you could do a favor for me. I hate to ask, but..."

"Uh, of course, if I can. What is it?" Jill felt guilty about sounding so hesitant, but she did have the group here and the dining-room table was spread with costume materials. Maybe she could tactfully refuse. Some other time, perhaps.

"I've never mentioned it when we've spoken over the fence, and mostly I do very well on my own. I have a weekly cleaning service, and of course I know the house so well, I've lived here so long...." She sounded diffident, embarrassed. "But I've been losing my sight. It's completely gone now, and there are a few things I need help with. My cousin, who usually helps me with this, is in the hospital, so I wondered—"

Jill was momentarily stunned. *She's blind. And I didn't know. And I didn't care enough to find out.* A wave of shame washed over her.

"Of course," she said quickly. "What do you want me to do?"

"Well, it's just that I've been getting those Meals-on-

Wheels, since I can't cook anymore. It really isn't safe. I pay for the meals, of course. But they come in a big box. They're frozen, each in its container…but I don't know which is which. I mean, the breakfasts from the lunches from the dinners. My cousin sorts them for me and puts them in the freezer in separate stacks. It makes it so simple. I just reach in and feel the right stack, you see. Do you think…?''

"Yes. Certainly. Do you have them now?"

"The man brought them a little while ago and they really should go into the freezer."

"I'll be right over," Jill said, and went back into the dining room. It was comforting to be able to just say to the group, "Sit tight a few minutes. I've got to run next door," and know that they would.

Jill was deeply shaken when she came back, and the other women were aware of it, as she explained where she had been. There was a jumble of images in her mind—the slow, patient groping of Mrs. Hopkins's hand as her gnarled fingers found her plain brown cane, the neat, foil-wrapped meal trays with the contents written on the cardboard tops in writing invisible to Mrs. Hopkins, the dust bunnies under the living-room couch where the cleaning service hadn't cleaned very well and which would embarrass Mrs. Hopkins if she could see them. And beneath Jill's explanation to the others, beneath the jumbled images, there seemed to be a silent voice in the bottom of her mind, repeating like a mantra, *I must do better. I must do better.*

That evening she would have liked to talk to Greg about it, but he elected to work down on the boat again. When had she and Greg stopped talking openly and freely with each other? She couldn't remember. There was always the invisible wall between them now. Pastor Bailey had talked about the walls people built between one another. She knew Greg was disappointed about being passed over for promotion, but she was his wife, his partner. He should have turned to her, not away from her. She tried to understand it, and failed. She thought she was being successful in hiding her sadness from the children until Ben approached her one afternoon. It had started to rain, a real lashing, slashing downpour, and the children came running inside. As she got them out of their sweaters and wool caps, Ben hugged her with a sudden fierceness.

"It's...okay, Mommy," he said almost pleadingly. "It's okay." With his four-year-old wisdom, he was doing the best he could to make her feel better.

"Of course it's okay," she responded, hugging him back. And she called Greg at the office, something she almost never did.

"Are you coming home to dinner tonight?" she asked bluntly.

"What? Dinner? I guess so, why?" He was obviously distracted, probably interrupted in the middle of something he was trying to concentrate on.

"It's just that—I don't know. The kids get restless when you're a no-show for three nights in a row."

There was the sound of a sigh. "Okay. I understand. I'll be there. And thanks," he added, as if she had done him a favor. She hung up the phone feeling guilty again.

Greg had shown up for dinner, but after the children were put to bed he had gone down to the boat for a couple of hours.

She talked to Pastor Bailey about it later in the week. She had learned that she had only to ask and he somehow found time for her. She took the children, because she could leave them in the church playroom where there were plenty of toys to keep them busy.

They sat in Pastor Bailey's comfortably shabby office, and she felt secure, cared for. He had told his secretary to hold his calls. *My friend,* she thought in gratitude. *This man of God is my friend.* She found it easy to talk to him, to tell him about Greg being passed over for the promotion he'd expected.

"It seems to bother him terribly," she said. "I've thought about it a lot, and I'm getting better at managing money. I don't think of it as the end of the world. He makes a good salary. But *he's* so defeated by it. Can you think of anything I can do that I'm not doing?"

He was silent a moment. "I suppose you've thought about going back to work, haven't you?" he asked finally.

"Yes. That's what I thought at first. I'm such a dead-weight financially...." She stopped at his lifted hand.

"No," he said decisively. "I think that would be the wrong thing to do. You've got a routine established now with the children. Don't disturb that, and upset them all over again. Because you have earned a large part of the family income in the past you feel guilty because you don't. And consider this. How much of your sudden impulse to go back to work is to help Greg, and how much is your own ego? If I read you right, giving up the excitement of working, and the feeling of self-worth, self-importance it gave you, was a tough decision for you to make. Have you thought about that?"

"No. And it's a good point," she answered thoughtfully.

"You see," he said, "we live in a materialistic culture. That's who we *are.* And we tend—God help us—to perceive personal achievement by how much we are paid for it. We don't have any price tags for, say, nurturing a child, or helping our mate. You've stepped aside from being co-provider and taken the role of helpmate. Leave it at that.

You'll find ways to expand the helpmate role as you go. Concentrate on that, on being the best helpmate you can.''

The old-fashioned word *helpmate* appealed to her and, smiling, she turned the word over in her mind for a moment. Then they had a good laugh when she told him the story of the unexpected guests and Felix's grand rescue.

Then she found herself telling him about Felice's open play for Greg, her face flushing with anger as she spoke. ''She's available,'' she said with bitterness. ''And she lets him know it and doesn't care who else knows it. It's an office joke. How can a woman do that to a man with a wife and children? She has everything, and yet she wants another woman's husband.''

He was shaking his head slowly. Then he surprised her again. ''Poor woman,'' he said softly. ''What an empty life she must have.''

Jill looked at him a moment in disbelief until she understood his meaning. ''I see what you mean. If a person has 'everything,' but still wants something else, then she doesn't really have everything, does she?'' Then she had to smile. ''I hope you aren't going to ask me to understand her and love her. I'm still working at trying to understand and love my mother-in-law.''

They laughed together. ''Actually, I was going to suggest something like that. I know it's hard for the human creature to understand that God loves *all* of us. Even the Lauras and the Felices of the world.''

''I'll give it a shot,'' Jill said, ''if you say so. But don't get your hopes up. I wanted to scream when she gave Greg 'the look'.'' It was so easy to unburden to Pastor Bailey. She was feeling a lot better.

She also told him, with some embarrassment, about not knowing that her next-door neighbor was blind.

''The odd thing is that Laurie knew,'' she said. ''When

I mentioned it to her, to caution her about it, she already knew. She had known it for some time. She said, if I remember correctly, as I was putting her to bed that night, she said, 'Yes, Mommy, she can't see. So I told her about the slide being yellow and red and stuff. She comes out by the fence sometimes and we talk.'" With the simple directness of childhood Laurie had accepted the fact that some people can see and some can't, and had done her five-year-old best to even things out and fill in the gaps. Even telling it, Jill felt a fierce sense of love for her little fusspot child. Laurie was going to be a good person. She needn't worry.

Greg came home from work early that night and seemed to catch Jill's upbeat mood, which she always had after she had talked with Pastor Bailey. He cleared up in the kitchen while she put the children to bed, and tossed aside the evening paper when she came into the living room at last.

"All secure for the night?" he asked.

"For the moment, anyhow, unless somebody gets up," she answered, sighing slightly. It was a relief to sit down. She had got up early and had spent most of the morning preparing some of Kate's last zucchini crop for the freezer. She was learning a lot from Kate, and every penny saved on the grocery bill helped.

"You…you're not going down to the boat tonight?" she couldn't help asking.

"No. Not tonight."

"I'm sorry about the boat thing," she said impulsively. "I know you were disappointed when I turned out to be such a rotten sailor."

He surprised her by laughing. "Yeah, but it's lucky we took that short trip to the San Juans before we set off on our honeymoon. Remember we were going to sail to Kauai for that.''

"Don't remind me," she said, laughing too. "We'd been out—what? Thirty minutes? When I got sick?"

"And sicker and sicker and sicker," he answered. "We can laugh about it now, but it wasn't funny then. Remember the wind got tricky and I couldn't leave the sails and there you were leaning over the side. I was scared to death you'd go over."

"Well, I recall you made up a silly limerick about it later after my stomach calmed down and we were in that quiet lagoon. So you couldn't have been too worried."

"Did I? Yes, I think I did."

"You bet you did. I can quote it for you," she said, and did.

"There was once a romantic guy,
Sailed off with his bride to Kauai.
But his beautiful bride
Gorped over the side.
Till he said, 'You win. Next time we fly.'"

"You remembered that." He seemed pleased and embarrassed at the same time. A rather comfortable little silence fell, and then he changed the subject.

"You know that little kid, Raymond something? He called me at the office today."

"Kate's little-waif neighbor? You're kidding."

"Waif is a good name for him. Yes, Raymond. He's a sharp enough little kid. I didn't talk to him but a couple of minutes out in the garage that night, but I guess he got my place of business from Laurie or Ben. Anyhow, he looked up the number and called."

"For goodness sake, what for?"

"Kids talk with each other," he said thoughtfully. "I'm so sorry for that kid. I guess he'd got it from Laurie or Ben that I come home—that is, I don't go off on business trips. He asked me about my job. He's…poor little guy is trying to find his dad a job that doesn't require travel."

"Oh, Greg, that makes me want to cry."

"Yeah, I got a little choked up myself. I asked about his dad's work. Apparently his dad's firm deals in security devices, surveillance cameras, bugs, night vision equipment and things of that sort. They work mainly with law enforcement. When a small town or rural police department wants to upgrade its procedures, he consults with them on it. Travel is built into the job. I tried to let the kid down as easily as I could, but I felt bad about it. It was frustrating, that powerless feeling when you want to help but there's nothing you can do. But it got me thinking about our kids. Kids do worry about things. I think…I hope things are okay with Laurie and Ben and Meggie." His voice softened as he said their names.

"I've been wanting to tell you something, Jill, but…it never seemed the right time. So I may as well just say it. You were right about this stay-at-home thing. It's different now. The kids are different. More secure, happier, it seems. I wanted to eat lunch alone today and do some thinking so I got a sandwich and went over to that little park near the office. There were kids playing there and it got me thinking about ours." He was looking off into the distance, his eyes thoughtful.

"It's different for them now. No more dropping them off or picking them up, rushing them from here to there. No more their having only one parent at a time because we had to take turns. I got to thinking of Meggie. Have you noticed that she's stopped pulling off her clothes and tossing them away?"

"Come to think of it, she does seem to have dropped that little habit," mused Jill.

"Maybe she just wanted to get attention from somebody, anybody, any parent available."

"You could be right." Jill answered slowly.

"We have to watch Meggie, though. She's the reckless one, the impulsive one. She's always been a bit fey, and some day—I hope it never comes, but she could get hurt."

Jill's heart went out to him. He cared so deeply about their children. The light from the lamp left half his quiet, serious face in shadow and gleamed on his fair hair, making her want to reach out and touch it.

"And Laurie," he went on. "She's changed, too. She's settled down, not so fussy anymore." He was silent for a while, his eyes dreamy.

"And then Ben," he added, smiling slightly. "Ben's our little plodder. I have the gut feeling that he'll have to work really hard to make it up to a B-minus grade level in school when he gets there. My bet is that both Laurie and Meggie will go sailing past him."

"Ben's not dumb," Jill said defensively.

Greg laughed softly. "No, but you must admit, Earth Mother, that our little Ben is always half a beat behind everybody else in the family. There's nothing wrong with being a plodder," he added. "Some of the best people in the world are plodders. What I meant to say before I got wound up like this is that you're doing one heck of a job." His voice was briefly unsteady. "I mean, I wouldn't want anyone else but you as a mother for my kids." He reached out and took her hand.

She couldn't speak for a moment, holding his hand, loving it, the strong, capable hand that could work through a delicate wiring job or put together great chunks of stuff that came unassembled in large boxes. She lifted his hand to her lips and kissed it.

But it was bittersweet. So she was the perfect mother, was she? Big deal. *But I'm your wife, too, Greg.* And she turned his hand over and kissed the palm, letting her lips linger. Long ago she had heard that in a love match there was a Lover and a Beloved. In this one Greg was the Beloved and she the Lover, always seeking, always reaching out.

"Ben is like my dad," she said softly, cradling his hand in both of hers.

"In what way?"

"Oh, somebody somewhere once said that there is always a Lover and a Beloved, and Dad was always the Lover. Mom—she's kind to Dad, cares about him, and, well, I guess she loves him in her way, but she's the Beloved." *Like you,* she thought. *Like you. Only you don't know it. I'm always here. I always will be. How does it feel to be the Beloved? To be the one granting love instead of giving it?*

Suddenly she felt a wave of sadness wash over her. *Oh, dear God, please help Greg see how much I love him. How I want us to be close again.*

"What's the matter?" Greg asked.

"Oh, I don't know. Nothing..." She shrugged and looked down at his hand in her own.

"Jill..." Greg began, his voice tinged with concern. But he didn't get to finish, because the phone rang stridently. Greg reached over and picked it up.

"Hello?" He listened for a long moment and then gestured to Jill. "It's for you. Your mother. She's calling from France. Lyon."

Jill leapt for the phone in sudden panic. Something was wrong!

"Hello? Mom?"

"Jill, darling. It's so good to hear your voice."

"Mom. Yes, it's me. Why are you calling? What's wrong?"

She could hear her mother's soft sigh, and almost see her mother's lovely oval face. She felt a rush of love. Oh, how she had missed them.

"Yes, dear. I'm sorry. There is a problem." Mom sounded tired.

"Well, what? What?" She could feel Greg watching her intently. He was very fond of her parents.

"It's your father, baby. He's gotten sick. Quite sick, I'm afraid. He's had a mild heart attack." Mom's voice shook. "But there's a serious problem and…he wanted to come home now. So we are."

"When? Mom, when? What's your flight number? I'll meet you with—"

"No, dear. It's all arranged. But I want you to go over and tell Katie. I can't…I can't just tell her on the phone." No, of course not. This was vintage Mom, watching over her chicks, protecting them, even in an emergency like this. Kate was Daddy's girl. She would be devastated.

"Yes, of course. I'll tell Kate. I'll handle it, Mom. But tell me your flight number. We'll be there with the van and—"

"No, Jill, listen to me." Mom's voice sounded desperate. "It's all arranged, darling. I've talked with our health care people and…it's all taken care of. *Don't* meet the plane. I'll…call you from Swedish Hospital. They've arranged…there will be an ambulance waiting at the airport."

Chapter Ten

~

Jill hung up the phone, her hands shaking.

"What is it?" Greg was right beside her, and she reached out and went into his arms.

"It's Dad. He's had a heart attack." She felt Greg stiffen, and she held on more tightly. "They're coming home. We...we aren't to meet the plane. Mom said there would be an ambulance waiting."

"Good grief. It's that serious?" Greg put her from him and looked down into her face. "Are you okay?" Then immediately "What about Kate?"

"I'm...I promised Mom I'd go over and tell her. Can you...I mean..." She stopped, confused. "What time is it?" She looked at her wrist and realized that she had left her watch on the kitchen window ledge, as she often did when she worked at the sink.

"Ten-fifteen," Greg said, looking at his. "You mean go over there tonight?"

"Oh, Greg, Kate would never forgive me if I didn't tell her as soon as I knew." She began to feel small tremors of shock go through her body and Greg held her close for a moment, as he would a frightened child.

"Yes, of course, you'd better go. I'll take care of things here. Take a minute to calm down. Take some overnight things in case you need to stay with her."

"But the kids... What..."

"I'll cope. Don't sweat it. If necessary I'll call Mother over. She's good in a crisis, and the kids won't mind too much if it's Gramma Laura."

"All right. All right," she said distractedly, pulling away from him. "I'll get my things." She started to the bedroom. The inward tremors wouldn't go away. *Oh, Dad, I love you so.* Somehow, not quite knowing how, she packed a small overnight case. Did she have everything? Gown. Robe. Slippers. Clean underwear for tomorrow. Panty hose. She could wear the same outfit tomorrow, couldn't she? She had on a shadow plaid skirt in dark green, with a turtleneck top. After Felice's visit she had begun changing in the afternoon from her tacky cutoff jeans and T-shirts. She wanted to look nice when Greg came home. If Greg came home.

"Here." He spoke right behind her, handing her the small plastic travel case she put makeup and creams and lotions in, on the rare occasions when she traveled anywhere. In his other hand he held one of her toothbrushes and the toothpaste.

"Thanks. There's more toothpaste in the bathroom cupboard, you know, with the extra supply of things." Thank goodness for Laurie and her coupon clipping. They were able to buy a lot of things ahead while they could get bargain prices on the coupon.

"You'll need your raincoat," Greg said, and she looked at him blankly.

"You mean it's raining again?"

"Afraid so." And even as he said it they heard a distant roll of thunder. "Jill, watch out on that West Seattle freeway, won't you?"

"Yes, of course, I always do. Don't worry. I'll... Do you want me to call you?" Would she have time? As soon as Kate saw her at this time of night she would know something was wrong.

"Here. Take my cell phone and give me a quick call from the van before you go in. Now, Jill!"

"Yes, what?"

"This is not the end of the world. Ralph is a strong, husky guy. He's never had any health problems that I've ever heard of. And Beth told you it was a mild heart attack. Maybe it's just a warning. What I'm trying to say is don't panic. They can do wonderful things now for heart patients."

"Don't worry. I'm okay now." She smiled bleakly. "Thank you." She raised her face and he kissed her gently.

She left in a drenching downpour, with her hooded raincoat zipped all the way up. Water was running down the driveway as she splashed out to it. Greg had backed the van out of the garage for her and she clambered in.

"Now watch that blasted freeway," he said, shutting the van door. She paused just a split second to watch him run for the shelter of the porch. When he reached it, he turned. The porch light was on and there were droplets of water on his hair and face. Then she shifted into Reverse and backed out.

Jill turned off the headlights just before she pulled to a stop in front of Kate's house, and picked up the cell phone from the seat beside her. She couldn't exactly recall getting here, but she was here. She punched in the number, and while she waited for the answer she looked at the big house next door to Kate's. There was one light on in an upstairs window, and a small, lonely figure stood there, looking out into the dark and rain. Raymond. Poor little waif.

Then Greg answered. "You okay?"

"Yes. Fine. I'm going in now. I'll...thanks."

"Okay. Take care. Good luck," he said. "And give Kate my love."

Just then Kate's porch light went on. She had noticed or heard the van after all. Jill got out and as quickly as she could, after grabbing her bag and overnight kit, hurried up the steps to the front door as Kate opened it.

"Jill. You're soaked. Come in here," Kate said. She hadn't gone to bed yet, but was still in her tacky denim skirt and faded blouse. "What in the world are you..." Then a faint look of alarm showed on her round face and the smile vanished. "Jill?"

"Here, help me," Jill said, her fingers fumbling with the coat zipper. *Anything to put off telling Kate.* She struggled out of the wet coat. "Kate, I had to come because, well, there's been...Mom called..."

Blindly Kate reached out to take the wet raincoat.

"Dad?" Kate said. "It's Dad, isn't it?"

"Yes. He's had a mild heart attack. *Mild,* Kate. Mom said mild. But he wants to come home, so they are, and—"

"When?" Kate asked, her voice tight. "Are you going to meet them? I'll go with you. We'll take your van."

"No, that's all taken care of." Jill made herself say it, reaching out her hands to Kate and noticing that her right hand was wet. "Mom will call us from Swedish. They...the health care people have arranged to have an ambulance waiting for Dad at the airport."

Kate looked at her blankly for a moment, then clutched

the wet raincoat into a ball against her chest, bending over in a kind of rocking movement. She was saying something softly. It took Jill another moment to make out what. She was saying into the wet raincoat, "Oh no, oh no, oh no."

Jill reached forward and embraced her, holding her close. Kate was so small, so short. She was the older of the two, but had always been the runt of the family.

"Come over to the couch," Jill said. "Sit down. I want to tell you about the arrangements." But it was no use. She doubted that Kate heard her. She had started to cry—deep, wrenching sobs, desperate, angry, trying to talk at the same time. Jill made out something of what she was saying. "Not fair...he's so good...worked so hard... waited...saved up...grand tour. You remember, Jill, grand tour...not fair..."

"Aunt Jill?" Jill looked over and saw seven-year-old Tommy, barefoot, in his rumpled pajamas. "How come you're here? What's Mom crying for? Is Mom sick?"

Jill beckoned him close, not wanting to leave Kate.

"No," she said gently, brushing back his shaggy brown hair. "Grampa got sick, and he and Gramma Beth are coming home. Your mom is...just sad because Grampa is sick."

"Will he die?" Tommy asked, his eyes wide. "Daddy died when he got sick." There was fear in his eyes now.

"Not if we can help it," Jill said firmly. "The doctors can do a lot for heart patients these days. Tommy, can you go get some tissues, and shut Joy's door so we won't wake her."

"Sure." Glad for something to do, he darted back into the dark hallway and was back in a moment with the box Kate kept in the bathroom. Jill handed them to Kate and reached out to Tommy. He came to her instantly, cuddling close, but watching his mother intently.

Kate was calming down. Her weeping had an exhausted sound. She was mopping her face patiently, tiredly, as the tears kept seeping out, but the deep sobs were gone now.

"I'm sorry to be such a crybaby," she said, her voice sounding hoarse, "but...something this, just out of the blue." She stopped and was quiet a long time. "It's such a blow," she said finally.

And Jill's mind echoed Kate's early comment—*not fair*. Kate, little short Kate, had taken too many blows already. Claude's long illness. Then Claude's death. Now this. It was too much. Too many blows. The three of them sat for long minutes on the couch, Jill with one arm about each, and after a time she knew she was praying silently, somewhere in the bottom of her mind. *Help us, God. Tell me what to do. Am I helping enough? I love them. Can they feel my love, God? Help me give my strength to Kate at this moment.*

After a while Kate pulled free and stood up.

"Tommy, you ought to be in bed. You'll never want to get up in the morning for school." But she didn't press it when he didn't move. "You ought to go home, Jill. I'm okay. I'm sorry about the outburst, but sometimes—" After a moment she could go on. "I'm all right now. It was good of you to come all the way over here. You're a good buddy."

"I'll stay the night. Greg said he can cope. He sent his love." She was watching Kate carefully and could almost see the dependable strength returning to her sister. There was a tightening of the muscles in the sturdy body, a stiffening of the short neck, and the head rose.

"No, really. I'm fine. When will they get here?"

"Mom said probably tomorrow, early evening. It was daytime when Mom called. They'll take him right over to the hospital and Mom will call us from there."

"Maybe we should be together, then," Kate said.

"Good idea. You're right. Let's be at my place. It's bigger." And they began discussing arrangements—who would drive, what, where. Who would take care of the children. Kate would keep her two home from school. And Jill volunteered Laura or one of her group members to sit when they went down to Swedish Hospital. It was comforting, the three of them together, on Kate's faded old couch, making plans. Tommy drifted in and out of sleep in Jill's arms. And the prayers continued in the back of her mind. *God, am I helping enough? And, oh, please help my dad. Some of the best people in the world are plodders, God.*

In the early-morning hours Kate insisted she go back home, and as she left Kate's house she looked up at the upstairs window next door, but it was dark. Too much trouble. Too much sadness. She hoped the little waif was in bed asleep now.

She slid into bed beside Greg at about three o'clock and got a few hours of restless sleep. When she woke it was to sounds coming from the kitchen. There was a moment of confusion and then the sharp memory. *Dad.* Mom and Dad were somewhere over the Atlantic now, coming home. Coming home. There was so much to do. She got up, struggled into a robe and slippers and went toward the sounds in the kitchen. When she entered, three sober little faces turned to meet her, and Greg was portioning out oatmeal.

"Grampa got sick," Ben informed her.

"They're coming home," Laurie added. "And Gramma Laura's coming over tonight."

Greg looked up. "Do you want some of this, or just toast?"

"Just toast, please," she said, sitting down in her place.

Greg was so good with the kids. "Did you call Laura last night? Can she come?"

"Yeah, she's got a meeting today, but she doesn't need to get here until early evening, and she's glad to do it. And look out the window. It's stopped raining for a while. We get sun breaks today, according to the weather guy on the late news last night. So the kids can play outside a while."

"I like wet sand in my sandbox," Meggie said complacently. "It sticks together when I pat on it." She was patting an imaginary sand shape by her oatmeal bowl.

"That awning over the sandbox doesn't do a lot of good," Greg said, putting bread into the toaster.

"The rain," Ben said, gesturing with his spoon, "comes sideways. See, Daddy, sideways. So it goes under there."

Jill tuned out the children's chatter and didn't tune in again until Greg put two slices of toast on a small plate in front of her. At some point he had also filled a mug of coffee, and the aroma rose enticingly.

"I don't know if you want butter on that or not," he said, sitting down to his own breakfast. "Sometimes you do, sometimes you don't."

Jill looked at the dry toast. "Today's a butter day," she said, reaching for the butter dish.

"I agree," Greg answered. "Be kind to yourself today, Jill. Don't try to do everything. How's Kate taking this?"

Jill felt a tremor go through her body. "It's hit her pretty hard, but she kind of…regrouped. She wouldn't let me stay the night. She sent me home. Kate may be little, but she's got a lot of…of…"

"Guts. Trust Kate to come through. What's the master plan for today?"

She began buttering her toast, at first lightly, then slathering it on, the way she really liked it. "She has a few things to do this morning, then she's coming over here. We have a bigger house, so when Mom calls we'll all be here and can go down to the hospital…if that's what we're supposed to do."

"They're coming over here?" Laurie was delighted.

"Yes, Laurie, then the grown-ups are going down to the hospital to check up on Grampa. Tommy and Joy will stay here."

"Are they sleeping over?" Ben asked.

"Maybe. Maybe not. We don't know that yet."

"I *guess* Tommy can sleep in my room, but he can't mess with my stuff."

Greg said, "When I get to work I'll clue Marshall in that I may need to leave early if I'm needed here. Okay?"

"Yes. Thanks."

It was a strange day, this waiting for a plane over the Atlantic droning toward home. It started out strangely when Kate came in with Tommy and Joy. She didn't look like Kate. She was wearing a suit, something about ten years old left over from the time she had done office work before her first pregnancy. It was brown tweed, with a short, boxy jacket in a slubbed weave that made her look almost stocky. And she had on panty hose and sensible brown walking shoes with barely one-inch heels.

"Well, I thought I'd dress up a bit since we're going down to the hospital later," she said in answer to Jill's surprised look. "I may need an extra pair of panty hose if you have any spares. These are about shot." She took off the jacket and sat down wearily on the living-room couch as both her children headed for the backyard and their cousins.

"Yes, I have spares," Jill said, knowing they would be

too long and wrinkle at the ankle and Kate wouldn't even notice.

"Jill, I hope you don't mind. I brought Raymond along. He's out in the car. But he's too timid to come in unless you say so."

"Raymond? For goodness sake! Don't we have enough to cope with today without—" At Kate's defeated expression, she made herself stop. Kate had forgotten to put on any makeup and there were dark circles under her eyes.

"Their housekeeper, Mrs. Cody, quit. She just gave in her notice and walked off. Ian's in town today, but he had to go to work and he's afraid Raymond might run away again. He didn't want to leave Raymond unsupervised today. Raymond is feeling guilty, I think, about Mrs. Cody leaving and putting Ian in a bind. And Raymond's good with the littler kids. He can kind of help baby-sit." Her voice was placating.

"Okay. Am I supposed to go out and invite him in?" Jill tried not to sound waspish, but she wondered how Laura would appreciate a sixth child added to the five she had agreed to stay with.

"Please, Jill. He's very vulnerable."

You're vulnerable, Jill thought. *You've had about as much as you can take.* But she put on a smile and went out front to get Raymond, who was slouched in the back seat of Kate's old Chevy, looking pitiful. The coaxing wave and smile she greeted him with were genuine.

The strange day dragged on, with both of them confused and distracted. Tasks were begun and left unfinished, forgotten. "Look, we didn't finish making the bed in here. We left off the spread." Things got lost and never found. "Did you see where I put that pot holder? I just this minute had it in my hand!" They followed one another around, talking in half-finished sentences, with lots of *Remember when…* as if to validate that they were still *family,* complete, whole and entire, and Dad was not somewhere over the Atlantic attached to odd little mechanical devices, with Mom and helpful flight attendants hovering over him. He would hate that, be embarrassed by it. *Hang in there, Dad.*

After the strange day came the strange evening. Laura arrived, brisk and smartly groomed, from her meeting, just in time to join them in an early dinner. Then she kissed Kate, something she had never done before, and gave Jill a peck on the cheek, something she almost never did.

"Don't worry about anything," she said. "As soon as the call comes, you folks go. Leave everything. I'll finish up here. Just forget everything."

Greg came in just as they were wondering if he would. As usual he picked up Kate clear off the floor and kissed her on the forehead, kissed his mother and then Jill.

"How'd we get Raymond again?" he murmured in Jill's ear, and she frowned him silent, which he accepted with the faintest shrug.

The telephone rang in the middle of dinner. It was six-thirty. Jill sprang to answer it, relieved to hear her mother's voice.

"Things have been moving pretty fast," Mom said, sounding tense and oddly strident. "But we've got him to Swedish and they're getting him settled. Are you coming down?"

"Yes, of course. We're all here at my place. Shall we come right now or—"

"Give it another half hour anyway, maybe a little more. These examinations take a while. His primary care doctor is here and the cardiologist and…I don't know, lots of people. You can take your time, really."

"Well, how is he? How did he handle the trip?"

"I...don't know. Okay, I think. He...looks sort of... tired and gray. I don't like his color at all." They talked a few minutes longer and Jill went back to the table.

"We can finish here and take our time. He seems to be doing all right, but the doctors are with him." She looked at her half-eaten dinner and couldn't eat any more.

They finished up hurriedly, despite what Beth had said, and left for the hospital as soon as they could. Greg drove the two sisters in Jill's van, and she was grateful. She felt oddly weak and boneless, wanting to lie down. They parked in the great gray mass of the parking garage across from the great gray mass of Swedish Hospital.

"Where in the world do we go?" Kate asked as they crossed the street and went through the main entrance.

"Don't worry about it," Greg said, in the middle, holding on to both of them. "Somebody inside will know. We'll have to walk about eight miles to get there when we find out where. This place is huge. I hope we can find the garage again when we come out."

He was right. Somebody knew and told them pleasantly. They rode in an elevator and tried not to look at the man on the gurney with them who was breathing with great difficulty. A male nurse was with him watching the drip. They walked along hallways, past nursing stations, past clusters of people talking, some in rumpled green smocks, some in white. People hurried by with clipboards. Around a corner somebody laughed. Everybody seemed to have pagers or cell phones. And a mechanical voice over their heads kept asking Dr. Simms to go to Pediatrics.

Then they saw Mom.

And Jill thought again how beautiful she was, with her pale oval face, magnificent dark eyes and the dark hair without a thread of gray. A few years ago she had started wearing it up, in a kind of swirled mass on top of her head, where it stayed, none of it ever falling down. So elegant. So neat. It showed off her lovely slim neck. She gave her sudden sweet smile and hurried toward them.

"Oh, I'm so glad to see you all." She tried to hug them all at once, and everybody was talking, asking questions that nobody answered. For the moment it was enough just being together, holding on to one another.

"What's the prognosis?" Greg asked when they were finally seated in a small group of visitors' chairs in a cul-de-sac in the hall. "Or haven't you got one yet?"

"Sort of, I think," Beth said with a sigh in her voice. She looked bone tired, as if she were pushing herself to go on, a minute at a time. "We had two really good doctors in France, but it cost the earth. Thank goodness for plastic. We'd run out of traveler's checks by that time. Actually, they knew what the problem really is and they told me, and the doctors here just verified it. As soon as we got here they used one of those—I can't remember what it's called. It's a big machine that slowly takes a picture of the whole heart. And two technicians sit in front of a kind of big TV monitor and mutter to each other.

"Well, Ralph's heart is very enlarged. You remember he played football in high school and college. Then he kept putting on weight and taking it off after he settled into being a librarian." Her voice shook slightly. "And we never knew. He'd been a little short of breath lately, and he was getting tired sometimes." She paused to glance at two men in hospital coats coming out of a patient's room, anxiously, as if the patient behind the closed door meant something to her.

"What does it mean? Enlarged heart?" Kate asked.

"Katie, I wish I understood medical things, but we've

always been so…healthy. We never paid much attention. They've used the term *congestive heart failure* a dozen times. They're going to keep him here in the coronary unit for a couple of days for observation. He's stable now. And I've got all these.'' She was gripping a handful of hospital forms. ''To get things going.''

''Insurance?'' Greg asked, reaching out. ''Give them to me. Filling out forms is one of my specialties. I'll ask you for anything I don't know.''

''Can we see him?'' Kate asked timidly. Her sturdy little hands were gripping her brown leather handbag. It was her best, and she seldom used it because it had been Claude's gift to her one Christmas when he couldn't actually afford real leather.

It was understood without saying that Kate would go in first when they got up to go back down the hall to Dad's room.

The pleasant but intimidating nurse said they could each have five minutes, no more. Kate stayed in the sick-room her five minutes and came out looking pinched, and somehow older. Mom motioned Jill to enter and she did, nervously. Even if it was Dad, she was always uneasy in a hospital situation. She never knew what to say after she had delivered the flowers or gift.

It was so strange to see Dad sick. All her memories of him were of a stocky, robust man who was always the one to volunteer to do any heavy lifting, or to twist off the stubborn jar caps with his strong hands. She had a quick mental image of him one year chopping down the biggest snow-covered tree they had ever had for Christmas, then hefting the trunk up over his shoulder to drag it down the snowy hillside. He had about him the look of a workman. People were always surprised to learn that he was a librarian. But Jill, and those who knew him, knew him as a quiet, thoughtful, methodical man with a good mind. At sight of Jill his homely face broke into a smile and Jill smiled back, trying not to see the machine nearby that registered the labored beating of his heart, or the needle that pierced his strong hand lax on the white coverlet.

"Dad, I'm…so sorry. What a rotten way to come home from your trip of a lifetime." Suddenly she felt choked up.

"How's your mother doing, Jill? Tell me." Even his voice didn't sound the same, but was raspy, with no strength behind it.

"She's holding up pretty well, Dad. Mom may look like a delicate flower, but underneath she's pretty tough."

"Good, I…wondered." The Lover, worried about his Beloved. There was a long pause, then, "Sit down, Jill," he invited, and she did. "How's it going with the stay-at-home thing? Your mother and I were stunned when we got your letter telling us about your decision."

"It's going all right, Dad. At first…I had doubts, but I'm sticking with it. And Greg agrees now, too."

"Good girl," he said, and closed his eyes for a time. She wondered if she should go, if he had lapsed into sleep. Then he spoke again, with his eyes still closed. "Did Greg come?"

"Yes. He's out in the hall."

"Good." It seemed more of an effort for him to speak. "I…want to see him before he leaves. Okay?"

She stayed a few minutes longer, and after Mom had a brief visit, she sent Greg in.

Mom talked with the two doctors for a while and they advised her to go home. There was nothing more she could do. If she was needed, someone would call her. Both Jill and Kate urged her to follow their advice. She looked ready to drop.

They rode home making plans and changing them. It was decided that their mother would go home to the big empty house near Kate's, which she and their father had left with such excitement a few months ago, on the grand tour they had waited a quarter of a century for.

"I want to sleep in my own bed," Beth had said. "Travel is great, but…"

It was decided that Kate and her children would go stay with Beth. Kate would drop Raymond off with his father, who would be home now. There was a lot Beth wanted to do tomorrow. She was planning to turn her downstairs sewing and hobby room into a downstairs bedroom for Dad. He mustn't climb stairs anymore. Kate would help her do that.

"I can help," Jill volunteered.

"I have other plans for you," Beth told her. "The airline checked all our luggage down at the airport. That has to be claimed. We couldn't very well take it with us in the ambulance. It has our camera in it. We got such great pictures. And we got presents for all of you and the kids, too. We found such delightful things."

She stopped suddenly and began to cry. Seeing Mom cry was so unusual that neither Jill nor Kate could think of anything to say. Jill's throat ached. It must have been a wonderful journey. She could imagine them poking around in shops, bazaars and marketplaces, finding this or that little treasure. *"Oh, wouldn't this be great for Tommy?"* Or being awed by the great museums or cathedrals or splendid views of strange places. *"We must get a picture looking from this high window."*

Since there was no food at Mom's place, it meant a stop at the supermarket. Jill and Kate went in to shop. Beth was just too tired.

Finally it was just herself and Greg, going home at last.

Jill felt limp with fatigue as they drove into their own driveway.

Laura looked at Jill with real concern when they came in. "Are you all right?" she asked, and Jill was so surprised that she couldn't answer for a moment.

"Yes, tired, but okay," she managed to answer.

"I know you are all...having a bad time," Laura said awkwardly. "So keep it in mind that I'm available to help. Call me. Call me any time. I mean that. Day or night." Then, all brisk efficient Laura again, she kissed Greg and left.

There was something nagging in the back of Jill's mind. She groped for it for a long interval. While they were preparing for bed, she found it.

"Greg, why did Dad want especially to see you?"

"Ralph and I are old friends," Greg said evasively.

"No. He wanted to talk to you. And you stayed a lot longer than five minutes. That nurse was looking at her watch and frowning. You had about one more nanosecond before she went in to get you."

"Oh, come on, Jill. Ralph and I—"

"Knock it off, Greg. What did he tell you? I'm not a child, so stop treating me like one."

"Sorry. I didn't realize I was," he said slowly. "Ralph is no fool, and...apparently he demanded and got some straight answers from the doctors. He's...he's in bad shape."

She had to sit down suddenly on the edge of the bed. "How bad?"

"An enlarged heart can be enlarged in different ways," he said carefully. "The heart is a muscle, and if you overuse any muscle it gets bigger and bigger. You know, we've kidded about those Mr. Universe guys whose back and shoulder muscles are so enlarged they can hardly lift their arms up. Well, the heart overused gets bigger. If you get an enlarged heart, you just hope and pray that it enlarges evenly all around. So that all sides are of uniform thickness. Then, with medication and care you can last a long time. But—''

''But what if it doesn't enlarge evenly?''

''If there is a thin wall, then it is much more vulnerable. Strain can cause the thin wall to…rupture. I mean— You can see I'm no medical expert. I'm trying to quote Ralph as accurately as I can.''

''You're saying that Dad's enlarged heart has a thin wall,'' she said numbly.

''I'm sorry, yes,'' he said gently. ''He can go at any time.''

Chapter Eleven

Jill took all three children with her to Sea-Tac Airport to claim Mom and Dad's luggage the next morning. It was a mistake and made things more confused than they need have been, but for some reason she wanted them near her. After parking in the vast airport garage, she carried Megan, and held on to Ben's hand. Laurie stayed close by, hanging on to Jill's car coat with one of her hands. In the other hand she gripped the baggage checks.

"I really don't like this place," Ben said more than once. "I want to go home."

On the other hand, Megan was fascinated and twisted this way and that in Jill's arms, trying to see everything around her, all the sights and sounds of a busy, over-crowded airport.

Finally it was accomplished, and the luggage loaded in the back of the van, the skycap tipped and the children secure in their car seats.

"I didn't lose the tickets," Laurie said proudly.

"No, you did a good job, and I appreciate it."

"The TVs didn't have any pictures," Megan complained, recalling the many flight monitors.

"Are we going home now?" Ben asked.

"No, we're going over to Gramma Beth's. They're going to fix lunch for all of us." And this Ben approved of.

It was a rather pleasant lunch. They'd come to terms with Dad's illness, each in her own way. There was almost an upbeat mood. Keeping busy had helped. In the midst of changing the sewing and hobby room into a downstairs bedroom for Dad, they had changed their minds. The sunroom was bigger. They were in the process now of reassembling the sewing and hobby room, and later would tackle changing the sunroom into the downstairs bedroom.

"Your dad's always loved that room," Mom said almost happily. "And it's big enough so that we can leave some of the wicker furniture in it." Forgetting how old the wicker furniture was, how faded the cushions and how the chairs squeaked when sat on.

After lunch the children clamored to stay with their cousins and Raymond. Apparently Ian McAllister hadn't yet found a new housekeeper. Jill welcomed the idea. She had a deep need to be alone for a while, to think things out. Obviously, neither Mom nor Kate knew how serious Dad's condition was. Dad, being Dad, had wanted to shoulder the burden alone and was keeping it from them.

"If you don't need me here, then, I do have some things to do," Jill said after they had put the lunch dishes in the dishwasher.

"No. Go ahead. We're okay," Kate said.

Home, when Jill reached it, felt like a sanctuary, and she sank onto the living-room couch. What was ahead of them? If Dad didn't make it...no, don't even think that. Don't even consider it. But if it happened, what about

Mom? It had never occurred to her to inquire into their finances. Mom and Dad were *there*. Did they have any money? Probably not much. Dad had worked as a librarian all his life, ever since he'd finished graduate school with his library science degree. And he was so open-handed.

They own the house. That thought sprang into her mind. From somewhere she recalled that at some point Dad had paid the last installment on the mortgage. So Mom would always have a home—most of which she wouldn't need. Mom, who had wanted half a dozen children, had persuaded Dad to get the big five-bedroom house, with the downstairs hobby room and sunroom and, yes, the large pantry between the dining room and kitchen.

Jill's head was leaning against the back of the couch, her eyes half-closed. The quiet of her home closed about her for an interval of near peace. Then she became aware that she was looking at the phone on the little corner table, and the light on the answering machine was blinking patiently. *Someone wants to talk to me.* She resisted this idea, let it blink. I'm not at home. *Oh, rats.* She got up with a slight groan. What now? She went over and pressed the button, and with little shivers of shock she recognized Dad's voice.

"Jill, dear. This is Dad." Then there was a pause. "It's ten-fifteen. I'd like you to come down and see me, if you can." How like Dad to add the *if you can.* "I need to talk to you. Okay? Love ya." Then the sound of the phone being hung up, with a fumbling and bumping noise, as if he was having trouble getting it into the cradle. Of course Dad could dial out. He had a phone on that table beside the bed. She'd seen it last night.

It was almost two now, and he'd called at ten-fifteen. She hurriedly looked up the hospital number and called.

The phone in his room rang five times and was answered by a nurse.

"Mr. Bennett is with his doctors now. Can he call you back?"

"No, thanks. He called me and asked me to come down. This is his daughter, Jill. Just tell him I'm on my way. I just now got his message. Thanks."

On the way to the hospital she made a quick stop at a bank machine. She used one so seldom now that she had to look up her *PIN* number, but she'd need parking money. She'd given the last of her cash to the skycap.

When she got to the hospital it was midafternoon and Dad was back in his room. He appeared to be sleeping, so Jill sat down quietly in a bedside chair. He opened his eyes and smiled his homely smile.

"Thanks for coming down. I find it kind of embarrassing to be a problem. I'm the guy who always fixed the problems. I've never been a problem myself before." His voice sounded somewhat stronger today. "Maybe that's not a bad epitaph for a guy. Ralph Bennett. He was never a problem. Not many men can say that. Sounds like something out of Auden's "The Unknown Citizen." Remember our poetry-reading phase? Jill, if you start to cry, I'm going to cancel this interview."

She gulped. "Sorry, Daddy."

"Good girl. What are your mother and Kate up to? They both stopped in for a short visit, and insisted in talking about nothing but the trip—our aborted trip."

"They're fixing up a downstairs bedroom for you, so you won't have to climb stairs anymore."

He gave a shaky sigh. "Greg called. He told me you pinned him down about my sorry condition."

"Yes, I did."

His big hand groped for hers and she took it, clinging to it as she had as a little girl.

"I think we both know that I probably won't be using the downstairs bedroom, don't we? You don't have to answer that. Just listen. Of all my womenfolk you are the strongest, Jill. And you're going to have to use that strength in the days ahead. I wanted to talk to Greg about this last night, but that pretty little blond nurse is a dragon in disguise. She thinks it's in my best interest to be alone in here looking at the ceiling. I don't want to look at the ceiling. When time may be running out, a guy doesn't want to waste whole minutes pondering the ceiling. I want to…" He paused, and seemed to rest for a long moment. "Back to business," he resumed. "If I have to look at the ceiling tonight instead of talking to Greg, will you tell him this. I, that is, your mother and I, own our home, free and clear. I paid that off. I've got some savings, which this hospital bill will probably wipe out, if it hasn't already."

"Dad. Don't worry about things like that now."

"I'm not worrying. I'm just filling you in on the facts. This is the way things *are*. These are the things you're going to have to deal with. When I go, your mother gets a modest pension from my years spent among Seattle's books. I have a $20,000 whole life policy. Your mother is the beneficiary. She can probably sell the house for a substantial sum. We've kept it up. Maybe she could get a small condo. Or team up with Kate. That's up to them. Now, Jill, listen carefully to this. I know your mother well. Don't let her blow all our limited assets on my send-off. That's what she'll try to do if you, or someone, doesn't stop her."

"I'll try, Dad. If you say so." Her voice sounded

wooden, she was trying so hard to hold on to her composure.

"Thank you. And always remember, Jill. Your old man had a good run. I married the best wife in the world. I couldn't believe my luck. And I was blessed with two wonderful daughters. My work in the world of books I loved. That was a very good deal. I couldn't have asked for better. Try to look after your mother. And...look after Katie. I do worry about my Kate."

"I do, too. And I'm working on that, Dad." She felt a weak pressure from his hand in quick understanding.

"Good girl," he said again and closed his eyes for a while. "What time is it?"

"Almost four."

"Better go now. Little Dragon comes on duty at four, and when she does I'd better be watching the ceiling. I think this ceiling is very important to her."

I can't leave him yet. There's so much I haven't said. "Jill?"

"I love you," she blurted. "I can't...there's so much to say and I can't...can't think...I love you."

"Oh, Jill, you just said it all. And I thank you for it."

She stayed a few minutes longer, but he seemed exhausted so she left, hurrying blindly down the hall to where she had seen a women's rest room. She plunged in and went into a booth before she broke down. Leaning against the door of the cubicle, she cried as quietly as she could, hoping nobody could hear. She didn't want to be a problem. *My father was never a problem.* She flushed the toilet a few times to cover any sounds she made, and slowly the sharp grief subsided and some sort of calm returned.

So, be strong Jill. But she didn't feel strong. She felt drained. She left the cubicle and washed her face in cold water at one of the basins and dug in her shoulder bag for some makeup. She thought by the time she got back to Mom's house maybe they wouldn't notice. Maybe her eyes wouldn't be so puffy.

What's for dinner, Jill? This would be the night Greg came home expecting something to eat. Well, she'd put it off until she picked up the kids. Maybe she'd stop at some deli. Hang the expense.

But the problem was solved when she got to Mom's house.

"We're eating here," Laurie announced. "Daddy's coming, because Aunt Kate called him and told him."

"Oh, good," Jill said, sinking into a living-room chair that gave her a good view of the dining room. Mom had kept a kind of *House Beautiful* home. Everything was old now but kept up, except in the sunroom, which everyone used most. Raymond was setting the dining-room table. He was really a rather nice child. Too bad Kate couldn't... She sat up straight. Raymond wasn't miserable when he was with Kate and her kids. Raymond was searching for a family. Kate needed another income. Ian McAllister needed someone to look after Raymond. It seemed so obvious and simple. And Dad had said, "Look after Katie."

Jill got up and went into the kitchen. Kate was at the sink putting together the salad.

"Kate, can Mom do that? I need to talk to you."

"It's not about your dad, is it?" Mom said in quick alarm.

"No, Mom," Jill said, hugging her. "This is something Kate and I have argued over, I mean, discussed in the past."

"Well, this better be good," Kate said, drying her hands. She followed Jill into the pantry.

"Maybe this is the wrong time," Jill said as the pantry

door to the kitchen swung shut. "But I just got a very sensible idea, and I want to run it past you. Why don't you offer to take care of Raymond?"

Kate looked at her blankly. "I am taking care of Raymond. Didn't you see him in the dining room? Ian hasn't got a new housekeeper yet."

"No. I mean take care of him permanently. For a fee. I mean a salary. He pays his housekeeper, doesn't he? Why couldn't he pay you? And Raymond is certainly happier with you—"

"You mean ask Ian for money! I would *never* ask him for money to look after Raymond! He's my neighbor! Neighbors help neighbors!"

Not always, Kate. Not always, Jill thought sadly, remembering Mrs. Hopkins and her Meals-on-Wheels and the unseen dust bunnies under her couch. And Kate was clearly appalled.

"Jill, for goodness sake! Haven't we got enough to worry about now, with Dad so sick? Why would you bring up a silly thing like that now? Forget it! Just forget it!" Angrily Kate pushed open the swing door and went back into the kitchen.

Well, you sure blew that one, Jill. Still thinking it was an excellent idea, Jill pushed open the swing door to the dining room and went in, where Raymond was surveying his very nicely laid table. He turned and gave her his most angelic smile. He really was an attractive child when he wasn't sulking. She heard Greg coming in, to the children's exuberant greetings, returned Raymond's smile and went back into the living room.

After dinner it was decided that Kate and Mom would go back to the hospital to look in on Dad. Did she want to come?

"No. I stopped in this afternoon," Jill said. "We can't tire him out."

"No," Greg agreed. "We'll just take our brood and go on home." As he kissed Beth goodbye, he added to her, "Call me if you need anything."

"I will, dear. Did you fill out those insurance papers?" Beth asked, patting his shoulder.

"Just about finished. You can sign them tomorrow," he answered reassuringly.

Later, in the haven of home again, with the children in bed, Jill went into the living room. Greg was sitting on the couch with the unopened evening paper beside him.

"Dad talked to me today about finances," Jill said, sitting down across from him. "They really don't have all that much." She gave him the sparse list of assets Dad had mentioned.

"I know," Greg said. "Ralph and I talked about this some time ago. Before they left on their trip."

"Do you think he had some sort of premonition?"

"Oh, no. It's just that Ralph is very much a realist. And they were going on a long trip, riding planes and trains and buses. He takes life as it is. You know, I was always the executor of his will."

"Yes, I knew that."

"Well, last night he wanted to give me a power of attorney. I don't know if it's really necessary but it might be helpful. So this morning I took one over, but that little nurse shooed me away before he had any time to talk much. The doctors wanted some test or other."

"You mean Dad expects you to take care of everything?" Jill felt again the sense of being beholden, of imposing. "Greg, I'm sorry."

"About what? This is family. We can't expect your mother to handle much. She'll be devastated."

"You talk as if he's already gone," Jill said resentfully.

"You insisted last night on knowing the worst, Jill. We have to face facts. This is hitting me hard, too. Remember, Ralph and I have been fast friends ever since I asked him for your hand. I'll never get over how pleased he was when I told him I wanted to ask you to marry me. I had Ralph scoped out from the get-go. I did it mostly tongue in cheek, thinking I could make a stack of brownie points with my future father-in-law. He wasn't entirely fooled, either, but he appreciated it."

"I know he's mentioned it often enough," she said fondly.

He waited a while. "Do you want to hear some more of the 'worst'?"

"I guess I'd better. Dad said today that I was the strongest of his womenfolk."

"You are. Which is probably why I fell for you in the first place. They say guys are attracted to women like their mothers, and my mother is a strong woman."

Stunned at being compared to Laura, something that would never have occurred to her, she missed the first part of what he was saying.

"...told me the best they could hope for is a transplant. He can get on a list—"

"Wait. Who told you what? I missed that. Start over."

"I said I talked with the cardiologist. The heart guy. He told me there are hundreds of patients waiting for hearts. Getting on the list is often an exercise in futility, but they put Ralph on. Ralph has ruled out any and all of those artificial hearts people get attached to. He wants none of that."

"He shouldn't rule out anything," Jill said desperately.

"Then I talked with the insurance people. They cover

quite a lot, but not everything, of course, so there's going to be a big bill.''

"Dad was afraid of that. He said it would probably wipe out his savings.''

"Probably. But let's cross that bridge when we get there.'' He started to say something else when the phone rang, and he reached over to the small table to answer it. He listened a moment, a half smile touching his mouth.

"For you,'' he said. "Raymond.''

"Raymond? You're kidding.'' She took the phone. "Hello?''

"Hi, Miz Rhys. It's me, Raymond. That was a real cool idea you talked to Miz Graham about. You know, in the pantry. I listened,'' he added without embarrassment.

"Well, Raymond, I tried,'' Jill said.

"Yeah, well, I just pitched the idea to my dad. He thinks it's a cool idea, too. And he's gonna pitch it to Miz Graham.''

Jill didn't know whether to laugh or cry. "Tell him good luck. I sure struck out.''

"I don't think he'll have that problem, Miz Rhys. I think it's a done deal awreddy. My dad walks away with the Best Salesman of the Year award at his company every year. So I don't think Miz Graham has a chance. Bye.''

She hung up the phone and turned to Greg. "Would you believe it? I think something is going to come out all right.'' And she told him about it.

"That would be a heck of a good solution to Kate's money problem. She looks after the kid most of the time, anyhow. Good for you.''

"Do you think McAllister will be able to convince Kate?''

"I hope so. Besides, it's so sensible. Kate's got to see the plain good sense of it."

"I sure hope you're right." Jill had a welling of relief. Maybe Kate was taken care of. Maybe just that one thing would come out right.

A silence fell between them and, strangely, Greg did not pick up the evening paper to read as he usually did. He laid his head back against the couch, and Jill studied his strong jawline and throat. He had reached up and pulled his tie loose. What was he thinking? Now, at this moment? She'd been married to him for more than six years. She had loved his body and his mind, his quiet humor, his decency, his kindness, his deep loyalties, but did she really *know* him?

"Would you do me a favor, Greg?" she asked.

"Sure. If I can." He spoke absently, idly, as if his mind was still elsewhere.

"Will you tell me honestly, even if you don't want to, what you were thinking about *just now,* looking off into space like that?"

He sat up straight at the seriousness of her tone.

"You really mean that?" He sounded startled.

"Yes, I do. I do mean it. Sometimes you are so shut away...so distant."

He frowned slightly. "I don't mean to be. I guess I was thinking." He paused. "I guess I was thinking that with Ralph as bad off as he is, that with a family crisis looming, I was thinking—you'll probably think this sounds dumb—but I was thinking that I can handle it."

"You can handle it?" she asked blankly, not understanding.

"Yes. You see, Jill—I'm not sure you are going to understand this, but a few months ago I think if this had happened, it would have flattened me. I don't think I could have handled it. I mean, everybody depending on me, all of a sudden.''

"I'm afraid you've lost me. I don't get it," Jill said.

He sighed. "I was afraid you wouldn't. I am exactly six feet tall, and I happened to get a very good set of genes, which gave me nice broad shoulders and a strong body. Looking at me, say, walking down the street, somebody might say, 'There goes a strong guy.'" The slight color of embarrassment rose in his face. "You see, you can't tell from the outside that inside maybe the guy is mush.''

"But you're *not* mush. You *are* strong."

"You could be right," he said with a slight smile. "I may be finding that out myself now. Who knows? I only know that a few months ago when you told me you were giving up the Shack to stay home…I was scared to death.''

"Greg! No! I'm so sorry. I didn't realize."

"I know you didn't. And I didn't want you to know. Guys don't want people, especially wives, to know things like that. It isn't the, shall I say, 'manly' thing. But you see, I wasn't really prepared for it. All my life, all my growing-up years, my mother was head honcho in our family.''

"I know she was in with your father's business, that property-management firm. They were in it together." Jill searched her memory for what she could recall about it. "I remember your mother sold the business when your father died.''

"She needn't have. She could have run the business on her own. She had been doing it for years. I guess…she wanted to keep up the illusion that it was my father's business and she was helping him. She worshiped him, Jill. You talked the other night about your parents, your mother being the Beloved. In my family it was just the reverse. My father was the Beloved. Everything and everyone in the whole household revolved around him. He wasn't really…a bad person, but it's just that, I guess, if you receive enough adulation for a long enough time, you begin to believe you're entitled to it, that you deserve it. He was very demanding, very spoiled. Everything took second place to whatever he wanted, at any given moment.''

Jill didn't know what to say. She didn't want to—couldn't dare—break the spell. The door shut for so long was opening. She moved from the chair to the floor in front of him, her legs curled underneath her, and reached for his hand. It was warm clasping hers.

''I know you have a hard time with my mother, and I'm always sorry, but I feel defensive about her. I've thought about her a lot, in connection with you. And I think now, this protectiveness she feels about me, this incessant *hovering,* is because she has some sense of guilt about me.'' He paused a long moment. ''When she was trying to make my father's life perfect, she didn't have much time for me. And I think now she regrets it…and tries to make up for it. She needn't, but she doesn't know that. When my mother loves, she loves very…fiercely.'' There was a soft apology in his tone.

''We—she and I—are getting along better now,'' Jill said hesitantly. ''I'm really trying.''

''I know. I see it. And I'm grateful. She hasn't had a…very good life.''

Suddenly Jill understood what Pastor Bailey had meant when he had said *To understand is to forgive.* And all the old angers against Laura seemed as nothing now. Laura, with what she had left of her life, was doing the best she could. Jill also remembered the words with which Pastor

Bailey always ended his Sunday sermons. *Love one another.* She laid her head down on Greg's hand.

"I'm so sorry you were afraid," she murmured.

"Well, I'm not now. I'm sort of…getting my bearings. Those first few weeks I always had the sensation that— any minute now—the sky would fall. The idea, the very *idea,* of my being sole provider of a family of five was terrifying. The only consolation I had was the conviction that I was keeping it to myself, that nobody else knew how I felt. How unsure I was that I could pull it off. I thought if I could keep it hidden, just maybe I could muddle through. You didn't know. I could tell that. You seemed to have perfect confidence that I'd make it okay. I think that sort of propped me up until I…felt I actually *was* coping. I had—always have had—such confidence in your judgment. If *you* thought I could make it, then…I just might cope."

"You *were* coping," she whispered fiercely. "You *coped.*"

"Not getting Marv's job was a blow, but I'll…deal with that later some time, after we…look after things for Ralph. First things first." He reached down and pulled her up onto the couch into his arms, kissing her gently, comforting her because her father was dying, and she was grieving. Oh, there was so much more to Greg than she had known.

She'd been married to Greg for more than six years, had lived with him, loved being loved by him, borne his children—but she hadn't really *known* him.

No wonder he had been distracted, preoccupied, taking extra jobs, working overtime. There was a far deeper meaning to Greg, going through the motions, than she had understood. Greg, accepting the stunning blow of suddenly being the sole family provider, with everyone depending on him. *And coming through.* And now, Greg taking over because she and Kate and Mom needed him.

This is family, he had said.

Greg, secretly afraid and unsure, was leading the way anyhow, whether he thought he could do it or not. Was this what marriage was really all about? Was this the *one-ness* they talked about? When "I" must give way and become "we," because one needed the other, because her needs were his needs, because of the oneness. She felt a deep sense of humility.

She had, somehow in the daily struggle, become a good mother. Could she, somehow, become a good wife? As good a wife to Greg as he was a husband to her? *Help me, God.*

She lay in his arms for a long time, resting against his strength, so that when the call came it was more bearable.

Gently he put her aside and got up to answer the phone. Only one call would come in this late. For some reason she stood, too. She wasn't sure why.

"Hello...? Yes, this is Greg Rhys." Then there was a long pause. "Thank you. Yes, I'll take care of it." He hung up the phone.

"Dad?" she asked, faintly surprised at how steady her voice was.

"I'm sorry. Yes. He's gone."

Chapter Twelve

It was a redbrick church, the church of her childhood, where she and Kate and Mom and Dad had attended all during her growing-up years. The Reverend Cyrus Ledbetter read the service for Dad. He didn't need to ask the family for any information, because he had known Dad as a faithful church worker for all the years he had been there.

Somehow the family had got through the days since Dad's death, making the necessary arrangements, trying to comfort one another, worrying about how Mom would get through it. The goodness of people helped. Jill had been confounded by the simple goodness of people.

Mom's, Kate's and now her own refrigerator and freezer were filled with prepared food from kindly people who would come and say, "You really won't have time to cook, so..." The women of the church were also handling the reception in the church recreation room after the service, to relieve Mom of this—so much kindness, such an outpouring of love.

Jill sat with the rest of the family in the section for the

bereaved and she could see the congregation as they came into the church, with the softest and most comforting of organ music in the background. "Abide with Me," "Rock of Ages" and all the old hymns that Dad had liked.

The church became full to overflowing. Some folding chairs were brought from somewhere by somebody and placed at the back, and here and there. And there were so many people who hadn't known Dad at all, but who came for those he had left behind. Jill saw many familiar faces among the others. The McAllisters, father and son, because they cared for Kate. And so many people from Greg's office. The Marshalls, Marv and even Felice, looking almost sad. What did Felice have to be sad about? Then, with a small lift of the heart, Jill saw Felix and Connie and, yes, even Angel. Which of his two jobs had he left today in order to come? And Pastor Bailey came, coming to hug her and shake hands with Greg and meet the others, before taking his seat with the congregation.

And there were Isabelle and Marijane, and a few rows in back of them was Daphne with—who? Mrs. Hopkins, her neighbor from next door, her head tilted back slightly, listening to the music. None of these people could do anything to help, because there was nothing left to do. But they were saying silently by their presence, *I'm here. I'm standing by.*

She and Kate had both brought their children to the service. She had asked Greg, "Should we take Meggie, too?" and he had said, "This is family. She's part of it. We can't shut her out." And Meggie, round eyed at the solemnity of the service, sat quietly on Laura's lap, perhaps not understanding, but taking it all in. Later she would remember and understand that this was part of her heritage.

She and Greg had discussed how they could best help through the service and afterward. "I'd better stick with Beth," he had said. "And you stay close to Kate." It had proved good advice during the hour or so the family stayed at the reception, and later at the grave site in the cemetery. Mom had retained an outer composure, looking elegant in her dark charcoal gray suit—but thinner, her lovely face almost gaunt. Kate did the best she could, but now and then tears rolled unheeded down her cheeks and she would apologetically mop them away with tissues handed to her by Tommy. He had brought packets of tissues, stuffed in the pockets of his too-short jacket. He outgrew his clothes so fast these days. Even in the too-short-suit he had a childish dignity that made Jill proud of him.

At one point, by graveside, Ben asked in an audible tone, "Daddy, is God here?" Greg's quiet "Yes" reassured Ben and he said firmly. "O--*kay*," as if that was that.

Greg drove them all back to Mom's house in the van, and they were filled with a kind of lethargy. It even affected the children. It was the letdown after an interval of emotion. It was almost lunchtime, so Jill and Kate went into the kitchen.

"Nobody's really hungry," Kate said as they put out a couple of the donated bowls of salad brought by friends, and some sliced meats and cheese. "I think Mom has about had it with the kids underfoot. So, as soon as we finish this, I'll take my brood and go home."

"But who'll stay with Mom?" Jill asked. "She can't stay here all alone in this big empty house. Maybe she'll come home with me for a few days."

"And you'll park your kids where?" Kate asked with

a tired smile. "No, Laura said she'd stay with Mom for a while."

"Laura?" Jill said, so surprised she put a plate down on the counter with a thump that almost broke it.

"Who better?" Kate asked, putting the lid back on a jar of salad dressing. "Laura knows what it means to lose a husband, and she doesn't come with two kids attached. Mom could use some quiet time, Jill. Travel is stressful even if it is fun, and Mom had several months of that. Then Dad... Laura's a quiet person. She said she'd look after things for a few days. You know, make the morning coffee, things like that. Talk with Mom, if Mom wants to talk. Or go read a book if Mom wants solitude. It seemed a good idea."

"Yes, it's a very good idea," Jill said softly.

She and Greg went home shortly after the lunch that nobody ate much of. Neither she nor Kate monitored what the children ate. It had been a strange day for children, so she wanted to let them do as they pleased. Tommy had said, "Mom, I really don't want this stuff. I'd really like to pig out on cake." And Kate had smiled wanly and said, "Pig away, Tom. Tomorrow we're back on the Program." It had been the one light moment during the somber meal.

Finally in her own home again, Jill put the children down for a delayed nap, with remarkably little argument. They were all tired. When she went into the bedroom to change her clothes she was surprised to see Greg in jeans, T-shirt and windbreaker.

"You're not going back to the office?" she asked in surprise.

"Nope. I couldn't concentrate if I did. I decided to rake leaves. I need to get outside for a while. I think that tree manufactures new leaves every night while we're sleeping."

"Mind if I come along?" she asked, shutting the closet door.

"Good idea. You can help. You sure don't have to cook anything for dinner tonight, assuming anybody's hungry."

"I'll bring the plastic bags," she said to his retreating back. Then she changed to an old sweat suit and warm jacket.

Outside it was a classic October day, cold and gray, with dampness in the air. The sky overhead held masses of gray clouds scarcely moving, as there was no wind at the moment. There were a few ragged chrysanthemums left in the garden, with a couple of valiant buds. The tree had shed a whole new layer of red leaves over the sodden leaves from the rain. Greg was coming out of the garage with two rakes, and they set to work.

"We can get this cleared if the wind holds off a while," he said. They stopped now and then when a pile of leaves was ready, to push them into a plastic bag. They had three bags full, which Greg took out to the alley for pickup, when the wind came back, at first teasingly, a gust here, a shiver among the tree branches there. They tried for a while longer near the fence on Mrs. Hopkins's side, but gave up. As soon as they had the beginning of a pile of leaves, a gust of wind would tear into it, scattering them wildly.

"Okay, let's give up," Greg said. "Can't fight Mother Nature when she wants to play games." They put the rakes back into the garage and sat down on the white-painted garden bench. Jill pushed her cold hands into her jacket pockets.

"We're going to have an aftermath, you know," Greg said quietly. "Are you prepared for that?"

"What do you mean?"

"The aftermath. After the funeral. I remember how it

was with my father. It was sort of a…dead time. Mother and I were sort of just getting through the days. Life was a very…dull gray."

Jill thought about it for a moment, remembering Claude's death five or so years ago. "And next month is Thanksgiving," she said.

Greg looked at her questioningly for a moment before he understood. "Wow, yeah." Family tradition had always been that both of Ralph's daughters gathered with their families at Ralph's home, with any stray relatives like Claude's father and Greg's mother. Mom had always done her homemaker best and Dad had always carved the great bird, with another one in the kitchen to provide what he called "leavings" for next day's snacks. Mom always sent everybody home with a leftovers bag.

Half the fun of Thanksgiving, Dad had always said, *is going back to the fridge later.* And eating gobbets of cold sage stuffing, or making a thick turkey sandwich and don't hold the mayo. Not necessarily because you were hungry, but because it was *there,* and it took you back in time to a day when all the family had been around the big table laughing and talking and together.

"And," Greg said, "Christmas, too."

They sat tiredly on the bench a while, not talking at all as the wind picked up. First it was there in little swirls and gusts. Then it was moving the tree's big branches, which groaned and swayed, raining down a wild scatter of leaves. As the wind got stronger, even the two empty swings swayed this way and that, their ropes twisting. Leaves darted up and flew through the air as if they had a life of their own.

"I think Mother Nature is winning," Greg said after a while. "I'm about to give up and go back inside."

"Me, too." They both got up.

In the kitchen they found Laurie had wakened from her nap and was looking into the open refrigerator.

"We have three kinds of cake," she announced. "I bet Mrs. Hopkins will be surprised."

"I bet she will, too," Jill agreed. "Greg, I could use a cup of coffee. How about you?"

"Good idea," he said, sitting down at the kitchen table. "Is Mrs. Hopkins a cake fancier?"

"Yes," Jill said, beginning to make the coffee. "After that Meals-on-Wheels incident, I began thinking about it. They provide a good basic nutrition for people who can't cook anymore, but it's a no-frills kind of thing. So I asked her if she ever missed the little treats, the sweet things. Turns out she does, so I've begun handing little things over the fence whenever something I make turns out well. And, of course, she gets a piece of *anything* Felix sends over." *My neighbor, Mrs. Hopkins.*

"I can't drink coffee yet," Laurie said pointedly, sitting down beside her father. Both Greg and Jill laughed, and Jill took the milk jug out of the fridge for hot chocolate. She took out a small pan, then put it back for a larger one. Might as well make enough for three, as the other two would come trailing out soon.

The aftermath began in the dull gray days that followed. The two sisters talked to each other more often on the phone. It seemed important about the condolence cards. Jill had never thought much of sending cards before now, but each sympathy card that came was another validation that Ralph Bennett had been here, lived his good life and gone on ahead. They passed the cards back and forth and guarded them almost jealously, keeping careful count. They'd had no idea how many people had known and liked their father enough to note his passing with regret and sorrow.

Mom had good days and bad. She was thinner, and they all urged her to eat more. "Mom, you've got to eat more. Try milky things. That puts on the weight," Kate had advised one day.

"I am. I really am," Mom had said valiantly. "I don't want to be a problem." And nobody understood why Jill, of all people, suddenly started to cry.

Laura, quietly competent, stayed on with Beth in the big house. The two older women had always gotten along well, but now a firm friendship seemed to be forming between them.

There came the time when they had to talk about money. It was the week before Thanksgiving, the holiday they all avoided planning for, except in little private asides. "What in the world are we going to do for Thanksgiving?" Or "I wish the Supreme Court would rule Thanksgiving unconstitutional for this year." Or "How about having something totally different? Like... like...enchiladas. Or all Italian. Or maybe Chinese."

Jill opened the subject of money one night after the children were in bed. There had been an early light snow, just a dusting.

"Do you think we'll have a white Christmas for the kids this year?" she asked, closing the curtains against the night. They were having a fire in the fireplace every evening now.

"In Seattle, who can tell?" Greg answered, putting aside the evening paper. "We take what we get."

"Have you finished all the business stuff? About Dad?"

"Just about. I haven't talked to Beth about it yet, because she seems so...frail these days. I didn't want to burden her.''

''What burden? Isn't it just paying off any bills and settling—''

''The hospital bill, even for those few days, was horrendous. And they had some credit card debt—everything costs so much more in traveling than you think it will.''

Jill sat down across from him so she could see his face in the firelight. *What a beautiful man.*

''Are you saying there isn't going to be enough money? Mom will get a pension from Dad's work, and he said something about she could sell that big old house and get a small condo.'' She stopped because Greg was shaking his head.

''I kind of ran that idea past her the other day and she looked horrified, so I dropped the subject. Jill, Beth's home is that big house Ralph and she bought thirty years ago and have lived in and raised their daughters in. I don't think it has crossed her mind that she might have to give it up.''

''Oh, good grief. And I know she spent a fortune on Dad's funeral,'' she said contritely. ''Dad specifically asked me to see that she didn't do that, but somehow...I couldn't.''

''No. I can understand that. People in grief want to do that one last thing. It's too bad. But yes, that was a bundle. Do you want to know the worst?''

''I guess I'd better.''

''When all the bills are paid, she's in the hole. And I don't see how she's going to go on living on that pension, in that house—or not for long, anyhow. That's prime Seattle real estate and, since the rezoning, the taxes have gone up.''

''I guess she could get a good price for it, then.''

"She could get a whopping price for it, but if it broke her heart to give it up, what good would a whopping price do?"

"Oh, Greg."

"We may have to help out financially for a while, just until she...comes to terms with things."

"Can we afford it?" Jill tried to keep the panic out of her voice.

"We don't have much choice, Jill," he said reasonably. "Kate can't help, at least not financially. And I, for one, don't want to go to Beth in her grief and throw this at her. I think she's had about as much as she can take for now. If worst comes to worst, we...can always borrow from the kids' college funds. They're not going to need that money for a long time, so we'd have plenty of time to put it back."

Jill was a long time getting to sleep after she went to bed. How right Greg had been about the aftermath. When would they ever get through the gray days? When would everything be all right again? *Which way, God? What now?*

Chapter Thirteen

Jill was looking after Posey for Daphne during the morning. She had her in a baby swing that was easy to move from room to room as she did her housework.

Felix called when Jill was grappling with getting the vacuum cleaner attachments back into their fitted case. They always seemed to get bigger when exposed to the air outside the case, so she had decided to let a message go on the answering machine. Then as soon as she heard Felix's voice, she dropped the attachment and rushed for the phone.

"Wait, Felix. I'm here," she said, keeping an eye on the baby swing, as Posey had discovered wiggling up and down in it, which made the whole frame wobble.

"Oh, hi. I guess this must be a bad time for you," he said apologetically. From the background noise, she could tell he was calling from the Shack.

"No, it's fine. I've been meaning to call you, anyhow. Thank you and Connie for coming to Dad's service. It meant a lot."

"Oh, well," he said, sounding embarrassed. He cleared

his throat and started over. "I was just wondering what you folks are going to do for Thanksgiving. I remember it's a big family do for you."

"Yes," she said dolefully. "It always has been. You'd know, of course, because last year I left you and Connie flat with one temp waitress to run the Shack alone while I went to the family feast."

"We survived. But seriously, is it going to be tough for you? And if so, why not do something different? Why don't I reserve the private dining room, and all of you come down here? You'd all be together—which I think is the purpose of the family festival thing—but you could each order something different, if the idea of the traditional bird gets to you."

"Felix! You're a genius!" She felt a great wave of relief.

"I was wondering when you'd notice," he said smugly. "How about it?"

"Yes! By all means! I'll talk it up, but I think I can give you a ninety-nine-percent-sure reservation. One condition!"

"What's that?"

"This we pay for. You're too openhanded, Felix. Business is business."

"Well, we can talk about it later if you want to, but business is better. I mean, we're managing better. I can take Angel or leave him—gladly—but he keeps a firm hand on the till. Incidentally, we can make the December payment, on time and in full. I'm afraid courtesy of Angel. I hate to admit it, but he has his uses."

Jill hung up the phone feeling a warm glow of gratitude. The fact that Felix, working rapidly and efficiently in the kitchen of the Shack—probably complaining that his feet hurt—could think of his friend's needs was very touching. *Thank you, God, for Felix's friendship. If Felix ever needs me, let me know it and help him whether he asks or not.*

She called Kate to run the idea past her, and Kate was very relieved. "And, incidentally, I can pay my share," she added.

"What do you mean?" Jill asked, half-knowing what was coming.

"Maybe I should ask Felix if he has any crow, and order that," she said ruefully. "The strangest thing happened. Would you believe that Raymond was listening at the pantry door at Mom's that day you came up with the idea that Ian should pay me for looking after the boy?"

"Yes, I could believe that," Jill said, suppressing a smile. "Raymond is a sharp little kid. He wouldn't miss much."

"Well, Ian came over last night. I think he waited what he thought was a decent interval after Dad's funeral. Anyhow, he is really so sensible, so reasonable, so practical. I'm sorry I flared up at you for making the same suggestion. But somehow, when he laid out the plain, commonsense reasons for us to get together for Raymond's care, I finally got it. It's a marvelous idea, for everybody concerned."

"How nice!" Jill said. "I'm so glad." Apparently being salesman of the year hadn't hurt.

"I think he's paying me too much, but he insists that's what it should be. Raymond will commute back and forth. The kids love the idea. He'll sleep over here when Ian is gone and take all his meals with us. I guess—oh, by the way, since we're having a different Thanksgiving, why don't I ask the McAllisters? A couple of outsiders might help take the edge off for us."

"Good idea," Jill said. "I'll talk to Mom."

It was less than an hour later that Beth herself rang the doorbell, surprising Jill because she hadn't called first as she always had before.

"Mom! Darling! What are you doing here? Come in. Come in," Jill said with delight.

"I really should have called first, but—" Beth came in. If anything, she was thinner and her face looked pinched and tired. "Who's the little baby?"

"That's Posey. She's Daphne Ingersoll's baby. One of my group, you know. I'm looking after her for a while today. Let me take your coat," Jill said, but Beth huddled closer into it. It was an interlined storm coat and should have been warm enough.

"I think I'll keep it on a while, dear. I just can't seem to stay warm." She hadn't worn a hat, and little wisps of her dark hair were trailing down around her wan face. She pushed them away. Her hands looked so fragile that Jill felt a lump in her throat. *Oh, Mom, please hang on.* Beth sat down in the chair Jill indicated and looked around the room, as if she were seeing it for the first time. "I've interrupted your work," she said, noticing the vacuum cleaner attachments, which Jill hadn't got around to putting away yet.

"No. Not all. I've finished," Jill said, scrambling to push them aside. "How are you doing? How is Laura?"

"Fine. She's busy today. You know, she's an officer in that professional women's group or club or something. She has a rather busy life." Mom's tone was absentminded, as if she wasn't really thinking about Laura's busy life. "I needed to pick up some...some..." She paused for a long interval. "Groceries," she added, huddling closer into her storm coat.

"Would you like something hot? Tea? Coffee? Hot chocolate?"

"No, thank you, dear. I was just out...and I thought since I wasn't far from here...I thought I'd just... Where are the children?"

How could she have been "not far from here" when she lived on the other side of the wide, sprawling city? "The girls are out back—at least, they will be until it starts to rain. And Ben's in his room playing with his vast collection of construction blocks."

"Yes, they said it would rain later today," Mom said, leaning forward and twisting her hands together. "I should have worn gloves. My hands get so cold. Your father gave me a pair of black pigskin gloves, knit lined. They were so warm. But I can't find them."

Jill sat down on a nearby ottoman, pushing it close to her mother's knees, and took the cold hands in hers.

"Mom, what's the matter? Why did you come?" she asked gently.

"Your sins always find you out, don't they? At least, I've heard that said. I guess..." Her hands clung to Jill's. "I guess I need to tell...somebody. I can't tell Katie. She'd be so shocked and hurt. I thought I could tell you. Because you're so...levelheaded." Her voice faded away, and her eyes drooped almost shut.

"Mom, what is it? What's wrong?" Jill's heart quailed. Mom looked so vulnerable.

"It's me. I'm wrong. I guess this was to be expected. It's just...difficult to get through. Pastor Ledbetter tried to help. But...I really can't tell him. I couldn't seem to say it."

"Say what, Mom?" What private demons could Mom possibly have to battle? Her eyes looked haunted.

"I wasn't a very good wife, Jill. Did you know that? I really wasn't...didn't..."

"Mother, how can you say that! The very last time I

saw Dad—when I visited him in the hospital—he said you
were the best wife in the world. He said he couldn't believe his luck. This is just your grief talking. After someone is gone and there isn't…any chance for those left to
mend fences—what did Pastor Ledbetter say?''

Beth pulled her hands away and unbuttoned the neck
of her coat, pushing it away from her thin shoulders. ''He
tried to explain to me about grief—seven stages, I think
he said. And one of those is guilt. The person left behind
starts thinking of all the…wrong things done, or things
left undone.''

''See?'' Jill said, almost pleading. ''It's just a natural
stage you're going through. It's hard, I know, but you just
need to stick it out.''

It was almost as if Beth hadn't heard her. ''Did you
know, I don't suppose you did, that I married your father
sort of on the rebound? I wanted to marry somebody else.
I was so foolish. I was so young. It was all so stupid,
looking back on it now. I was in with this group of four—
all four of us. We'd been through high school together
and we were all in the same college. I think Betsy started
it. She got engaged. We were all so excited. Then Rowena
got engaged. It was summer. We were having parties and
bridal showers and weddings. Before the summer was
over I'd conned your grandparents into buying me three
expensive bridesmaids' gowns.'' Silent tears had started
down Beth's gaunt face. ''I don't even know those people
now. I lost track of all of them years ago. Isn't that stupid?
But at the time it all seemed so *important*. I changed my
whole life—and Ralph's—because of it.''

''Mom, darling. We all make mistakes. But the life you
lived with Dad—''

''I'd been dating— This is really ridiculous—it took
me five minutes the other day to remember his name. It

was Brad Muller. I wanted desperately to marry Brad, but his parents had more sense. They pressured him to break the engagement and finish college. I was so humiliated. And...Ralph was always *there*. Ralph wasn't in the group—he was an older student, a neighbor, but *there*. Anyhow, I was sick of college. I'm not a big brain. I just wanted to get married and have my children. I wanted...actually, I guess what I really wanted was all the parties, the bridal showers and a big wedding, and Brad was gone and...Ralph was available. I *used* him. He didn't deserve that.''

''Oh, Mother, don't do this to yourself,'' Jill pleaded, aching for both of them. For Dad, so loving, so faithful, so grateful, and for Mom, too. Maybe the Beloveds of life didn't have it so easy, either.

''I...could have been so much kinder to him,'' Mom said softly. ''He...he made the best of it. Ralph wasn't stupid. He knew. He was never fooled. But he was capable of so much love. He could *give* unstintingly even if all he got back was crumbs. Now, of course, it's too late. I can't...make up for anything.''

''You don't have to make up for anything. Dad was happy with what he had, with his marriage. Even if...you didn't love him as much as he loved you, you gave him the marriage he wanted. He wouldn't have wanted any other.'' Jill dug in to her pocket for a tissue and handed it to her mother. Beth took it and blotted at her thin cheeks.

''I suppose this will...pass,'' she said tiredly.

''Of course it will pass, Mom. This is just something that has to be survived when you lose someone.'' Despite her effort, her voice quavered. If only people knew what they did to each other, carelessly, heedlessly, selfishly.

Love one another. Pastor Bailey's Sunday closing words lay in the bottom of her mind.

Posey broke the mood of sorrow that held them. She was wriggling up and down in her swing, rocking it precariously, and Jill had to get up to steady the frame. When she turned, Beth was standing. She had a pair of black gloves in her hand.

"Would you believe it?" she asked in wonder. "The pigskin gloves were in the pocket of this coat. How odd." She lifted the gloves and pressed them against her pale lips. "Oh, Jill, we make so many awful mistakes."

The swing steady again, Jill took Beth in her arms.

"Mom, it just *seems* like a bad mistake. Dad would have been miserable with anyone else. Even if you think you weren't a good wife, *he* did. That's what matters. You just have to hold on to that."

Beth looked at her, her great eyes filmed with tears. "But his life could have been so much better and now there's no way I can change that. It's done." She began to put her gloves on slowly, stroking the leather up over her fingers. "I must go," she said dully. "Since I'm here, does Greg have anything I need to sign, or anything?"

"I don't think so. Anyway, there's no hurry. He's taking care of things. He'll get to you when he needs to."

"Yes, thank you. Give him my love. Kiss the children for me."

Jill saw her out, her heart aching. She seemed so fragile, so defenseless against her guilt. Jill was praying silently, intensely. *Please God, help my mother forgive herself.*

Later, when Daphne had picked up Posey and her own children had been given lunch and were down for their naps, Jill took a chance and called Laura's cell phone number.

When Laura answered, Jill asked. "Did I get you at a

bad time?'' There seemed to be a lot of background noise. ''You aren't at Mom's, are you?''

''No, I'm at my hairdresser's appointment now. I'm just about to go under the dryer. What's wrong?''

''I need—'' Jill paused in surprised wonder, as this was the first time in her life she had ever said these words to Greg's mother. ''I need to talk to you. Can we...is there any way we can get together today?''

''Of course,'' Laura said. ''It's about Beth, isn't it? I've been wanting to talk to you about it, but... I'll tell you what, when I get through here I'll stop by your place. That's where you are, isn't it?''

''Yes, about what time?'' Jill asked. ''Not that it matters. I'm anchored here all day every day.''

Laura laughed. ''It'll be close to four. Is that all right?''

''That's fine. And thank you.'' She hung up the phone, realizing that she had forgotten to tell Mom about the new Thanksgiving Day plans.

Laura rang the bell at almost four exactly. It had started to rain, and after they had got through the children's greetings at Gramma Laura's sudden appearance, Jill settled them down in Laurie's room to watch, once again, one of their favorite videos, with a firm request that they stay there, as she and Gramma Laura would be having grown-up talk.

''Mom stopped by today,'' Jill said after they were seated. Then she paused, not knowing how much to say, since Beth hadn't said whether or not she had confided in Laura.

''And she seemed depressed, didn't she?'' Laura asked.

''Very depressed,'' Jill agreed. So Mom hadn't spoken to Laura as openly as she had talked today.

''I've noticed this coming on. Something is bothering her. I know what it is to be widowed,'' Laura said, her face tightening with remembered grief. "And I worry. I'm glad you called, because I've wanted to talk to you about it. I like Beth so much. I try to observe her tactfully, judge how she's doing.

"She forgets things. She wanders around aimlessly. Sometimes in the evening, when there's nothing much on TV and we're reading, she will look down at her book for minutes on end and not turn a page. She makes odd little comments that don't seem to have any meaning—at least, to me they don't. For instance, this morning at breakfast, she said out of the blue, 'Ralph liked cinnamon toast, but he was always fighting a weight problem so I didn't encourage it even on special days.' She's deeply troubled. I guess, when someone you love is gone, you keep thinking of things you could have done better." Wise Laura, she was close to the truth, without realizing it.

"I don't know what to do," Jill said helplessly. "What can one do?"

"Well, for one thing, grief is something each person has to work through alone. Nobody can do it for you. But I've had the beginning of an idea."

"What?" Jill asked, willing to clutch at any straw.

"I think if she could get interested, really interested, in something. Your mother was—still is—a really dedicated homebody. She's never worked outside her home—never wanted to, according to what I've picked up. When Kate and you married and left, she avoided the empty nest syndrome by what she calls her 'good works,' at the church, the food bank and all sorts of useful things. But her main focus, her hub, was her home. She and Ralph entertained rather a lot, didn't they?"

"Yes. Dad was a very gregarious soul. He had dozens of close friends, it seems. And for years they had foreign exchange students living with them. We're still getting sympathy cards from faraway places. Then, of course, when Dad retired, they went on their grand tour...." Jill's voice dwindled.

"Let me think about it," Laura said. "I'd hate to see Beth sink into a serious state of depression. Maybe I can come up with something."

"I'd—we'd all—really appreciate it," Jill said humbly. "And I want to thank you for...for staying with her. It's about the kindest thing anybody could do."

"Nonsense," Laura said briskly. "Beth's a lovely person. Think how many Thanksgiving dinners and Christmas dinners and Easter breakfasts she's invited me to. And I've enjoyed them all. Beth is a born hostess, and that's a real gift." Laura stood up.

"Incidentally," Jill said, "we thought we'd avoid the family festival thing this Thanksgiving. It's too soon after Dad. So we're going over to the Tacky Shack. Felix will reserve the private dining room for us. We'll all be together, but not in a home setting. What do you think of that?"

"Pure genius," Laura said, smiling her rare smile that was so remarkably like Greg's.

"May I tell Beth? Or is it a surprise?" Laura asked. "She's been worrying about that, too. She simply hasn't the heart to do it herself this year."

"Yes. By all means. I meant to tell her, but when she was here I simply forgot."

Jill talked with Greg about it later that night, after the children were in bed.

"Well, that does it," he said. "I can't possibly bother her with finances at a time like this. I'll just have to take care of things." They were sitting in front of the dying fire in the fireplace.

"You mean pay the excess bills?" Jill asked in a weak voice. "Didn't Dad have a good insurance policy?"

"It was only twenty thousand, and Beth spent about half of it on the funeral. The rest went the same way as Ralph's savings account. In Beth's present distracted state it won't be too difficult. I mean, she won't know. I find if I put a paper in front of her and say, 'Sign here,' she signs. She's so…shattered," he added sadly.

"I'm so sorry about this," Jill murmured.

"Don't be sorry. I can get the money—that's no problem. We're going to need a bit more anyhow, with Christmas coming up. Did you know Laurie says she wants a computer?"

"You've got to be kidding. Where'd she get that idea? She wouldn't be able to use it yet."

"She's not going to get it. I put her off. She picked up the idea by watching some TV documentary about kids and computers. But the kids are getting older, and as they do, Christmases cost more."

"Good grief, what happened to the olden times? When kids were happy with an orange and popcorn?"

"You must have been reading one of those nostalgia books. You and I were never satisfied with an orange and popcorn. And I don't think our parents were, either. Ben wants a bicycle helmet. He knows precisely which one. He showed me a picture of it in the Sunday paper."

"But he hasn't got a bicycle. And he's not going to get one yet. He's too little."

Greg shrugged. "I know, but he wants that helmet. I guess that's Ben's way of preparing for the time when he *will* have a two-wheel ten-speed. Ben's ways are not always the ways of the rest of the world. Ben's his own man."

He was relieved when she told him about the Thanksgiving plans. "Good. I was wondering. I don't think I could have sat through a big family dinner with everybody being careful not to say the wrong thing. And say," he added, "since we're inviting the McAllisters, maybe I'll invite Marv. I think he might enjoy it. Since his wife died he doesn't do much of anything on holidays."

So it was decided, and the gray days moved dully on, one after another. Thanksgiving dinner at the Shack was not only bearable, it was a rather pleasant break for all of them. Both Kate and Jill thought Beth looked better. She wore a soft sheer wool dress in a hazy shade of heather, with a high neck that covered the thinness and hollows of her throat.

Now there was only Christmas to deal with, and then maybe next year this time the healing would have taken place, or at least enough healing. *Please help us, God. Help my mother.*

Felix couldn't help them out for the Christmas dinner, because the Shack would be closed, although he questioned Jill about it.

"Don't be ridiculous, Felix. You and Connie want to have your own Christmas, with your kids." They were sitting in her living room. It was Monday, so the Shack was closed and they had time to visit a while. Felix had brought over the December payment, in full and on time.

"Yeah," he agreed, nodding. "Even Angel takes off work for Christmas. *Navidad* is very big in Mexico. So, what are you going to do?"

"Well, I've got a fairly large dining room, so we thought we'd have Christmas dinner over here. I was wondering about a turkey, though. I was thinking something different, but we have ham for Easter. Do people ever have a Christmas goose anymore?"

"You've been reading *A Christmas Carol*. You wouldn't like goose. Too gamey. Too greasy. Nobody would eat any of it. The American palate is slowly becoming fat free." He said this with regret, as Felix firmly believed that fat free was taste free. "How about a nice prime rib? That's kind of festive."

"Prime rib! That would do it!" And before he left, she got his recipe for Yorkshire pudding. That took a while, because he had to reduce it from thirty servings, and Felix's math was always a little shaky.

As soon as he left she called Greg to tell him they had the December payment in full and on time, and she heard his sigh of relief over the phone. Were they really getting short of money? She was certain that she would be the last to know, because he thought she would feel guilty about not working. As soon as Christmas was over, she would sit down with him and demand some straight answers. Although what she could do about it wasn't clear.

Almost as soon as she hung up the phone it rang again, and she picked it up.

"Hello?"

"Hell-*o!* This is Felice." And at Jill's surprised silence, Felice added, "Felice Fletcher. You know, from Greg's office."

"Yes, of course, Felice. How are you?"

"Ah, fine. Are you terribly busy right now?"

"No-o," Jill said warily. "Not terribly, why?"

"Well, I picked up a few little gifts for your kiddies. And I thought I'd...stop by and drop them off. I'm leaving the office early today. Will you be home?"

"Yes, of course, but you really didn't need—"

Felice cut her off. "I'll see you in about half an hour, then." Her tone held a forced cheerfulness, and Jill put down the phone slowly. Felice playing Santa Claus?

Oh, sure. And pigs will fly.

Chapter Fourteen

It was almost five when Felice came. Jill had already changed from her housekeeping clothes into a softly pleated forest green skirt and vest, over a long-sleeved white blouse, so she didn't feel too shabby when she saw Felice's soft gray suit with a hint of pinstripe.

"Come in," she said cheerfully. What was it Pastor Bailey had said? Something about Felice being a very troubled woman in need of understanding. Okay, she'd give it a shot.

"Thank you," Felice said, not looking at all troubled, but very confident, very upbeat, with a kind of suppressed excitement, which might not be difficult wearing a suit like that.

"I like your suit," Jill said by way of an icebreaker. Wearing a suit that made anyone seeing it wonder how much it cost would be a good confidence builder.

Felice came in carrying a large shopping bag from the biggest toy store in town, which she put down on the entry-hall chest.

"Please don't say I shouldn't have. I just fell in love

with your little ones and had to add something to their Christmas.''

''Well, it was very good of you,'' Jill said. ''Do you mind if we keep them for Christmas morning?''

''Not at all,'' Felice answered, walking into the living room as Jill put the bag into the hall closet and then followed Felice.

''Would you mind if we talk a bit in the kitchen? I have a couple of things to do. It's that time of day.''

''Of course not. I love your kitchen,'' Felice responded, and followed Jill into the kitchen, where she sat down at the kitchen table.

''Would you like a cup of coffee or something?'' Jill asked, pushing up her sleeves. *Watch this, Felice. The perfect homemaker, homemaking.*

''No. Nothing, thanks,'' Felice said as Jill took salad bowls from the cupboard and put them in the refrigerator to chill.

''As a time saver I often cook things ahead,'' Jill explained, taking a frozen quiche out of the freezer. ''The kids love anything with cheese in it.''

''You really enjoy this, don't you?'' Felice said in an oddly thoughtful voice.

''I've learned to,'' Jill said truthfully.

''But at first you didn't?''

''It took some getting used to. I had to change my whole way of working, of thinking, actually. I have completely different goals now.''

''Then why did you do it?'' There was genuine curiosity in Felice's voice.

Jill turned from the freezer and looked at her, sitting there at another woman's kitchen table, asking personal questions.

''I did it because I thought I should,'' Jill said simply.

"Because you thought you should," Felice echoed, a look of faint puzzlement in her lovely eyes, as if Jill had said something in a foreign language.

You don't get it, do you, lady? Well, it's the helpmate thing.

"Yes," Jill said, turning on the oven and setting the dial to the correct temperature. The quiche was too big for the microwave. Then she sat down opposite Felice to wait while the oven heated.

"When people take on obligations, like having children, there's a kind of unwritten contract they have to fulfill. Our youngest girl, Megan, almost died in a freak accident at her day care center. I had been thinking for some time that our two-career family, plus three children, was one of those situations where—at some point—something had to give."

"I see," Felice said, and Jill had the feeling that she might have a glimmer. "I like you," Felice added, as if speaking to herself. "Under other circumstances...in a different setting...I think we might have been friends."

"And we can't now?" Jill asked, surprising herself, and was dismayed to see Felice's eyes film over with tears, so that she turned away abruptly and got up to cross the room and look out the window over the sink into the backyard. Jill got up hesitantly. The backyard view wasn't a cheerful one now. The maple tree, bereft of all its leaves, would be swaying its bare branches coldly in any wind that passed, looking naked and cold. The remaining leaves lay in sodden piles here and there.

"I shouldn't have come," Felice said, reaching over to take a paper towel from the roll. She turned from the sink to face Jill, carefully blotting her eyes. "I feel like a fool."

"Do you feel like talking about it?" Jill asked, astonished at herself. *That's a line out of Pastor Bailey's book.*

Felice sighed. "I don't know. Maybe that would help. I've never done anything like this before. I'm carrying around this stupid load of guilt, that's all that's the matter. And I really have no reason to!" she added with an attempt at defiance that didn't quite ring true.

Jill glanced at the oven and twisted the dial. The temperature was almost right, so she put in the quiche. "Come into the living room. I've finished here for the time being." She set the timer. "I want to lay the evening fire in—" She stopped herself. She had been going to say that she and Greg always had a fire in the fireplace evenings. It sounded a little too cozy.

In the living room Jill let Felice take her time. She knelt in front of the fireplace, putting on the first layer of crumpled newspapers, then the small sticks of kindling, and on top of that she arranged three of the small logs from the brass log holder. Then she sat back on her heels and looked at her handiwork. That should catch nicely.

"You're so capable, Jill," Felice said. "I never saw a woman lay a fire in a fireplace before. I'm so impressed."

"Well, there's not much to it," Jill said cheerfully, getting up to take the chair opposite Felice.

"I wish you wouldn't be so nice," Felice said ruefully. "You see, I just cut your husband out of his promotion today. The trusty office grapevine has it that Greg's always expected to take over Marv's job. Now he…won't." She looked like a little girl waiting for a smack on the face.

Her bald announcement sent a shiver of shock through Jill. *Don't lose your cool, Jill.*

"Congratulations," Jill heard herself saying calmly.

"Thank you," Felice said, crossing her arms over her

chest and shrinking back in the chair, making herself look somehow smaller. "You see, I'm a very ambitious person." She was speaking awkwardly, an apology of sorts. "I've been on the fast track since...since kindergarten. And I must tell you this is the first time I've felt *guilty,* of all things, about, well, anything I've had to do. Business can be a pretty cutthroat, backstabbing deal, you know. And...well...I thought about it a long time because Greg is such a...nice guy. I mean, but business is business and one simply can't let one's career go stagnant. Not moving up is moving down."

"Oh, don't worry about Greg," Jill said smoothly. "With his abilities he won't have a problem. Seattle is a business hub. Did you know that a lot of national businesses started in Seattle? And there aren't nearly enough truly qualified and experienced people like Greg to go around. Why do you think Marshall's had to go to a head-hunter firm to recruit you from out of state? Don't worry about Greg. Just enjoy your promotion. Use your opportunity. Greg will be fine." *What am I saying!*

"Do you mean...you think Greg might *leave* Marshall's?" Uncertainty had crept into Felice's tone. A flash of sheer panic showed in her eyes. She's in love with him, and she wants him there, Jill thought.

Jill spread her hands. "Why would he want to stay there? I can't speak for Greg, of course. He makes his own decisions. But when he has so much to offer, why would he stick with a dead-end job? The VP slot was the only advancement opportunity coming up at Marshall's, and if that's gone, well." She shrugged. "Are you sure you don't want a cup of coffee or something?" *That's your exit line, lady. Pick up on your cue.*

"No. Really. Thank you. I must be going." Felice

sounded almost distracted. "I hope...everything is...I mean, I hope you have a lovely Christmas."

They both got up and started toward the front hall. "We always do," Jill said. "We're a little downbeat this year because of my father's death, but—" She paused, opening the front door, feeling a wave of sadness. "But there are always Christmases to come."

"I was sorry about your father," Felice said, and Jill had the feeling that she actually was.

"Thank you. It was kind of you to come to the funeral. We appreciated it. And Felice—" She stopped. What could she say to this strange driven woman, so ambitious, so mixed-up, going through life demanding things she couldn't have?

"Have a Merry Christmas, Felice."

"Thank you," Felice said, and there was between them for just an instant a sense of reaching out, then quick withdrawal. Felice shivered and then said brightly, "I should have worn a topcoat. Well, goodbye for now." And then she was gone.

Now, why in the world should I feel sorry for Felice? She'd better run that one by Pastor Bailey. Maybe he could explain it. Jill shut the door thoughtfully. What was she going to tell Greg? Had she interfered too much in what was his own business? Had she put something on the office grapevine that would embarrass him if he had no intention of leaving his firm?

She opened the subject with Greg that night as soon as the children were in bed. He had been unusually quiet during dinner.

"Greg, I have something to tell you. Or maybe confess is the better word. Felice stopped by today." She blurted it out.

Greg sighed. "I'm not surprised. Nothing that woman

does surprises me anymore. What was on her mind?'' He lit the fire she had laid, and sat back on his heels while it caught and flared up.

"Well, at first it was to bring the children some Christmas gifts. They're in the hall closet.''

"Yeah, but what was the real reason?'' He got up and pulled the ottoman over in front of her and sat down on it. "If she by chance dropped a little hint that the VP job is filled at Marshall and Associates, it's already on the office grapevine.''

"Has Barry picked it up that fast?''

Greg nodded, half smiling. "Sometimes I think he's got the place bugged. Or else he's got the clerical staff working as his moles.'' The fire was crackling and popping now as the kindling burned hotly. It would die down in a few minutes, and they both watched the leaping flames.

"There's more,'' Jill said. "I may have said a few things I shouldn't. I guess I hinted…actually, I said outright that if the VP slot was gone you'd probably start looking elsewhere. I may have overstepped…'' She waited anxiously. She didn't want to put him on the spot.

"Not really,'' he said slowly. "You're fairly well on target. I followed your advice and updated my résumé. And you know what? It looks good. I surprised myself. I put my finger over the name Gregory Jason Rhys and said to myself, 'Would I hire him?' And my answer was a resounding 'Yes!' I don't want to sound too conceited, but good is good. And I'm not being facetious here. I've had some pretty broad experience at Marshall's. I've got real skills to offer in the market for real skills.'' There was an underlying tone of confidence that was new with Greg, usually diffident and self-deprecating.

"You wouldn't want to stay at Marshall's if Felice is

VP?'' Jill asked. She kept her voice steady with an effort. *I'm not working now. You're the only breadwinner.*

He looked thoughtfully into the fire and then answered slowly. "I've given that a lot of thought over the past weeks, ever since Felice arrived on the scene. I wouldn't mind working for a woman. I've had a lifetime of being comfortable with strong women, but I *would* mind working for Felice." He looked up at her, his eyes candid.

"Because she's…attracted to you?" Her voice sounded rather small.

"And she never fails to bring it to my attention. It would be…uncomfortable. I guess that's the best word to use here." His eyes held hers, willing her to understand.

"You see, love," he went on, "I'm a person of the male persuasion, which you are well aware of, and we male persons have certain…reactions. It's built into the male genes." He let it rest there.

She swallowed. "You…you mean having her flirt with you all the time is…difficult?"

"Now and then, yes," he admitted. "I'm sorry. It means nothing real. Nothing at all." He waited a moment, then went on. "She can't understand why I don't go along. You see, I don't think she's ever been…resisted before. I think she pretty much always gets her man, and maybe I've become a challenge of some sort. And she just doesn't get it that this is a no-win game for her." He reached over and took her hands.

"You see, Jill, when a guy has a code of conduct, or…a creed or, in my case, a faith, he *has* to play by those rules. He *has* to go by that book. And in my book there's a definite set of rules spelled out. Number seven states very clearly that a guy stays faithful to his wife. If you're a Christian, you're subject to certain standards of behavior. Period. I'm sure other faiths have similar rule books, but

I only know my own. So, yes, when the lady gets the job, I'll have to move on. It's not only a get-thee-behind-me-Satan move, either, it's just common sense. Marshall's is a small firm. There was only one way for me to go up, and if that's taken, I'm dead-ended. I'll probably try some of the larger companies.''

"When do you think…" She tried to push aside a sudden very real fear.

"Not until after the first of the year. We've got Christmas coming up. It won't even be announced until the office Christmas party, and that's—let's see, I don't have a calendar handy, but I think in about ten days. Marshall will announce any staff promotions then.''

"Will you mind awfully?'' she asked. "I remember you were so keen at Marshall's in the beginning.'' She wanted to cry, but held it back.

He reached over and took the poker to push at one of the logs, causing sparks to fly up the chimney. "A year ago I'd have been crushed, but in these past few months, so much has happened…'' He paused for a long while, looking into the leaping fire. "No. I don't mind all that much. Maybe I'm ready for a change. Thinking through and updating the résumé helped.'' He turned to her again. "It'll be okay,'' he said with his slow smile. "Trust me.''

She tried to hold on to that confident *Trust me,* during the cold December days that followed. Most of the time she had to keep the children inside because of the weather, and finding things to keep them occupied tested her patience and ingenuity. The group helped, as they could pool resources, getting all the kids together to make Christmas cards and gifts. Some of the childish efforts touched the heart and lifted the spirit.

Somehow, trading off child care, the members of the

group got their Christmas shopping finished. Small good things happened to add cheer at odd and unexpected moments.

Felix called in something of a panic. "Jill, you haven't bought your Christmas prime rib, have you?"

"No. Not yet. Why?"

A gusty sigh of relief came over the phone. "I thought maybe you already had it in your freezer! Don't—repeat don't—pay butcher-shop price! It'll cost you the earth. I'll get you one at my restaurant price."

What a nice thing to do! It made her day.

And somehow or other, during the time since the last office party, something strange and wonderful had happened to her hips. She took the ivory satin sheath out of the closet and held it up, looking at it longingly. *Do you suppose? Na-a-a. Not yet.*

Five minutes later she was standing in front of the fulllength mirror smoothing it down over her hips. She turned this way and that, exulting. She pushed her dark hair up on top of her head. Maybe she would put it up, the way Mom did. She had tried it once before, with disastrous results. Yes. At this office party she'd try an updo. *Today the sheath. Tomorrow the hair stays up. Anything is possible.*

A few days before the office party she took the children over to her mother's house, and while they were immersed in the old family photo albums, which always fascinated them, she had a serious hair discussion with Beth.

Her mother seemed better, brighter somehow. They had time to talk for a while after the styling session and before the children tired of the photo albums.

"You're looking better," Jill said fondly. "You may have even put on a pound or two." And Beth smiled her lovely smile.

"I think it's called coming to terms," she said. "I've been meaning to talk to you and Kate about it. Would you girls have any...I was going to say objections, but that's too strong a word. Would you girls have any reservations if I decided to run a small business?"

Jill was stunned. "Mom," she said gently, "you don't, uh, you haven't..."

"I know, I don't and I haven't," Beth said with a laugh. "But, well, dear, Laura has come up with what I think is a really good idea. She's thought of a way I can market skills I already have, skills I've used all my life."

Jill stared at her, completely confused.

"I'm a homemaker. It's something I've done all my life. And if I do say so myself, I'm pretty good at it. Plus which—" she ticked the pluses off on her slim fingers "—one, Seattle is a tourist mecca, and two, I have a beautiful five-bedroom house with a superb view of the Sound. And three—so Laura says—I'm a born hostess. She and I have been boning up on how one runs a bed-and-breakfast place. It doesn't look that difficult. I mean, the business end of it. Laura is an experienced businesswoman. She doesn't want to be involved in a B and B— she has too much else on her plate—but she will help me get started, and you know a lot about feeding people. What do you think?"

"Oh, Mom, what a wonderful idea!" Jill was almost crying. *Thank you, Laura. Thank you.* "I can't wait to tell Katie. She'll be thrilled."

Jill went home on cloud nine and told Greg about it as soon as he came in the door.

"What a great idea! It's a natural," he said. "It's just exactly what Beth needs."

By mid-December Jill had the front hall decorated with evergreen boughs and holly, and the children were living for Christmas, counting the days. They all had special places to hide their accumulating gifts. There was a lot of whispering and giggling, and secrets that other people guessed and pretended they hadn't. Meggie understood things better this year and entered into the spirit of the season with abandon.

The office party was the only downer.

"You look terrific! What a knockout!" Greg said as Jill turned this way and that in the ivory sheath, Grandmother Bennett's ruby necklace, borrowed from Beth, glittering at her throat.

It was part retirement party for Marv, who was leaving for Wyoming just after the New Year. And Marshall announced that Felice would be the incoming vice president of Marshall and Associates. Greg was the first to congratulate Felice, closely followed by Jill with her brightest smile. *Trust Greg,* she kept telling herself, but the hollow feeling in her stomach wouldn't go away. He couldn't possibly stay on at Marshall's now.

They put up the tree a week before Christmas so the children would have a while to enjoy it. Greg had gotten such a tall one that he had to cut a piece out at the top and splice the top spire back on to accommodate the angel who always perched at the very top.

"Next time I'll take the yardstick," he said. "You said this was too tall," he admitted as they decorated it. They had additional ornaments this year, some of them very old. Beth had decided that her big Christmas trees belonged to Christmases past.

"I've divided them as fairly as I can," she said, giving boxes of ornaments to both Jill and Kate when they were all together one day. "I'll just enjoy them at one remove, on your trees." Some were old and very fragile, collected through all the Christmas years of the Bennett family, each wrapped in its own memory. Jill took her box almost reverently.

Felix and Connie stopped by the day before Christmas to leave their gifts and pick up those Jill had got for their family.

"Don't leave these under your tree," Connie said, her eyes full of laughter as she strained to lift up a tote with two fat gift-wrapped packages in it. "You know Felix has this passion for feeding people."

Felix had gift wrapped two ten-pound prime rib roasts for their Christmas dinner, and Jill put them in the refrigerator to be roasted Christmas morning, filling the house with their delicious smell. *Love one another,* she thought, hugging both Connie and Felix together.

Greg was a last-minute shopper, so there was always plenty of late-evening gift wrapping on Christmas Eve, after the children were in bed. The only gift he wrapped himself was his gift to her, which had to remain a secret until Christmas morning.

"It's a sacred family tradition," he said, his eyes glinting with laughter. "You made the mistake of wrapping all the presents the first year we were married, so now it's tradition."

They finished about one-thirty Christmas morning, and looked around the living room with satisfaction. The tree shimmered in all its glory, and there seemed to be a hundred bright packages banked around the base.

"I'm beat," Greg said. "Let's take a break. Merry Christmas."

"Merry Christmas back," Jill said. "Could you use a snack before we go to bed?"

"I sure could. Are there any of Kate's cookies left?"

"Are you kidding? Dozens. You know how it is when

Kate makes cookies. Would you like some milk with them?''

"Perfect," he said, sitting down on the floor in front of the tree, the glow from the many Christmas-tree lights illuminating the planes and hollows of his face. "You did a great job on Ben's helmet," he added, moving it an inch to the left for some reason.

They sat on the floor in front of the most-beautiful-tree-we've-had-yet, which they said every year, and munched Kate's cookies and sipped cold milk.

"I got a little surprise present today," Greg said. "I really don't know quite what to make of it."

"What is it?" Jill asked, putting back the fifth cookie because she suddenly remembered the ivory sheath.

"A card and a very brief note in it from Felice. Would you believe she's decided to dump Marshall's job and take that one that's been dangling in front of her for weeks? And it wasn't in Cincinnati like I thought. It's in Detroit."

"Why!" Jill asked, astonished, but on second thought she felt she might know why, and a feeling of sadness pervaded her. "I...hope she finds what she wants," she said quietly.

Greg was looking at her intently. "You handled all that very well, my lady," he said softly. "It was an odd situation."

"Very odd," she agreed. "What are you going to do now that she's gone? That leaves the VP slot open again, doesn't it?"

"It does indeed, and Marshall with egg on his face. As to what I'm going to do at this moment in time, as they say, I don't have a clue. I'd made up my mind to move on. I've even got an appointment on January second with a placement firm. I'll have to think about it."

A feeling of relief engulfed Jill. Either way he had it made.

He picked up another cookie and turned it this way and that, the way a person does who doesn't really care whether they eat another cookie or not. "There are good arguments for both staying there and for going someplace else, but I'll ponder that one after Christmas. A lot has happened in the last few months...a lot has changed. Things are sort of...working out for us now." He was quiet for a time, his eyes on the brilliant tree and its glittering ornaments.

"Mother talked with me today about Beth's B and B. That's going great. There's a small investment to be made in the beginning. Beth needs to have some renovating done to meet city codes for that kind of business, but we can handle that okay."

"Are you sure?" Jill asked, as the caution she had learned about money rose in her mind.

"Yes. There's something I want to tell you. We have quite a large stash of cash in the bank, so you don't have to sweat it so much about money."

"How'd we get that?" she asked in astonishment.

"Okay. Now, when I tell you I don't want you to go into cardiac arrest. It's something I should have done...a long time ago. And it finally dawned on me."

"What!"

"Jill, don't freak out on me, but I've done some growing up in the past few months. And when people decide to grow up, it means they put aside their toys, their playthings." His eyes held hers. "Please don't go all protective of poor little Greg the way Mother did, but...I sold the *Far Horizon,* I sold my boat." Despite the bantering tone, his voice shook as he said it.

"Oh, Greg," she whispered, burying her face in her

hands to hide the sudden rush of tears. She felt his arms around her, drawing her into a close embrace. He let her cry a while, murmuring into her hair words of comfort that she couldn't hear. "Oh, Greg, couldn't we have done something else? The boat meant so much," she asked miserably, wiping at her wet face with the handkerchief he had handed her.

"It was something I had to do. It was only common sense. Not only did I have a hefty investment tied up in it, there were the ongoing monthly costs, insurance, moorage fees, upkeep, yacht club dues—all of it. I think people can become independently wealthy by *not* owning a boat."

They were quiet for a long time, sitting in the glow of the tree. "You know," he said, "I told you before how scared I was when you gave up working. But in looking back over the past months, I think it was the very thing we needed. I don't know if you ever realized this or not, but…I was getting pretty burned out on marriage in general and ours in particular. I was…fed up." There was a hint of hesitation now in his voice.

"Oh, I knew," she said softly. "That night out at the marina, when I went down to the boat. I knew you were going to stick it out, but…"

"Well, yeah," he said. "That's a given, according to my rule book. But things were really bad for me. There wasn't any joy in it anymore. Maybe I shouldn't be saying this…"

"Yes. You should. We mustn't build walls."

He smiled, letting his finger trail over her cheek, wiping away a stray tear. "That sounds like something Brian Bailey would say."

"It is. I think it's a direct quote."

"Okay. If we're not building walls, I'll be honest and

say that—for just a little while—I wanted out. I'd go down to the boat and just wish I could…I mean, there was the Sound and beyond that the whole *Pacific*…but I got over that. Do you know when I think my turnaround point came?''

She shook her head, unable to say anything.

"Laurie. She came to me one evening to show me her box of grocery receipts. She pointed out all the money she was saving on our grocery bill with her coupons. And I thought a *five-year-old kid* had more family loyalty than I, a supposedly adult male, did.'' His voice shook. ''I did a lot of thinking.

"Then I started observing you, watching how you were working, trying so hard to cope…and *coping*. Making the kids feel more secure, teaching them things, getting by on less and less money—and giving up the work you loved to do it. It was what we needed, and I finally got the message.''

She touched—briefly—the side of his face, almost breathless with the wonder, feeling the *oneness* with him.

"So that's what I mean when I say I grew up. Men have been taking care of their own for centuries, but you have no idea of the *satisfaction* I began to feel at being able to do it myself. Me. Greg Rhys, breadwinner. I don't know exactly what we're going to do next year, but whatever it is, it will be good. We're going in the right direction. Things have…evened out for us and I think, I know, most of it was your doing.

"A lot will happen next year. Beth will find her way. I'll move ahead in my work. Laurie will start kindergarten—it's all out there for us.''

They sat for a while longer in front of the glittering tree, not wanting to leave, not wanting to break the spell, but finally he moved.

"Look who's here," he whispered. And Jill lifted her head from his shoulder to see Meggie standing in the doorway.

"Is it Christmas yet?" Meggie whispered.

"Not yet, punkin," Jill said, getting up. "Mommy will put you back to bed."

Greg got up, too. "I'll clear up this stuff," he said, gathering up the remains of the cookies and the milky glasses and going toward the kitchen.

After she had put Megan back to bed she found him in the kitchen. He had finished washing their two glasses and was drying them. He put them into the cupboard and, looking at her, tossed aside the dish towel. She went over to him and put her hands on his shoulders.

"Merry Christmas, Greg," she said softly, kissing him gently. He held her closer and she saw the love in his eyes. The word *helpmate* came and went in her mind. *This is the good life, Jill.*

"Shall we go upstairs now?" he asked, his voice husky.

"Yes. Let's do that," she answered, and reached over his shoulder to shut the cupboard door.

* * * * *

Dear Friends,

I hope you enjoyed reading *Helpmate*. It was a statement I wanted to make. So many women are leaving the workplace now to become stay-at-home wives and mothers. It is a growing trend. The women's movement, in which I was active as a young woman, opened the door for women who wanted a career outside the home, or in addition to marriage and motherhood. The women's movement had real successes, but for a time I feel that the pendulum swung too far, and women who did *not* choose an outside "career" were looked down upon for "wasting" themselves.

Now there is an increasing realization that choosing a career outside the home is a right choice for *some women,* but *not* for others. Only now are women starting to know that the Open Door may—or may not—be entered. It's a choice each woman must make for herself.

Whatever your choices have been, or will be, good luck and Godspeed. I wish you a wonderful rest of your life.

Faithfully,

Virginia Myers

Take 3 inspirational love stories FREE!

PLUS get a FREE surprise gift!

Special Limited-time Offer

Mail to Steeple Hill Reader Service™
3010 Walden Avenue
P.O. Box 1867
Buffalo, N.Y. 14240-1867

YES! Please send me 3 free Love Inspired™ novels and my free surprise gift. Then send me 3 brand-new novels every month, which I will receive months before they appear in bookstores. Bill me at the low price of $3.19 each plus 25¢ delivery and applicable sales tax, if any*. That's the complete price and a saving of over 10% off the cover prices—quite a bargain! I understand that accepting the books and gift places me under no obligation ever to buy any books. I can always return a shipment and cancel at any time. Even if I never buy another book from Steeple Hill, the 3 free books and the surprise gift are mine to keep forever.

103 IEN CFAG

Name	(PLEASE PRINT)	
Address	Apt. No.	
City	State	Zip

This offer is limited to one order per household and not valid to present Love Inspired™ subscribers. *Terms and prices are subject to change without notice. Sales tax applicable in New York.

ULI-198

©1997 Steeple Hill

Available in
September 1998 from
Love Inspired.®..

FOR THE SAKE OF HER CHILD

by

Kate Welsh

Amanda Powers's prayers were finally answered when she was reunited with her missing son. But her beloved boy needed her now, more than ever. As did widower Garth Jorgensen, the man who had raised her son as his own. Was a marriage for the sake of their child part of the Lord's mysterious plan?

Available in September 1998
at your favorite retail outlet.

Steeple
Hill™

ILIFSHC

Love Inspired® presents...

THIS SIDE OF PARADISE
by
Cheryl Wolverton

Adventure. Excitement. Romance.

Mild-mannered Jennifer Rose was stranded with a
stranger! On a mission to save three orphaned children, she and cynical pilot Gage Dalton had crashed
in the dense jungle. Struggling to survive, Jennifer
soon found herself on the adventure of a lifetime. For
not only was her life in jeopardy, her heart was in dan-
ger of being lost to one very handsome man.

*You won't want to miss this wonderfully
uplifting story coming in September 1998...
only from Love Inspired.*

Available at your favorite retail outlet.

ILITSP

Steeple
Hill™

**Remember the magic of the film
It's a Wonderful Life?
The warmth and tender emotion of
Truly, Madly, Deeply?
The feel-good humor of *Heaven Can Wait?***

Well, even if we can't promise you angels that look like
Alan Rickman or Warren Beatty, starting in June in
Harlequin Romance®, we can promise a brand-new
miniseries: GUARDIAN ANGELS. Featuring all of your
favorite ingredients for a perfect novel: great heroes,
feisty heroines and a breathtaking romance—all with a
celestial spin.

Look for Guardian Angels in:

June 1998: THE BOSS, THE BABY AND THE BRIDE (#3508)
by Day Leclaire

August 1998: HEAVENLY HUSBAND (#3516)
by Carolyn Greene

October 1998: A GROOM FOR GWEN (#3524)
by Jeanne Allan

December 1998: GABRIEL'S MISSION (#3532)
by Margaret Way

**Falling in love sometimes needs a little help
from above!**

Available wherever Harlequin books are sold.

The author of over fifteen inspirational
romances, Irene Brand brings
Love Inspired® readers a poignant and
heartfelt story.

HEIRESS

by

Irene Brand

After discovering that she was the sole heiress to her
uncle's vast fortune, Allison Sayre embarked on an
amazing journey. She never imagined she would
uncover a shocking family secret. Or be drawn back
into the life of Benton Lockhart, a man whose
powerful spiritual convictions had once
inspired her....

Available at your favorite retail outlet from
Love Inspired.®

Continuing in
August 1998 from *Love Inspired*...

SUDDENLY!

a delightful series by
Loree Lough

*Celebrate the joy of unexpected parenthood in this
heartwarming series about some very unexpected
special deliveries.*

You enjoyed the romance and excitement in
SUDDENLY DADDY (June '98). Be sure to
catch the next wonderful book in this series:

SUDDENLY MOMMY
(August '98)

Jaina Chandelle's mission was to inform a lonely
bachelor that she has been caring for his orphaned
nephew. She wasn't supposed to become emotionally
involved with the fledgling father. But how could she
ignore the pull on her heartstrings for handsome
Connor Buchanan...or deny the longing to help raise
the boy who had become the child of her heart?

Steeple
Hill™

Available at your favorite retail outlet.   ISM